## "I'm a realist, Carrie. You're a..."

"I know what I am! Go ahead, be cynical." She glared at him, an inner fire now lighting her eyes. "You were a good reporter. Heck, you're even famous. But here's what I think. I think you got some kind of kick out of seeing the awfulness of mankind. I think it confirms what your dark, brooding soul has always believed— that our world is a miserable place. And that, Keegan Breen, is just plain sad, and that's why I feel sorry for you."

"You know what I think, Carrie?"

She scowled. "I think you've made it quite clear."

He smiled, because in truth he was enjoying this moment more than many he'd experienced in a long time. He more than liked this fighter Carrie. He more than admired her. "I think we've pegged each other pretty accurately. We haven't been together two weeks yet, and we know each other as well as if we'd been friends for years."

Secretly, he was starting to hope they could be more...

Dear Reader,

This is the final love story about three sisters, The Daughters of Dancing Falls. I hope you've enjoyed the journey of each of the unique women, who are bound together by their love for each other and their caring father. No family dynamic is perfect. It takes work, patience and love to nurture the bond of parent and child.

In this book, Carrie's story, this youngest daughter flexes her independence muscles despite having challenges to face. All her life she fought against her father's overbearing concern, and only when she meets a man who seems her complete opposite does she learn what it means to see the world from another person's point of view—even her father's. I sincerely hope that Carrie's struggle to be herself while recognizing her special gift to help another person heal will be a satisfying end to a series I loved writing.

*Cynthia*

PS: I enjoy hearing from readers. You may contact me at cynthoma@aol.com or visit my website, cynthiathomason.net.

# HEARTWARMING

## Rescued by Mr. Wrong

—

*Cynthia Thomason*

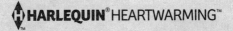

Recycling programs
for this product may
not exist in your area.

ISBN-13: 978-0-373-36826-6

Rescued by Mr. Wrong

Copyright © 2017 by Cynthia Thomason

All rights reserved. Except for use in any review, the reproduction or utilization of this work in whole or in part in any form by any electronic, mechanical or other means, now known or hereinafter invented, including xerography, photocopying and recording, or in any information storage or retrieval system, is forbidden without the written permission of the publisher, Harlequin Enterprises Limited, 225 Duncan Mill Road, Don Mills, Ontario M3B 3K9, Canada.

This is a work of fiction. Names, characters, places and incidents are either the product of the author's imagination or are used fictitiously, and any resemblance to actual persons, living or dead, business establishments, events or locales is entirely coincidental.

This edition published by arrangement with Harlequin Books S.A.

For questions and comments about the quality of this book, please contact us at CustomerService@Harlequin.com.

® and TM are trademarks of Harlequin Enterprises Limited or its corporate affiliates. Trademarks indicated with ® are registered in the United States Patent and Trademark Office, the Canadian Intellectual Property Office and in other countries.

Printed in U.S.A.

**Cynthia Thomason** inherited her love of writing from her ancestors. Her father and grandmother both loved to write, and she aspired to continue the legacy. Cynthia studied English and journalism in college, and after a career as a high-school English teacher, she began writing novels. She discovered ideas for stories while searching through antiques stores and flea markets and as an auctioneer and estate buyer. Cynthia says every cast-off item from someone's life can ignite the idea for a plot. She writes about small towns, big hearts and happy endings that are earned and not taken for granted. And as far as the legacy is concerned, just ask her son, the magazine journalist, if he believes.

## Books by Cynthia Thomason

### Harlequin Heartwarming

*The Bridesmaid Wore Sneakers*
*A Boy to Remember*
*Firefly Nights*
*This Hero for Hire*
*A Soldier's Promise*
*Blue Ridge Autumn*
*Marriage for Keeps*
*Dilemma at Bayberry Cove*

### Harlequin Superromance

*The Men of Thorne Island*
*Your House or Mine?*
*An Unlikely Match*
*An Unlikely Father*
*An Unlikely Family*
*Deal Me In*
*Return of the Wild Son*

### Harlequin Special Edition

*His Most Important Win*

This book is dedicated to anyone who ever felt that true love was just beyond their grasp. Don't ever stop reaching.

# *PROLOGUE*

"WHITEOUT CONDITIONS." Those had been the radio forecaster's words just a few minutes ago as Carrie slowly navigated the lakeshore route to her home in Fox Creek, Ohio. She couldn't recall ever driving on such treacherous roads before, but now she knew exactly what was meant by "whiteout." The paleness of the snow-covered asphalt seemed to blend with the white of the air around her as flurries mounted in intensity. The horizon had been obliterated, making the lanes of the highway indistinct and the sun only a gray, hazy memory. Her surroundings were muddled together, a vacuum of white, starkness and cold.

The sudden blizzard wasn't the only frosty aspect of this holiday season. Her chilly conversation with her father last night was still fresh in her mind.

"I'm very disappointed, Carrie," her father

had said. "This is the first time you've missed Christmas, and I can't imagine what is more important than being with your family."

Once again her father had used the guilt factor to persuade her to do what he thought was best. Carrie was tired of explaining all her decisions. Besides, no one in the Foster family understood Carrie's devotion to trees, especially the shoreline birches of central Michigan lakes that were showing serious effects of pesticide treatment.

Even worse, her father had followed up by announcing, "I've made you an appointment with a brilliant new allergist, Dr. Hower, for December 26. I don't want to cancel."

"Not another allergist, Dad," she'd said. "We all know what I'm allergic to—nearly everything. I won't be prodded and poked anymore!"

"Fine. Have it your way." He'd been angry, but after a moment his tone had leveled. "Honey, I am the doctor in this family, and I'm only thinking of you."

That statement had calmed her since it was true. Unfortunately, her father's concern and medical expertise had left her longing for independence her entire life and a lot less mothering from her caring father. This time she was determined to chart her own course, which meant monitoring the experiments with her trees and refusing more asthma treatments.

Dr. Martin Foster had ended their uncomfortable conversation with a warning. "If you change your mind…"

"Daddy, I won't."

"If you do, don't set out in the morning. Bad weather is predicted for Christmas Day." As if he didn't trust her to do anything he told her, he'd added, "I mean it, Carrie. Don't drive if the forecast is unfavorable."

When would he ever stop treating her like the baby of the family? Even babies grew up, and she was thirty years old. However, by that evening, Christmas Eve, she'd mellowed. With promises from her crew to continue her work, she'd decided to tackle the five-hour drive in the morning and arrive at her father's estate, Dancing Falls, in time for Christmas dinner. She'd loaded her car with gifts and headed south for the normally easy drive. Hopefully she'd miss the worst of the weather.

But typical of Ohio winters, a freak blizzard, worse than predicted, had blown in off Lake Erie. The turnpike closed almost immediately, but the traffic app on her iPhone showed that the local two-lane roads were being cleared, leaving her route along the lake passable. That was a few hours ago. Now, in midafternoon, she still had more than two hours to drive in rapidly deteriorating conditions.

Carrie slowed her small foreign car, impractical for blizzard conditions, to a crawl, and was still unable to determine where the road ended and the shoulder began. She hadn't seen another pair of headlights in miles, so she wasn't worried about hitting another car. She gripped her steering wheel and plowed ahead. This storm couldn't last forever. She pictured her father sitting in his chair by the fireplace, secure in the knowledge that his daughter wouldn't dare ignore his warning and be foolish enough to set out in a storm. He would be furious if he knew she was out in this weather.

Vapor collected on the inside of her windshield, so Carrie lowered her window a few inches to let in fresh air. Just in case, she reached inside the pocket of her purse where she always kept her inhaler. Sometimes, thank goodness not often, a sudden blast of frigid air could bring on an asthma attack.

This was obviously not her lucky day. The wind rushed around the knit stocking cap over her head and seemed to flow downward and settle directly in her lungs. She felt her airways constrict with a tingling pain that signaled a problem. She put the inhaler between her lips, depressed the button and breathed in the lifesaving medicine.

Several seconds later she found herself staring into a pair of bright gold eyes. She braked suddenly, and her heart raced as she realized she was sliding toward a deer, a beautiful fawn-colored creature who stood in the road and was probably as shocked to find herself out on a day like this as Carrie was. Carrie swerved. The deer took flight.

Before she could contemplate the miracle that the deer's life had been spared, Carrie's car skidded on a patch of ice. She braked with a slow and steady pressure as she'd been taught by a driver's education instructor. The car began to fishtail. Turn the steering wheel in the direction of the skid or away from it? She couldn't remember. She lost control. The car veered off the road as if it had a mind of its own and spun in a complete circle before plowing into a bank of snow and hitting something solid.

Carrie felt the impact in every bone. A sharp pain sliced up her right leg as the car's air bag exploded around her chest. Her forehead connected with a bone-rattling jolt against the top of the steering wheel. Carrie thought of her family snug and safe at Dancing Falls. Images of her two sisters, her niece and nephew, her dad, swirled in her mind before she lost consciousness.

# CHAPTER ONE

LATELY, KEEGAN BREEN was the last person anyone should count on to run an errand of mercy. And he was just fine with that. He didn't ask anyone to do anything for him, and he appreciated the return consideration. However, this Christmas Day was something of an emergency. His neighbor Duke struggling to cope with memory loss associated with his eighty-six years, had forgotten to order his heart medication, and he needed to take it every day, or... Well, even Keegan didn't want to be responsible for that.

So Keegan had called Duke's doctor and discovered that the MD had some samples of Duke's meds in his home. Keegan then ventured out in the snow to pick up a couple of pills. What had started out as a short twelve-mile journey to town in light snowfall had now become an hour's pain-in-the-neck trek in blizzard conditions.

"Lake-effect snow," Keegan muttered to himself. A person never knew when it would do its worst, but that was the chance he took living on the shore of Lake Erie. Thank goodness his seven-year-old Chevy Tahoe—with its 350 horses, V-8 engine and two tons of steel on a truck chassis—could barrel through almost anything.

He slowed for the curve about a mile from the abandoned Cedar Woods Campground where Keegan lived in the old camp store and Duke lived in a small trailer. Through the whiteout conditions, Keegan managed to see a pair of red taillights glowing faintly from a mound of snow left by an earlier plow. He braked to a crawl and stopped behind the motorist who'd obviously lost his mind to be out in this weather on a holiday. Especially without a "blizzard beast" like the Tahoe.

Getting out of his vehicle, Keegan walked around to the driver's side of the compact car. A few more minutes and the ridiculous little two-seater might have been buried in a mini avalanche, leaving the driver to become a human popsicle.

Pulling his jacket collar around his ears where his ball cap stopped short of providing protection, Keegan approached the driver's window. Snow had accumulated, but it was light and dusty, not the kind that sticks the moment it lands. He brushed off the snow with his heavily gloved hand and peered inside.

Besides a mound of wrapped packages, only one person was in the automobile—a woman, slumped over the limp remains of an air bag, and one who apparently didn't have the sense to listen to a weather forecast before venturing out on a day like this. Even more astounding, the gal had left her window partially opened and snow was settling on her shoulders and head.

"Lady!" Keegan called. "Lady, are you okay?"

She wasn't. Keegan saw a faint stream of red coming from her forehead. He'd seen enough head injuries in his day to know the possibility of serious complications. He tried the door. Locked. With about four inches of opening to work with, he slipped off his glove and stuck his hand in the window, wiggling his arm downward to the door lock. Thank goodness he was able to reach the button and pull it up.

He opened the car door. The woman didn't move. Her breathing seemed labored. "Darned air bag must have knocked the wind out of her," Keegan said aloud. He'd never thought they were a good idea. He wasn't crazy about seat belts either, especially now when he had to work his fingers through deflated nylon to free the woman.

The seat belt latch clicked, and the woman moaned and tried to sit upright. She managed to turn her head and stared with partially closed eyes at Keegan. Those eyes popped wide open instantly. Visibility was poor, but he figured she'd seen enough to be freaked out by his appearance, so he backed up a step. Meticulous grooming wasn't at the top of his list of priorities these days.

She stuck out her hand and pounded his chest with a weak fist. "Leave me alone," she said.

Keegan leaned in the car door. "If I do, you'll freeze to death out here. And you have a head injury."

She struggled to take a breath. "I do?"

"Yes, and who knows what else is wrong. You've driven your car into a snowbank and hit one of our scenic telephone poles."

She continued staring at him as if he were her worst nightmare. "Call an ambulance," she said.

"You don't want me to do that. If I call for an ambulance, it would take forever in this weather for it to reach us. Plus, we'd be putting the drivers at risk. Your best bet is to go with me."

"Go with you? I don't even know you."

"I don't know you either, but I'm willing to take the risk," the man said. "Now, let's get you out of that car, so we can get you medical help. You could have serious injuries."

"I do," she said through gritted teeth. "I think I broke my leg."

CARRIE FELT LIKE a knife had sliced into her calf. She touched her head and stared at the sticky red mess on her fingers. Definitely bleeding, but the cold was slowing it down some. What was she going to do now? Miles from nowhere, a broken leg, a damaged head, an asthma attack, and no one but this large, grisly-looking man to help her. His hair reached his shoulders, and he looked like he hadn't shaved in a month.

Mr. Grisly leaned on the roof of her car. "Do you live around here?" he asked.

She could honestly answer that she didn't. She was still at least two hours from home and four hours from her Michigan address. But maybe she should lie. What good would that do? Even if her car wasn't wrecked, she didn't know if she'd be able to drive anywhere. Why couldn't it have been her left leg that was injured?

"No," she said. "I live in Michigan."

"No one you know in this area?"

She shook her head, knowing if she gave her father's name, he would never let her forget her foolish decision.

"Then I guess you're stuck with me." He reached his arms into her car, pushing back the remains of the air bag. With a skillful and surprisingly gentle touch, he probed her arms and legs. "I don't think anything else is broken. So come on. We're going to the hospital."

Did she want to add stupidity to her list of problems? She didn't know this guy. *Think, Carrie.* Drawing in a sharp breath of pain, she said, "I don't even know your name."

He exhaled a frosty breath. "Keegan Breen."

"I don't know if I trust you."

"Look, I'm not going to hurt you. Truthfully, I'm not that crazy about helping you. I was on my way home and looking forward to a fireplace and roasting some hot dogs." He gave her a lopsided grin. "It is Christmas, you know."

"How far is the hospital?" she asked.

"Twenty minutes, maybe more in this weather." He looked out her windshield. "I think it's let up a little in the time we've been talking." Wiggling his fingers, he added, "Let's go, buttercup. Grab hold."

There was something calm about his voice, almost soothing. And anyway, what other choice did she have but to trust him? She couldn't stay in an automobile that didn't even have a working heater anymore. She wrapped her hands around each of his forearms and let him do the heavy lifting. He pushed his hand under her rump and had her out of the car and safely tucked against his chest in a matter of moments. The change in position made the pain in her leg worse. She bit her lip to keep from screaming out.

He started walking toward a monster car of some type. "Wait," she said. "My purse. My inhaler. My glasses. They probably fell off the dashboard when I hit the pole."

He trudged back, leaned her against the car and reached for her purse on the passenger seat. She took it, scrambled to find the inhaler where she'd dropped it in the bag. He found her pair of dark-framed reading glasses on the floor of her car and handed them to her. Then she allowed him to lift her again. This time she wrapped her arms around his neck and buried her hands in the fleece underside of his collar. Ah, warmth... and something else, too. The scent of hickory, like kindling from a fire. Nice. Maybe he wasn't kidding about the fireplace or the hot dogs.

Just before they reached his vehicle, he glanced down at Carrie's face, probably his first good look since he'd found her. His jaw dropped a bit. "You're just a kid," he said. "Why did your parents let you out on a day like this?"

*Once again the baby of the family gets treated like a baby.* All her life people had been telling her she didn't look old enough to be out of grade school or middle school. Just recently she been aged to the high school level. *"I swear, Carrie Foster, you don't look old enough to even have a full-time job..."*

Well, she did have a job, a very responsible one as an agent with the US Forest Service. And she had a master's degree in natural sciences. And she was an adult! "I'm not a kid," she said. "I'm quite old enough to know better than to drive in this weather, thank you!"

"Knowing and doing are obviously two very different things to you." He deposited her in the roomy passenger seat of what she now recognized as a Chevy Tahoe, similar to the vehicles her coworkers drove in the Service. After this experience, she'd have to seriously consider trading in her cute French car and getting a four-wheel drive of her own.

"I'd put you in the backseat, but it's full of fire logs," he said. "I can help you elevate your leg onto the dashboard."

"No. I'm okay. Just drive."

He went around to the driver's side, got in

and pulled his phone from his pocket. "I've got to make a phone call before we go."

"Okay."

"Duke? It's Keegan. I've got your meds, but I won't be back at the camp for a while. How soon do you need them?"

The camp? Was this guy a survivalist of some kind?

He paused while Duke answered. "No problem. I should be home by then." Another pause. "I'm fine. Just came across a stranded motorist who needs some medical attention. I'm dropping her at the hospital."

Carrie relaxed her shoulders into the seat back. Once she was at the hospital she'd be safe, and the twenty-minute drive with Keegan Breen was better than alerting her father to her problem and enduring his criticism. Besides, there was something comforting about the conversation she'd just heard, and she realized that she was beginning to trust him. Keegan was apparently doing something for a friend. And right now he was her only hope of getting out of a snowbank and getting her leg looked after. It was nice to know he was accustomed to helping people. Although she couldn't get the image of his idea of a "camp" out of her mind.

And getting to the hospital was only the beginning of her problems. What would she do after he dropped her off? She didn't want to call her sisters. Even if she swore them to secrecy about this event, they would ignore her and immediately tell their father, claiming it was for her own good. Everyone just assumed that Carrie needed help, and rules of independence didn't apply to her. Her best bet was to see what the damages were and what the hospital suggested. Then she'd make a decision.

"So, what were you doing driving on a day like this?" His voice brought her back to the present and the throbbing pain in her leg.

"I was hoping to surprise some people today."

He stole a quick glance at her before focusing on the road. "They should be surprised all right. A call from the hospital should knock their socks off."

So true. If the hospital called her family, someone would definitely hop in a car to come get her, which could easily end in another vehicle disaster. And if they even made it safely in this blizzard, she'd never hear the end of it.

"I'm not going to tell them," she said, deciding at that moment that she would handle this situation on her own—somehow.

He stared at her a bit longer, his face serious. "That's your decision, I guess. But you are in somewhat of a mess here."

She shifted on the seat, trying to relieve some pain. There didn't seem to be a comfortable position. "How much longer?"

"About ten minutes I'd say." He stared up at the gray sky. "As long as another flurry doesn't start."

She appraised his face, which seemed perpetually set in a stern profile. Despite his growth of beard, she could tell his features were strong and weathered, as if he'd spent time in the sun and wind. Maybe he was a farmer or a construction worker, something like that—or, there was the image again, a survivalist. She'd heard stories about these rugged, gruff men who lived in compounds. Anyway, she figured he wasn't a businessman driving an old monster vehicle. The gray in his beard indicated that whatever he did, he'd been at it awhile.

His hair was a different story. Once he'd removed his cap, she saw just a sprinkling of gray at his temples where the strands flowed back to a shoulder-length mass of thick, dark brown waves. Good, healthy hair. She brushed her fingers through her fine, baby blond hair with its professionally colored darker tips and realized she envied him for his apparent lucky-from-birth gift.

"What's your name?" he asked suddenly.

Jolted back into awareness, she said, "Carrie. Carrie Foster."

He stuck out his hand, and she briefly grasped it. "I've never heard the name Keegan," she said. "It's Irish, isn't it?"

"Through and through. Mom and Pop and all the grandfolks."

Keegan swung into the parking lot of a building Carrie identified as Trumbly County Medical Center. The lot was nearly empty with snow packed up against car bumpers. He didn't bother with finding a space, instead, stopping at the emergency entrance. He came around to her side and lifted her out of the vehicle.

"I can walk," she said.

"Sure you can, but humor me. I like to flex my muscles once in a while."

Inside, he called for a wheelchair. A nurse brought one immediately, and Keegan gently lowered Carrie into it.

"What have we got?" the nurse asked, tenderly probing the wound on Carrie's head.

"Car accident. Besides the obvious, I suspect a broken leg."

The nurse wheeled Carrie into a smaller room where a staff member asked her a number of questions about medications, the level of her pain. She took Carrie's blood pressure and pulse before someone with a clipboard came in and asked for Carrie's insurance card. Thank goodness she had her purse, and thank goodness the card didn't show her Ohio address. If there was any way to avoid alerting her father about this trouble, she wanted to do it. She and Dr. Martin Foster had had so many arguments over Carrie's health, her asthma, her stubborn resistance to listen to reason about being out in nature for her job, she figured this incident might make her dad chain her to Dancing Falls forever. But seeing her family at Christmas had prompted her to set out in this weather despite facing a certain argument with her dad. She'd thought he'd mellow once he realized she had arrived safely. But now…

"Your vitals are good," the nurse said. "But we're going to do a CT scan of the head and take an X-ray of the leg. Both tests will just take a few minutes." Turning to Keegan, whose presence had become surprisingly comforting to Carrie's peace of mind, she said, "You can wait in the lobby."

For the first time since Carrie had met him, he seemed indecisive. Stay or go? What would he do? He had no obligation to stay, but for some reason, Carrie wanted him to. "It's just a quick X-ray," she said. "I'd appreciate it if you'd wait."

He shrugged. "Sure. I can wait as long as it doesn't take too long."

A half hour later, Carrie was wheeled into an emergency cubicle. A nurse went to get Keegan, and they were told the doctor would be in shortly with the test results.

When the doctor arrived, he stood next to Carrie. "Well, young lady, you were lucky this time. This could have been much worse. As long as I've lived in the snowbelt, I've seen foolish people try to drive in our crazy weather and come in here with all sorts of…"

"Doctor, I know I shouldn't have been driving," Carrie said, trying not to resent the doctor's parental tone. "What did the X-ray of my leg show?"

"You have a simple fracture. We're going to put a soft cast and a boot on it. Should be okay in a month or so."

"A month? I can drive, can't I?" Carrie asked.

"Drive? Heavens, no. You fractured your right leg. You won't be driving until you can do it without a cast or boot. Unless you want to get in another accident and maybe take someone else out with you this time."

She was going to be stuck here for a month? Where would she stay? Would she have to call her father after all? Could she expect someone from her crew in Michigan to come after her? They were operating on limited man power through the holidays.

"You can come into my office in a week, and I'll x-ray your leg again," the doctor said, handing her a business card. "Right now a nurse will bandage your head and apply the cast. You do have a slight concussion, which means someone will have to watch you through the night." He focused on Keegan. "You can do that?"

His eyes widened. "Me? I don't know…"

"Yes, he can," Carrie said. "I'll be fine."

"You can't leave the hospital without a responsible party to drive you home and take care of you." He stared at Keegan. "You're a relative?"

Keegan started to speak, but Carrie interrupted. "Yes, yes, he is. This man is my husband."

# CHAPTER TWO

"Why in the name of everything that makes any sense at all did you tell that doctor I am your husband?"

Thank goodness Keegan had kept quiet while the nurse bandaged Carrie's head and provided her with pain meds to get her through the next few days. Now, as they were leaving the hospital parking lot, Keegan's patience had obviously reached its limits.

"I certainly couldn't monitor my concussion symptoms by myself, now could I? I needed a husband at that moment, and you were the only candidate." She waited for him to say something. He merely continued seething. "I could have said you are my father. Would that have made you happier?"

"What you could have said is that I'm nobody to you, that I don't even know you. You could have avoided a blatant lie somehow."

"And what would that have done for me? They weren't going to let me leave the hospital. And even if they did, I would have been on my own in a town I don't know, in a snowstorm, without a car, with a broken leg and again…a concussion…"

"You're darn lucky the doctor didn't ask my name. He'd have noticed that our last names are not the same."

"I thought of that," she said. "I had an answer ready."

He shook his head. "I'm sure you did. I'm starting to feel like you rammed your car into a pole, and I'm the one dealing with the consequences."

"Don't you think you're being a bit dramatic? Besides, you can hardly say that you don't know me. We've been together for—" she glanced at her watch "—almost four hours now. I feel like I know you as well as I know most…" She couldn't come up with a word.

"Strangers?"

"We're not strangers. You saved my life."

"I wouldn't go that far. And anyway, if I had it to do over again…"

"You're saying you wouldn't help me

again? For heaven's sake, Keegan, I could have frozen to death."

He didn't say anything. Maybe he was thinking that was a very real possibility.

"If it makes you feel any better, I would do the same for you."

He gave her a skeptical look. "You'd pull me from a wrecked car, take me to a hospital in a blinding snowstorm and sit with me for three hours?"

"Of course. I don't know about getting you out of the car, but the rest I would do." She leaned forward, grateful that the pain injection had started working, and it no longer hurt to move. She could clearly see into Keegan's face. "I hate to suggest this and give you any ideas, but unless you come up with a place to dump me, I'd say you're more or less stuck with me for tonight at least."

"I'd say you put it just about right."

"I could go to a motel, but I need someone to watch me. Do you have family, a wife, perhaps? She could check on me."

"I don't have a wife. I live alone, which makes this whole situation even worse."

She might have preferred hearing that a motherly Mrs. Breen would be present, but she'd make this work. For some reason she was no longer afraid of this man. She didn't suspect an ulterior motive in his begrudging acceptance of her overnight stay. If anything, she figured he'd just continue to brood and finally ignore her. "It's one night, Keegan," she said. "Tomorrow I'll call a tow truck and have my car brought to your house, and I'll be on my way back to Michigan."

He gaped at her. "Are you so drugged up you can't remember what the doctor said? You can't drive for a month."

She waved her hand dismissively. "Oh, I don't think that's true. He was being overly cautious. I can manage."

"Carrie..." This was the first time she could recall him using her name. "You weren't able to manage an automobile with both your legs working!"

"Look, just let me stay with you tonight. Tomorrow we'll work something out." His silence was deafening, so she took a different approach, one she didn't really believe. "I'm taking more of a chance than you are," she added. "I'm a defenseless female. You could obviously do whatever..."

He held up his hand. "Stop right there. Do you actually think I'd touch a girl that doesn't look more than about seventeen years of age…?"

"I'm thirty! I'll show you my driver's license."

He took a moment to let her pronouncement sink in. "Okay, maybe you are, but what if you suddenly go all wonky on me and call the police? How will it look, you, incapacitated, and me in a cabin alone together?"

"First of all, don't give me any reason to call the police, and second, you'll look like what you are, a Good Samaritan whose only crime is helping a needy traveler." She grinned, hoping he saw it that way. "Why, it's practically biblical in moral righteousness."

He didn't seem convinced, but at least he kept driving toward whatever mysterious place he lived.

*How DID I end up in a mess like this?* Keegan kept going toward the campground where he inhabited a cabin that seemed to grow smaller by the mile. What choice did he have? Carrie was right. She couldn't stay alone with a concussion. He'd seen enough battle injuries of that type to know that concussions could be serious. But she'd flat out lied telling the doctor he was her husband. Recalling his shock, he almost smiled now. If she only knew. Keegan Breen was not husband material. He'd tried it once. He'd failed. Right now he wasn't even confident that he should be lifesaver material.

But he could get through one night. He'd let her bunk in his bed with her leg elevated and the pain pills taking her to Neverland. He'd sit up in a chair and watch her, and then this would all be over. Tomorrow they could get her car towed, and then maybe she'd call someone to come drive it for her.

Yes, the perfect solution. He would only be inconvenienced for a few hours. Feeling confident with a plan, he looked over at her. "So, you have family?"

"Of course."

"Someone who could come and drive your car for you?"

She gave him a sideways glance. "I'm a good driver, you know."

"Hmm…" He pointed to a mound of white

in the road ahead. "Your car, exactly where you left it."

She stared at the lump of frosty carnage. "Oh, my poor car. But that could have happened to anyone," she argued. "It was a terrible storm."

"I don't drive a tin can, so it didn't happen to me," he said smartly. "And aren't you glad?"

"I was reaching for my inhaler," she said.

"Why do you have an inhaler? Do you have asthma?"

She didn't answer but nodded her head slightly.

Oh, great. Another wrinkle to add to his list of nursing duties. *Stay on topic, Breen.* "Now, about those family members…"

"I have two sisters. Each of them would come here to get me. I have one father who would come also." Her voice tensed when she mentioned her father. "And I don't intend to tell any of them about this."

"Why not?"

"My father has issues about my asthma. I won't go into that now, but he would somehow turn this broken leg into an example of how I don't take my asthma seriously. And

I don't want my sisters on the road in these conditions."

"Okay. What about a husband?"

She shook her head. "Just you, and you're only temporary."

"You got that right." He felt obligated to point out the obvious. "Carrie, you can't stay with me indefinitely. I live in a Cracker Jack box. You've got to go somewhere."

"I know I do. Why would I want to stay with you? You obviously don't want me." She paused as if waiting for him to argue the point. When he didn't, she said, "I'll figure it out tomorrow. Right now my head hurts too much to think."

She leaned forward. Her hair fell straight as an arrow around her shoulders. Her thick bangs caught a waft of air from the heater and blew away from her forehead, revealing more of her face. Such a young face, Keegan thought again. She could pass for a teenager. Maybe, just to keep things honest, he would ask to see her driver's license.

Now that he studied her, he could detect some subtle signs of age. She didn't have that rosy glow that healthy teens had. She was pale, but maybe that was due to pain.

There were a few tiny lines around her full mouth and a couple at the corner of her eye. But all in all, it was a cute face, Keegan thought. Darned cute.

*Hold on, Breen*, he said to himself. You're forty-one years old, old enough to be her jaded uncle, so don't let your mind go off-kilter about having a houseguest for one night, especially one with her problems. In fact, who knew how many problems this lady had? Physical ones—those were obvious, but why wouldn't she call someone in her family to rescue her? What was she hiding? He wouldn't put it past her to start telling a whole new series of lies.

He'd noticed the label on her coat. Top of the line. Her gloves were the finest leather. Her boots probably ticked out at a couple hundred bucks. And he didn't know much about hair color, but it couldn't be cheap to keep that two-tone look fresh. It was like she didn't know if she wanted to be a blonde or not.

Maybe she was a rich brat, though she didn't seem like it. Yes, she was opinionated, pragmatic to a fault and way too bold for his tastes, but overall he'd peg her as level-headed even though she wasn't quite realistic enough about her current predicament. And she was brave. She was staying with an older, unshaven guy who could... Well, she was lucky in that regard. He hadn't lost all direction in his moral compass.

And she was *cute*. There was that word again, one that hadn't been evident in his personal vocabulary in a long time.

"How much longer?" Her voice jerked him back from private thoughts.

"For someone who's not going anywhere, you sure are concerned with miles. But you're in luck. See that sign up ahead?"

She squinted into the darkening dusk and light misting of snow. "Yes, I see it."

"Home, sweet home." He turned on his blinker and slowed.

She placed the flat of her hand on the car window and said, "You live in a campground? Wow. How interesting."

He grunted a response before saying, "You think that's cool or something?"

"Not cool I guess, but you certainly are close to nature, and that can never be bad. I don't understand how you could live in nature and still be so grumpy."

He ignored the grumpy remark. "Believe me, I've lived—and slept—in nature much more than I care to remember. And I only leave the sign up here by the road so people can find where I live. This isn't a working campground. No one has stopped here for at least fifteen years."

"You did, obviously. You live here."

He pulled around a circular path to stop in front of a log-sided building which appeared as a hulking shadow in the darkness. The Cracker Jack box, she assumed. "I own this property. My grandfather left it to me a year ago. I still don't know if it was a test of my endurance or a joke."

She couldn't see much of the surrounding land. Nightfall had reduced the landscape to vague images of a smattering of trees, a few concrete pads mostly covered in snow. "You certainly aren't very grateful," she said.

"I will be, come spring, when Cedar Woods becomes only a bad memory in my rearview mirror."

She wondered what he meant. This had to be a prime piece of property. As far as she could determine, Lake Erie was still just across the road, and there were no buildings to obstruct the view. Since the massive cleanup of the lake several years ago, this property had to be a potential paradise.

Keegan's phone rang. "Hello, Duke. Yeah, I'm back." He paused. "I can bring your medication over in a few minutes." He nodded. "Okay, if you think you can make it over here on your walker. The fresh air will do you some good."

He disconnected and turned to Carrie. "Hang on a sec. I've got to switch on the outside lights so we both don't end up flat on our butts on an ice patch."

He did more than that. He flipped on a bright light and brought a snow shovel from behind the structure. In a few minutes he had a clear path from the cabin to the Chevy. Carrie had never shoveled snow. Her father had a service, a nice middle-aged guy who came out with his plow to lay salt and do the driveways at the first sign of snow. And the US Forest Service always maintained the roads for its employees.

She watched Keegan's movements—sure, strong and practiced. She didn't doubt he could shovel his way to the main road if he had to.

Keegan left the shovel against the house and came to the Chevy and opened her door. Spreading his arms, he said, "Let's go, princess. Your humble servant awaits."

His condescending way of speaking to her prickled. She'd been called "princess" many times in the past, often from males who were suffering from what they called her cold shoulder. And sometimes from folks who referred to her as the favored third daughter of Martin and Maggie Foster. She hadn't liked the reference then, and she liked it even less now. In truth, the Martins loved all their daughters equally, never showing favoritism of one over the others. Despite his problems with her lifestyle, Martin was a wonderful father, and Maggie once was a caring and loving mother. Unfortunately her advanced Alzheimer's disease had robbed her of the ability to even communicate with her children now.

"Don't call me that," she said to Keegan. "I'm not a princess. I spend most of my time outdoors, where I'm a hard worker. I know what it's like to have dirt under my finger-nails."

"Sorry." He almost looked appropriately chastised. "It's just a logical assumption. I mean you're wearing a three-hundred-dollar coat and designer boots…"

"That means nothing. You own a piece of lakefront property and this castle made of logs, and I certainly wouldn't make the mistake of calling you Prince Charming."

He smiled, showing nice white teeth below the scrub of moustache on his upper lip. "You're right," he said. "I'll try to be more careful with the princess references."

He scooped her into his arms and began carrying her to the cabin. "I'll come back for the crutches they gave you."

"Good. I'm sure I'll get used to them quickly."

"Oh, yeah. They're a piece of cake. You ought to be running a marathon any day now."

"You don't have to be sarcastic, and you don't have to treat me like a baby." Truthfully, she hadn't felt so secure in a long time. Keegan had strong arms, a comfy broad chest and a sure step. What more could a princess want?

A cackle of laughter permeated the quiet air. It was followed by the raspy voice of an elderly man. "Hey, Keegan, what you got there? I sent you in for a couple of pills and you come back with a woman. When I send you to have my oxygen tank refilled, you'll probably come back married!"

Keegan stopped, his hand on the doorknob, and whispered close to Carrie's ear. "Do *not* tell this man that I'm your husband."

"I wouldn't dream of it. I only did that so I could get out of the hospital."

"Hello, Duke," Keegan said. "You going to make it?"

Carrie tried to see the visitor over Keegan's shoulder, but either Keegan was too tall or the man was too short. His voice and a soft metallic squeak of the walker indicated that he was closer. "Yeah, just a few more feet to go."

Keegan took Carrie inside and deposited her on a large comfortable sofa. "I'll be right back," he said, "just as soon as I get Duke his pills and fetch your crutches. You know what they say, a caretaker's work is never done."

She thought he might have smiled at her, but if so, he turned away quickly, pulled up his collar and went back into the cold.

Thirty minutes later Carrie had mastered the crutches well enough to make it to a small but tidy bathroom and back to the sofa again. The doctor had told her to use the sticks for a short time and then rely on the walking boot. The transition couldn't come fast enough. Walking with crutches wasn't for sissies, and neither was going over eight hours without a meal.

As if reading her mind, Keegan said, "We should eat. What do you want?"

What was he going to do, show her a menu? How much food could he have in this place? She decided to make it simple. "I usually have grilled cheese and tomato soup when I'm not feeling well."

"I can manage that." He headed to the kitchen and began opening cupboard doors. "One Christmas dinner coming up."

Oh, yikes! Christmas! Carrie had left all the presents in her car. And she'd promised to call her family. She dug her cell phone out of her purse, settled into the sofa cushions to muffle her voice in Keegan's small living room, and dialed her father's number. She had to be careful with her words so her father wouldn't conclude that she was having a problem or that she'd disobeyed his very strict orders. Thank goodness her young nephew, Wesley, answered the phone. Carrie adored the six-year-old.

"Hey, Aunt Carrie, this is the best Christmas ever, except you're not here."

"I know, sweetie. I miss everyone so much."

They talked about his gifts and the giant tree that her sister Jude's friend had brought them. Jude had been furious at first when Liam Manning had carried the tree into her small apartment above the barn at Dancing Falls, but she'd quickly adapted to the Christmas spirit once she realized that she was crazy about the man who'd brought her the tree.

Wesley passed the phone around and Carrie spoke to everyone. Her sister Jude seemed so much more cheerful than usual. And her sister Alexis's newlywed status made her positively euphoric. Last, Carrie spoke to her niece, Lizzie, and then her father. Their conversation was especially brief, and she ended it with asking her dad to give her mother a kiss for her.

When she finally hung up without telling her family any of the events of her day, Carrie realized she truly did miss them all. But she wasn't about to make her misfortune a reason for her sisters or father to start out on icy roads, or for her father to keep her at Dancing Falls forever.

"Everybody okay?"

Keegan's voice cut through her melancholy. "Who? What do you mean?"

"Whoever you were talking to. I hope he had a nice Christmas."

"If you mean my first-grade nephew, then, yes, he did."

Keegan set a tray with two meals on an ottoman, and handed Carrie a napkin, a glass of water and a pain pill.

"This looks wonderful," she said, breathing in the scent of melted cheese and warm tomatoes. She took the pill, and ate a few bites before saying, "Thanks for this, Keegan. And don't worry about the sleeping arrangements. I'll be fine on this sofa."

"You'll take the bed tonight," he said matter-of-factly. "Can't have you thrashing about on the sofa and maybe falling off."

"What will you do?"

"I'll probably just sit up all night and stare at you."

She widened her eyes at him. "Now, that's just creepy."

He pulled a sheet of paper from his pocket. "I know, but that's what these instructions from the hospital say I'm supposed to do. So take up the creepiness factor with the doctor." He picked up his sandwich and the TV remote. "You watch the news?"

"Sure."

They settled back to engage in world events and images of Christmas cheer until Carrie finished her dinner and fell asleep on the couch.

A few hours later, she didn't know how many, she heard someone call her name. "Carrie, Carrie, wake up."

# CHAPTER THREE

"I'M SORRY," a man's voice said. "I didn't mean to startle you."

She tried to erase the fog in her brain by taking deep breaths and sitting up. Unfortunately, nothing in her body seemed to be working. She heard herself moan.

"I figured you'd be sore," the man said. "Usually takes a few hours after an accident for the muscles to tighten up."

The past hours were slowly coming back to her. And the fact that she was in a cabin with a man she'd only just met. "Keegan?"

"Who else did you think it would be?" he said. "Don't try to get up. I'm just checking on you. I'm supposed to wake you through the night."

"I'm a little confused…"

A small lamp burned in the corner of an unfamiliar room. In the dim light, she attempted to acclimate herself to the surroundings. The last she remembered, she'd been watching an orchestra perform at the White House on a huge flat-screen TV. She'd been on the sofa. Now she was definitely in a bed. The room was cool and quiet.

"How did I get here?"

"Not on those crutches."

"You carried me in here?"

He responded with a nod and withdrew a small metal cylinder from his shirt pocket. A flashlight. Carrie realized he'd changed clothes, trading his long-sleeved Henley shirt for a warmer flannel one. Apparently he'd showered, too. A fresh pine scent drifted to her nose. She loved the smell of pine.

"What time is it?" she asked.

"One a.m. I've got to give you a pill and check your pupils."

"What for?"

"I'm not sure." He looked at the paper he'd held earlier. "One might be larger than the other, or they both might be big. Or, hopefully, they both will be normal-sized. I've got to ask you some questions, too."

He pushed a button, turning on the modern LED flashlight. She allowed him to hold up her eyelids and shine the light in her eyes.

"They look okay to me. Do you think you're going to throw up?"

"What? No."

"What's your name?"

She frowned. "We don't really have to do this, do we?" When he simply stared at her, she said, "Carrie."

"Do you remember how you got here to my place?"

"Of course. I'm not confused anymore. My whole body hurts, and I'm tired. Can I go back to sleep now?"

"I'm supposed to ask you when you were born and who the president of the United States is."

"I can put your mind at ease," she said. "I was born thirty years ago, and the president is my boss. You can go because I'm quite fine, really." She moved and pain sliced up her leg. "But not before you give me that pain pill."

He handed her the pill and a glass of water. She pushed herself up in the bed and leaned against a pillow. And noticed that she wasn't wearing her clothes. A soft cotton T-shirt fell loosely around her torso. "This shirt is yours?"

"It is."

"How did I end up wearing it?" she asked. "Tell me you didn't…"

"I did. But don't get your princess panties in a twist." He frowned. "Oops, sorry about the princess thing. You're still wearing the underwear and socks you showed up in. There were blood stains on your sweater. I've washed it and hung it up to dry. You can reswaddle yourself appropriately in the morning."

"I will." She didn't know whether to be embarrassed, angry or grateful. Or resentful of the way Keegan talked about undressing her as if it were an everyday occurrence for him.

He nodded toward the glass. "Drink up. My guess is the pain won't be so bad in the morning, and we can cut down on the dosage."

She did as he instructed. The water was cold and refreshing and felt good going down her throat. "I don't have a fever, do I?"

"I don't think so. I felt your forehead earlier."

He was taking his nursing duties seriously. She noticed a wooden armchair next to the bed. "Have you been sitting there all night?"

"Pretty much."

"That chair looks very uncomfortable."

"It is, but don't get carried away with gratitude. I remembered that you said you'd do the same for me, so I'm just paying it forward. I've got your phone number on speed dial for when I break a bone."

She smiled. There was no way he could know her phone number unless he'd gone through her purse. He didn't seem the sneaky type. Suddenly alert and wanting to talk, she said, "Have you ever had one?"

"One what?"

"Broken bone."

He thought for a moment, a reaction she found strange. Either a person had suffered a broken bone or he hadn't. It wasn't the kind of thing anyone would forget.

"Oddly," he said, "I haven't. Sprains, pulled tendons, a bullet hole, that sort of thing, but no breaks."

She leaned forward. "Bullet hole?"

"Only one. I consider myself lucky, and I think that if they ever take an X-ray of my skeleton, they'll discover that I'm made of titanium."

"What do you do for a living that you get shot and wounded all the time?" She didn't really believe him about the bullet. "Or do these injuries come from jealous boy-friends?"

"Nope. Generally speaking, no one has a reason to be jealous of me. As for my work, it did involve an element of danger. But I don't do anything dangerous now. In any case, we all have a past, don't we? Even you, I bet."

"Sure. I've been bitten by spiders, got a raging case of poison ivy and once I got a giant splinter. But I work in the forest. You didn't tell me what you did before living here."

"Nope, I didn't. I traveled a lot." He took her glass. "Do you need to go to the bathroom?"

"No, I'm okay for now."

"I'm going into the living room, but I'll be back to check on you."

She couldn't help noticing that he'd strategically ignored her question about his occupation. Was it because he was lying about the injuries? Or ashamed of how he'd gotten them?

"Call if you need anything," he said as he shut the door, leaving her alone and wondering.

A few minutes later a smoky odor crept under the bedroom door. Carrie coughed, feeling her lungs constrict. "Keegan, what's that awful smell?"

He opened the door. "A cigar. I have one every so often—mostly after really difficult days—or when I have unexpected company."

"You can't do that when I'm in the house. I have asthma."

"You're allergic to cigar smoke?"

"Among other things, but especially cigar smoke."

He expelled a long breath obviously meant to convey his extreme self-sacrifice. "Fine, I'll put it out. If anything else bothers you, I'm sure you'll tell me."

She smiled and snuggled into her pillow. She didn't believe he was half as tough as he wanted people to think, especially when he whispered, "Merry Christmas."

MONDAY MORNING, DECEMBER 26, Dr. Martin Foster's family and home had pretty much returned to normal. His housekeeper, Rosie, had agreed to watch Wesley while his mom, Jude, went to the hospital to see the man she would soon marry. Alexis, her husband and her daughter had gone home to Columbus. Presents that hadn't already been worn or played with were displayed neatly under the tree. The leftovers from a big meal were stored in the refrigerator for Monday night's supper. And everyone agreed that it had been a nearly perfect holiday but would have been better if the Fosters' youngest daughter, Carrie, had been home.

Dr. Foster's breakfast was interrupted by a knock on the front door. He went to answer and was delighted to see Aurora, who owned Aurora's Attic Bed and Breakfast, his immediate neighbor and Fox Creek's newest enterprise.

Martin wiped a few toast crumbs from his chin as he opened the door. "Why don't I just give you a key, Aurora?" he said. "It's not like you aren't as much a member of the family as the girls are."

Dressed in her typical attire of jeans and a flannel blouse, she breezed by him carrying a white box. "Well, I'm *not* a member of your family, Marty, and to come in without knocking would just be rude, at least the way I was raised." She smiled at him. "Besides, you can use the exercise that walking from the dining table to the front door gives you."

He patted his stomach and thought about putting in an hour at the hospital gym later. At sixty-five, he was in great shape, but his own personal stuffing had settled around his waist since yesterday's dinner with all the trimmings. He didn't know how Aurora maintained her wiry, thin figure, especially when he smelled the contents of the box she was carrying. She must not eat her own cooking.

"Are those cinnamon rolls, or are you just trying to break my heart?" he asked her.

"They are cinnamon rolls," she said, handing him the box. "I thought there might be enough family left to enjoy them this morning."

"Oh, there is," he teased. "Wesley and I will polish these off in no time, and Jude will be back from the hospital soon." He started toward the kitchen. "I've got a few minutes. Come on in and have a cup of coffee."

They sat at the kitchen table where Martin enjoyed a still-warm-from-the-oven roll.

"Did you hear from your son last night?" he asked Aurora.

She shook her head. "I didn't expect to. After he stole that money from me and took off, I figured I wouldn't hear from William until he'd been arrested or—" her eyes clouded over "—worse."

Martin wished there was something he could do to make Aurora's situation with her son easier. She'd taken him in a few weeks ago when he'd gotten out of rehab, but the thirty-year-old had disappointed her again by taking cash and jewelry from her bedroom dresser. At least Aurora had convinced Martin that she'd come to terms with the kind of person William was, and she no longer held out hope that her baby boy would change.

He patted Aurora's hand. "But yesterday was Christmas. I just thought…"

She gave him an aching sort of smile. "I doubt William even knew it was a holiday. Besides, I had your family to celebrate with. It was a wonderful Christmas with Alex and Lizzie, and Jude falling in love."

"Yes, it was, but Carrie should have been here. I don't know what I'm going to do about that one, Aurora. I want her home where I can take care of her. It's almost like she resents having a doctor in the family."

"I know how you feel, Marty, but Carrie doesn't want to be taken care of."

"She thinks she's invincible, but I've seen her during those times when the asthma attacks severely limited her breathing. Her mother and I watched her carefully her whole life when she played or did chores, or, God forbid, even got near an animal or ragweed. And what does she do? Studies natural sciences and forestry in college and takes a job with the Forest Service where asthma triggers abound."

Aurora smiled, which always worked to take the sting out of her words. "Marty, you say that as though her decision was her way of rebelling against so much parental interference."

"I've thought about it. You know kids."

"I'm not saying there couldn't be an element of truth to your theory, but from what the girls tell me, Carrie truly loves trees and wants to care for the environment."

"I suppose. But what she chose to do with her life defies all logic. If she should forget to take her pills, or can't find her inhaler in an emergency…" He ran his fingers through his thick gray hair. "I'm surprised I haven't lost every hair on my head worrying about that girl. Maggie and I thought she'd eventually outgrow some of her allergies, but they've only gotten worse, and Carrie has only gotten more stubborn."

Aurora took a sip of coffee. "I'm sorry you worry so much about her, Marty."

He smiled. Of all the people he knew, perhaps Aurora was the one who most understood. "One of these days, if I can pin Carrie down long enough, I'm going to make her do the sensible thing and stay here with me full-time."

Aurora looked at him a few moments. "Oh, that should work well," she said.

He chuckled. "I can dream about it at least…"

"Dr. Foster?"

Recognizing the voice of Maggie's nurse, Martin stood and rushed to the bottom of the stairs. "What is it, Rebecca?"

"Maggie is refusing her food. She's okay for now, but I thought you might want to come up and have a look."

Martin turned and nearly ran into Aurora who had followed him from the kitchen. She nudged him forward. "Go. I'll see myself out."

He gave her shoulder a little squeeze as a goodbye and headed for the stairs. His life was caught in this awful middle ground. He was committed to the woman upstairs whom he loved beyond reason, and yet he had some strong feelings for the elfish, red-haired sprite of a woman he'd just watched leave. Aurora had come into his life as if she'd been sent to become a rudder for the difficult years he was having now.

And there was no denying the truth any longer. He cared deeply for her.

Less than a minute later, Martin sat at Maggie's bedside. He took her hand and looked into her eyes, though her gaze was focused, as usual, on an indeterminate spot on the ceiling. "What's this I hear, Maggie Mine? You don't like your breakfast this morning?"

His wife looked pale, but otherwise she seemed as she did every morning, caught in the vacuum of her mind, a condition from which there was no escape. Alzheimer's disease left struggling family members with far more questions than answers, like why did the heart keep beating strong when the mind seemed to have shut out every sound, sight, touch? It wasn't fair, and to a healing man of science like Martin, it was fate's dirty trick.

Martin pressed a spoon to Maggie's lips. "It's tea, darling, just the way you like it." Her mouth twitched, but it was more an effort to keep the liquid from going in than a desire to taste it. Martin set the spoon on the nightstand. "That's all right. You're just not hungry. We'll try later."

Martin checked his watch. He was due at the hospital in forty-five minutes, and yesterday's snow would make driving difficult. "I have to go, Maggie, but I'm planning to call Carrie in Michigan later today. I told you we all talked to her last night, and she seemed fine, but, I don't know, I just feel that something's not right."

He fluffed Maggie's pillow. "I'm sure it's nothing to worry about. What do I know about intuition anyway? It's just that, of all our daughters, she is the one most removed from us and the one who most keeps me awake at night. Jude is barely a half mile away in the barn. Alex is a mere three-hour drive away in Columbus. But Carrie, she travels the country, determined to save the forests while I sit here and fret."

He bent and kissed his wife's forehead. "I can well imagine what you would say to me, Maggie darling, what common sense advice you would give me. But I can't change who I am any more than you can change who you are." He smoothed a hand over her forehead. "It's up to me now, to worry for both of us. And I'm doing a bang-up job of it."

CARRIE OPENED HER eyes to a dull throbbing in her head. The room was still mostly dark, but it was morning. She could see sunlight streaming around the heavy window shades. A digital clock next to the bed read eight thirty. Surely she could take another pain pill now.

She sat up and carefully moved her booted leg to the edge of the mattress. The crutches were against the wall within her reach, so she stood on one leg, tucked the aluminum torture sticks under her arms and headed out the door, aware that the T-shirt she wore barely covered her fanny. Well, no time for modesty now. She had to use the bathroom.

When she had accomplished that task, including rubbing a bit of Keegan's toothpaste over her teeth, she went into the living room. A fire still burned in the fireplace, turning the chill of the bedroom into a cozy warmth. She next needed to see to another necessity—food. She was starving.

She poured coffee into a mug left on the counter, and, fearful of spilling it while trying to reach a chair with her crutches, she stood against the counter and took a long, welcome sip. And wondered where Keegan was.

The question was answered promptly. The front door opened. A man's heavy steps pounded the porch, an obvious attempt to rid his boots of snow. And then Keegan appeared with her suitcase in his hand.

"Good morning," he said, whipping off his ball cap and shaking snow from the brim. "I thought I'd be back before you woke up."

She blinked. "You have my bag."

"I do. I remembered that we hadn't locked the car yesterday, so I went to see if I could get your things. Luckily the bag was in that small area behind the seats."

"What about all the presents? Were they still there?"

"Yes, I think so. Did you want me to bring them here?"

"No. They'll be all right. You locked the car?"

"I did."

"Thank you. I can't wait to put on clean clothes." She cringed before asking the next question. "How did the car look?"

"Still mostly like a pile of snow."

"Great."

"I scraped some of it off so the tow truck can at least find the vehicle."

"Have you called anyone yet?" Considering that it was Monday, and Christmas was officially over, businesses should be operating as normal.

"No. We're going to have to get someone from Sandusky where the hospital is located. That's the closest town. I don't want to make decisions for you. It's only right that you talk to them and get the charges first."

She recalled the salesman's words when she bought the car. "It won't be easy to get repairs," he'd said. "But that's true for all foreign makes."

And then there'd been her father's warning. "Don't buy that car, honey. It offers no protection. Get something sturdy and solid instead."

As usual she hadn't listened. She had to have the adorable thing. "Like it matters what the charges are," she said to Keegan. "I have to pay it." She drank more coffee, relieved that the headache had abated some and she was beginning to feel more like herself.

Keegan took a skillet from under the stove and set it on a burner. "One thing though, Carrie... If the car won't start, there really isn't any reason to have it towed here to the campground. It should go back to the shop where it can be serviced. I use a guy named Grady. He knows engines and all the diagnostic tests they use on cars these days, and his prices are fair."

"Does he know foreign cars?"

"I'm sure he does, though models like yours are a rarity around here."

"I'll call him." Carrie stared longingly at the skillet. "What are you planning to do with that?"

He removed a tub of butter from his refrigerator. "After I get you settled in a chair, I plan to make bacon and eggs. If you behave yourself and put your leg up, I just might share."

She could almost taste what she imagined would be the best meal of her life. "Keegan?"

He peeled a few slices of bacon and dropped them into the skillet. "Yeah?"

"After breakfast I'd really like to have a shower."

"Sure. If you think you can manage."

She smiled as innocently as her mischievous sense of humor allowed. "I thought you'd help me."

# CHAPTER FOUR

HE ALMOST DROPPED the spatula he was using to flip the bacon. Without looking at Carrie, he said, "You want me to help you take a shower?"

Her laughter was infectious and at the same time intimidating. "Not in the way you're thinking."

He grunted under his breath. "Take it from someone who knows a bit about words, little girl. You should watch what you say to avoid finding yourself in a heap of trouble."

"Quit calling me little girl and princess and all those other demeaning names."

He scrambled three eggs. "Sorry. You're right."

"Why do you know so much about words? Do you do crossword puzzles?"

"Never. My interest goes beyond knowing what *q* words don't have a *u* following them."

"So, you're a writer?"

"I write a bit." She was curious this morning, and he was just as determined to keep his anonymity. Once a person realized who he was, who he had been, the questions began, and so did the reliving. Unless he was writing, Keegan had no interest in remembering his past.

She shrugged, accepting his succinct answers. "About the shower, I meant what I said. I certainly need help. You can get me into the bathroom, turn on the water, lay out some clean clothes and then leave. Oh, and maybe put a plastic bag over this soft cast."

He turned the bacon once more. Concentrating on cooking was not as simple as it had been a minute ago. Maybe he'd allowed his mind to wander to inappropriate places. "I can do that," he said.

He brought a plate to the table and escorted her to a chair. "Toast is coming up."

"This looks great." She took the paper towel he'd left by her place mat and settled it on her lap. "Where did you learn to cook?"

"You call this cooking? I call it survival training. Some of the places I lived, I'd have to prepare a meal and eat it before the insects could carry it off the plate."

"You make it sound like you lived somewhere in the outback."

*Close. Though the outback would have been easier.* He went to get her toast, and brought his plate to the table. He took the only other chair available and sat across from her. The third chair, the one his grandmother and grandfather had used when he visited, was still sitting by Carrie's bed. She looked refreshed this morning, like maybe the pain had subsided and she could make a decision about her immediate future. But the bandage on her swollen forehead was surrounded by a sickening purplish color which he knew must be tender to the touch.

"How are you feeling?" he asked after they'd both consumed most of their breakfasts.

"Pretty good. I slept well, but that's because I had the bed. Tonight we'll switch. I don't want to take up your bed when you need it. I'll be fine on the couch."

*Tonight?* He stared at the top of her head. Had that been a slip of the tongue or was she planning to stay another night? And another? He thought she'd be gone by this afternoon. Well, okay. He could deal with one more night if he had to. Heaven knew, he'd dealt with worse situations than this. But what did she think would change after the second night? She'd suddenly be cured?

After breakfast he helped her into the bathroom, lowered her to the closed toilet lid and set out a washcloth and towel. He then brought a large black plastic bag which he used to wrap her leg from her foot to her knee and secured it with duct tape. "That should work."

"Where did you put my bag?"

"In the bedroom."

"Okay. Would you pick out some clean clothes for me? My shampoo and conditioner is in a zippered case on the right side of the suitcase."

"What clothes do you want?"

"I don't care. Anything is fine."

"Be right back." He went into the bedroom, transferred the suitcase to the bed and opened it. A pleasant scent wafted up to his nostrils, and he resisted the urge to see where the floral fragrance originated. *Not your business, Breen*, he told himself.

He picked out a pair of sweatpants, a shirt and some underwear, and went back to the bathroom.

Carrie gave him a strange, almost critical glare when she saw his choices.

"You told me to pick something," he said. "Do you have a problem with this stuff?"

"Not with the sweatpants. The boot will fit around the ankle with no problem, but…" She held up a jersey knit shirt that had been embellished with silver beads. She'd brought it along in case her family wanted to go out to dinner. "Are we going someplace fancy tonight?"

"Which is why I asked what you wanted," he said. "I just grabbed the first things I saw."

"I understand. Just bring me a simple T-shirt. They are rolled up at the bottom of the case."

He reached for a small bundle, held it up and wished he hadn't. "Your underwear?" The miniscule thing hardly seemed to fit its description. Keegan was not comfortable around lace, especially when there was such a small amount of it connecting two triangles of nylon.

"Well, yes, but I wear that when I want to achieve the three *f*'s."

"Which are?"

"Feminine, fancy and fun. I don't think this situation applies."

Darned right. Keegan would have felt better holding up a cotton brief he could have used as the jib sail on his boat. "I'll put it back."

"Never mind. It will do." She waved her hand to dismiss him. "If you'll just bring another shirt, I'll manage."

He set the bottles of shampoo and conditioner in the shower, brought a different shirt for her and left. As he picked up the breakfast dishes, all he could think about were those tantalizing scraps of lace.

She came out of the bathroom a short while later wearing the sweatpants and the green T-shirt which said Save a Tree, I Value My Job. Keegan smiled at the shirt. "I guess you really are a tree hugger."

"I like things that grow and bloom and change with the seasons. Always have. I guess I believe that if people are close to nature, they can change, too."

"Is there a human person in your life you love as much as you love trees?"

"A few," she said. "But overall, I find it much easier and more comfortable to cultivate relationships with nature, *cultivate* being the definitive word. Trees adapt to their environment. Too many people don't even bother trying. They settle into lives of stagnation."

Keegan cringed inside. He'd been basically living a stagnant life for over a year, and he'd been fine with it. He wondered how her job choice fit in with her illness. Keegan didn't know a whole lot about asthma, but he did know it was not curable. Once you had asthma, you had it forever. "So how do you manage your asthma out in the wilderness?" he asked her.

She sat on the sofa and patted the damp bandage on her forehead. He reminded himself to change the dressing for her.

"With medications and common sense. Asthma can be controlled if a person is aware of their triggers."

"And what are your triggers?"

Her full mouth twisted in a frown of acceptance. "Almost everything. I have allergic asthma along with the standard one-size-fits-all variety. But I medicate every day and always keep a bronchial dilator handy for emergencies. And just so you know, I don't live in the wilderness. I work in urban reforestation. There's a big difference. The most remote areas I get to are acreage around lakes, public parks, that sort of thing."

"And exactly how does a person reforest an urban area, with tree houses?" He thought he'd made quite the clever joke. At least she smiled. Oddly, he was truly interested in her answer. But he'd always been a fanatic about learning what he didn't know.

"By choosing the right trees for a particular area. Just because a property is urban doesn't mean it can't use trees for beautification. We call them 'working trees.' Some we plant for shade, some for soil improvement, some to prevent erosion… The list goes on."

"So your job is not just a matter of 'there's a good spot for a tree?'"

"Hardly. For instance, if I were to reforest this patch of ground you live on…"

"Hold on," he said. "This property is as is and where is. I suppose there are a few dead trees and shrubs, but for what I have planned, it doesn't need beautifying." *I'm selling it just like it sits, dead trees and all. It won't matter once a five-story hotel occupies the acreage.*

She frowned at him. "Obviously I wasn't planning to go outside with a shovel and get to work. Do what you want. It's your property. Besides, I haven't even seen it in the daylight. There may have been so much neglect that it would be too costly to regenerate the soil."

Now she was just being contrary or trying to make him feel guilty. *So much neglect?* Granted, no one had taken care of this place in years. But surely it was still salvageable. *Doesn't matter, Breen,* he said to himself. When the hotel is here, when all the tree roots had been removed...

Wanting to change the subject, he put the last of the washed dishes in a cupboard. At that moment a persistent scratching sounded on the cabin front door, followed by a bump and a thump. "I suppose I should warn you about something..."

Before he could explain, the door opened, and a large dog bounded inside, leaving snowy paw prints on the floor. The animal headed straight for Keegan, tongue hanging out and tail twisting with wild enthusiasm.

"...about the dog," he said.

She laughed. "Glad I took my medication this morning. He's beautiful."

"She. Flo is a female Irish setter."

"Is she yours?"

"No. Belongs to Duke, but she likes to split her time between the two of us."

Flo picked that moment to shake vigorously, sending snowflakes fluttering around the cabin.

"I'd love to pet her," Carrie said. "But so not a good idea."

"Yeah, among the triggers you talked about, dog hair must be a biggie."

"Yep, it is. My sister has a dog, but she always keeps Mutt at least a hundred yards away from me."

Keegan took a dog treat from a canister, teased Flo with it a few moments and finally let her win. Then he walked to the open front door and snapped his fingers. "Out now, girl. Go find a chipmunk to chase."

The dog obeyed. If only all females were as cooperative as this Irish setter. He closed the door. "Are you ready to make that phone call to Grady?" he asked Carrie.

"Oh, right. Sure."

"Just remember, even if he gets your car running, you can't drive it. You'll have to get two people to come and get both you and the car."

"So you keep telling me."

He brought her the number, and she dug her cell phone out of her purse. Once she'd made the arrangements to have her vehicle towed, he unpacked the supplies a nurse had given him at the hospital. Ointment, gauze, sterile tape. "Let me put a clean bandage on your forehead."

She sat still, letting him do his clumsy thing. *Good grief, Breen, your hands didn't shake this badly when you were in a war zone with IEDs exploding around you.* But then, embedding with a bunch of military guys was far different from cohabitating with this one delicate female. At least his world, as unexciting as it had been pre-Carrie, would go back to normal once she called in her own personal troops to get her out of here.

As unexciting as it was… Keegan lived

with the reality that his life now was un-
eventful. When he wasn't working on his
book, he watched television news broadcasts.
He still couldn't quite get his fill of news.
Now, since Princess Carrie had plowed into
a snowbank within shouting distance of his
cabin, he felt like he was approaching the
starting gate of a wild roller coaster ride,
which might involve facing feelings again.
There were too many feelings he didn't want
to relive except on a computer screen.

What was it about Carrie that intrigued
him? He didn't want to be intrigued. She
was all smiles and hope and consumed with
nature. Keegan was the exact opposite. And
he was growing accustomed to a low-energy
existence. Yet, he was intrigued. He figured his all-but-forgotten libido would settle down once she headed to wherever home
was. And he could go back to sleeping in his
bed and the nightmares that plagued him
every night. Now if he could just get rid of
that recurring pain…

She lightly touched her forehead where
he'd just applied the bandage.

He occupied his inexperienced hands with

putting away the amateur doctoring equipment. "How does that feel?" he asked.

"Fine. You do good work, doc."

He huffed a disbelieving breath. "Hopefully you won't get gangrene. Want me to help you to the sofa and turn on the TV?"

"Sure. I could watch something, I guess."

He started to help her to her feet when he heard a knock on his door.

"Geez, Breen," she said. "Aren't you a card-carrying hermit?"

He frowned. "I thought so, but it's a bit like Times Square around here this morning." He went to the door and opened it to a rather large woman with a heavy winter coat and a scarf around her frizzy gray hair. She held a basket in her hands.

"Oh, it's you, Delores," he said.

She thrust the basket toward him. "Scones. Just made 'em warm from the oven."

He hesitated. "Take them," she ordered. "I can't eat a dozen scones."

No one could, he thought. But maybe Carrie could help. He glanced at Carrie. Her bright eyes told him that Delores's English accent might have mistakenly indicated that the woman actually knew how to make a good scone. Wait until Carrie tasted one. She'd learn soon enough that accents do not automatically hint at good bakers.

He raised the cloth around the biscuits and pressed on one with his thumb. Yep. Dry and hard as ever. "Thanks, Delores."

She stuck her head inside the cabin, looked around, spied Carrie and said, "Hello there, darling. I heard Keegan had some company."

"That makes you, Duke, Flo and me who know about this arrangement," Keegan said, nodding at Carrie. "This is Carrie. Carrie, Delores. Now all the people that matter know that I have company, and I don't see any reason to tell anyone else."

She narrowed her eyes at him. "Are you implying that I'm a gossip?"

"Ever since you invested in a cell phone," he said.

"Why are you trying to keep this lovely young lady a secret, Keegan? What have you got up your sleeve?"

"Nothing but my arm," he said attempting to close the door and send a clear message. But Delores was too quick for him and had apparently just noticed the walking boot on

Carrie's leg. She was inside and removing her scarf before he could step out of her way.

"Oh, my, you poor dear," she said, casting a disapproving glare at Keegan. "You didn't do this to her, did you?"

His jaw dropped. "You know, Delores, I should start charging you rent. Sometimes your conclusion jumping is just too much!"

Carrie quickly came to his defense. "I had a car accident. Keegan has been a perfect gentleman and a fairly good nurse. In truth, he more or less got stuck with me after pulling me out of a snowbank."

Delores patted Carrie's hand. "Well, that's fine, then. He could use a little company in this place. I live just out back in the yellow unit by the tree line. If you need anything, just open the bedroom window and holler. I'll hear you."

Carrie smiled. "Thanks, but I'll be okay. I'm only here temporarily until my car is fixed."

Now she was staying until her car was fixed? When would that be? A couple of days? A week?

"I'll be on my way, then," Delores said. She rewrapped the scarf and headed for the door. As she left, she called back, "*Ta-ra*, then, see you cozy couple later."

One glance at Carrie's round eyes confirmed that she had heard the comment.

When he'd shut the door on the latest visitor, Keegan set the basket of scones on his table and grumbled. "Neighbors. Never liked 'em. Never will."

Carrie responded as casually as her telltale grin allowed. "Except one you risk your life for to get his medicine. And the other you let live here rent-free."

"They both live here rent-free," he grudgingly admitted. "They sort of came with the property when I moved in."

She nodded slowly. "I see. Then what choice did you have?"

Not much. And when the property sold, he thought, both of those decrepit trailers and their nosy old residents would have to go. And he sure wasn't taking them with him.

THE CLOSEST CARRIE had gotten to fresh air on this first full day of confinement had been when she stuck her head out the kitchen window. Ordinarily she never went a full twenty-four hours without being in the open, communicating with the trees and plants she loved so much. But unwilling to test her walking boot in the snow, she'd had to settle for a deep breath of cold, crisp Ohio winter air from the windowsill. Cold almost didn't describe the outside temperature. Frigid, freezing, approaching zero was more accurate.

Her decision to test the environment had almost caused an asthma reaction. When she felt the first signs of laboring lungs, she quickly drew her head back inside and closed the window. Bitter cold temperatures were not kind to asthma sufferers, which was why Carrie had recently made plans with the US Forest Service to send her for the worst of the winter to Tennessee where the temperatures were fairly moderate. Now, of course, with this broken bone, she might have to reconsider.

So, as darkness settled around the cabin, she thought about her future. If she didn't go to Tennessee on her next assignment, and if she didn't go back to Michigan where temperatures could be almost as severe as Ohio's, what would she do? Swallow her pride and go home to Dancing Falls where her father would pamper her until she felt like a near invalid?

While she was growing up, her father had constantly checked the outside temperatures to determine if his youngest daughter could go out and play. If the thermometer dropped below thirty-five, she was bundled in a snowsuit, mittens and a hat. And still her father watched from a window.

And he wondered now why Carrie had chosen to work in nature and a lifestyle that allowed her to choose for herself when she could go outside. Independence was a wonderful thing, and the Fosters had encouraged all their daughters to be independent, even if their teaching backfired occasionally. The Forest Service had been an understanding employer, allowing Carrie to move assignments according to climate changes. But her father still believed that he, and only he, knew best.

Blocking the low drone of the television, Carrie continued thinking about her father. She loved him dearly. He was sweet, caring and brilliant. His current life was divided between his career and his responsibilities to his ill wife. And yet he still found time to fuss over Carrie. Every phone call, every visit was always punctuated by questions on her health, reminders to take medicine, gentle urges to get her to come home. And she couldn't convince him that she was fully capable of making her own choices and monitoring her health. She didn't even want to think of his reaction to her foolish decision yesterday. Embarking on a five-hour trip in a snowstorm had not been such a good choice, as it turned out.

How different her life would have been if her mother, Maggie, were still the vibrant, funny, sensible woman who'd raised the girls into early adulthood. She would have understood Carrie's need to be herself, her striving for normalcy in the career she'd chosen. She would have balanced Martin Foster's obsessive worry with calm rationality. Maybe their new neighbor, Aurora, who'd become a trusted friend to her father and sisters, could provide the support her father so desperately needed.

Carrie's thoughts were interrupted by the local weather report. She sat up straight on the sofa and hit the volume button on the TV.

"Fairer temperatures, a slow warming trend…lots of sunshine with highs tomorrow in the upper thirties."

Carrie smiled. Practically bathing suit weather in northern Ohio. Tomorrow she could go outside and investigate these seven acres which seemed to not matter to Keegan Breen. The prospect made her almost giddy.

She turned off the television, leaned into the comfortable sofa cushion and closed her eyes. Keegan had been stuck at his computer most of the afternoon, doing what, Carrie didn't have the faintest idea. Now he was in the bedroom with the door partially closed. But she could hear his voice, low, peaceful…almost loving. The mellow timbre of his words vibrated deep inside her in a soothing, comforting way, as if she could listen to that voice all night.

"Sounds like you had a good Christmas," he said. "Did you do anything special to celebrate?" There was a pause after which he said, "No, I don't need to talk to her. The check arrived, I assume." Another pause. "You're welcome. I love you, Taylor."

Keegan uttered a few more words which Carrie couldn't make out. Then she heard him disconnect with a simple, "Take care of yourself." Carrie opened her eyes as he came into the living room rubbing the back of his neck. He suddenly seemed tired.

Carrie sat up. "Everything okay?"

"Sure. Why would you ask?"

"I heard part of your conversation," she said.

"You were listening to my phone call?"

"Not intentionally, but you didn't close the door all the way."

"I thought you were watching TV."

"I turned it off." She waited for him to say something else. He went into the kitchen and started making a pot of coffee. "If you'd like to talk about anything…" She laughed softly. "I am the perfect captive audience."

He turned away from the coffeemaker to stare at her. "Carrie, if you want to know who I was talking to, why don't you just ask?"

"Okay. Who were you talking to?"

"My son. He lives in Seattle. And again I just spent another Christmas away from him."

"That can't be easy."

"It's not, but over the years I've missed

plenty of holidays, and I've got no one to blame but myself." He pressed the button on the coffee brewer. "You want a cup? It's decaf."

"Sure, thanks. And, Keegan…?"

"What?"

"You must be divorced from the boy's mother, right?"

"That's a logical assumption."

"Did she not invite you to spend Christmases with your son? Did she keep him from coming to see you?"

He frowned, and she hoped she hadn't crossed a boundary of privacy. But he seemed like he was having a tough time with missing his son.

"My ex-wife isn't an unreasonable person," he said. "I'm just not Daddy-of-the-year material. Let's leave it at that."

Wow. Keegan's conversation with his son had been short and almost awkward. Yet his voice had been comforting, his tone almost sweet. If she had to guess—and since he wasn't going to say anything else, what other choice did she have—she concluded that he had genuine feelings for his son.

"Okay," she said. "Conversation closed. You take the bed. I'll sleep fine on the sofa."

"Never mind." He took a long sip of coffee and brought a mug to her. "I won't be sleeping much tonight anyway."

# CHAPTER FIVE

KEEGAN'S CELL PHONE rang early the next morning. He answered it right away and spoke in a near whisper, obviously trying to keep from disturbing Carrie in the bedroom. His voice was alert, as if he'd been awake a long time, or perhaps, as he'd said, hadn't slept much at all.

"Oh, hello, Grady," he said. "No, she's not up yet, and I don't want to disturb her."

"It's all right," Carrie called out. "I'm awake." She glanced at the bedroom clock. Eight o'clock. Sunlight streamed through the window blinds promising a beautiful day, just what she'd hoped for.

Keegan's head appeared in the opening of the bedroom door. "Can I come in?"

"Of course."

He entered the room, and she sat up against the pillows. She pulled a comforter over her sleeveless nightgown and placed her arms over the top, wrapping herself in a modest cocoon. The only times she had been this underdressed with a man had not turned out well for her. She lightly clasped the amethyst amulet she always wore around her neck, appreciating its smooth familiarity.

Keegan smiled while his gaze grew more intense. "Warm enough?" he said.

She brushed bangs from her eyes and tucked a strand of hair behind her ear. "I'm good. That's the car mechanic on the phone, isn't it?"

"Yep. Hold on. I'll put him on speaker." Keegan pressed the appropriate button. "Go on, Grady. Carrie's listening."

"We've got a problem," the mechanic said. "I checked the car out thoroughly yesterday but couldn't figure out why it wouldn't start. Finally found the problem. The impact destroyed the steering box."

Carrie leaned forward in the bed. "That sounds bad."

"It's not good," Grady said. "Without a steering box, you can't...well, I guess it's obvious. Unfortunately this is not a universal gizmo. I've had to contact the foreign automaker and order a replacement. Once it gets here, I don't know how long it will take me to get the car running again. I've never exchanged this particular part before."

"I see." Carrie stared at Keegan, trying to judge his patience barometer. Was this news already ruining his day? She'd taken a week off from her job, so she wouldn't be expected back in Michigan until after the coming weekend. But that might be too long for Keegan to put up with her.

"When can we expect the part to arrive?" she asked.

"Depends how far they have to look to find one. Apparently these things never break down."

"But mine did," she said.

"Yes, yours did. Plus we're still in the midst of holiday season. Car-part places may be closed or at least working with partial staff, the mail might be slow. Worst-case scenario, we might have to order one from France. Still, I can't imagine not having you on the road by the end of the week."

A nice prediction, but Grady didn't know that she wasn't supposed to drive with a broken leg. Keegan was obviously thinking about that diagnosis. Why else would he be frowning? Maybe he was thinking that since the roads were better today, she had no reason not to call her family—no reason that he knew anyway.

Today was only Tuesday. Maybe, by some miracle, her leg would heal well enough for her to drive. She believed she could handle a car using the foot with the walking boot attached. But apparently she wouldn't have a chance to try until week's end. She was content to stay in the cabin until Friday or Saturday at least and then determine her course of action. Drive or not drive? She stared at Keegan again. The frown was gone, but she feared he might be doing a mental ten count.

"Do what you have to do," she instructed. "I can give you a credit card number if it will help."

"No need. I'll order the part and try to put a rush on the shipping. If you're a friend of Keegan's, I'm sure you're good for it."

*A friend of Keegan's?* Was she, or was she fast becoming his worst nightmare?

"Thanks, Grady," Keegan said. He disconnected, slipped the phone in the pocket of his flannel shirt. She thought he would have a comment on what Grady had said, but instead, he asked, "Are you hungry yet?"

"I could eat. Actually, maybe I could even cook breakfast for both of us today. I don't like to be waited on." She was willing to do anything that might make her appear less of a burden.

He took a step closer to the bed. She instinctively tightened her arms over the comforter. He smiled. "Let me fix breakfast this time," he said. "Maybe tomorrow you can do it."

"That's very nice of you." How formal! She sounded like she was talking to a waiter in a restaurant. But in reality she was talking to a man who stood mere feet from her bed, *his* bed. For all her innocent flirting, and too many men had accused her of just that, she'd never been this close to a man in his bedroom before. Flirting was one thing. But she'd always been careful not to let it go too far. As much as she liked men, she'd learned the hard way that she wasn't ready for an intimate relationship.

Seemingly unbothered by her discomfort, Keegan came closer. When he reached the side of the mattress, he leaned down and lightly touched the bandage he'd put on her forehead the day before.

Carrie flinched, drawing away from him.

"Did that hurt?" he asked, concern thick in his voice.

"No. It's okay. I just…" She didn't know where she was going with that sentence.

"I have to change the bandage again," he said. "Unless you think you can do it. But you'll have to use a mirror, and the only one I have is in the bathroom. You'll have to stand."

*Don't be ridiculous, Carrie*, she told herself. She'd thrust herself into this man's life, basing her hasty decision on intuition and about thirty minutes of conversation. He'd done nothing to indicate that he wasn't the man she'd believed him to be—a bit grumpy, a loner, but basically a moral individual.

She sighed, relaxed. This was Keegan's house. She wanted to stay here, but she'd have to stop acting like she was afraid of her own shadow. When was she ever going to forget the past…or at least learn to live with it? "No, you change it, please."

He raised a corner of the gauze, his finger grazing the skin above her eyebrow. She sucked in a quick, panicky breath.

"What's the matter?" he asked. "You seem so jumpy." He stood straight. "Good grief, Carrie, you don't think I'm going to hurt you? I would never..."

"No, of course not. I don't think that." *It's just that someone else did.*

"I'll get started on breakfast," he said. "And change the bandage after we eat. You come out when you're ready." He left, closing the door to give her privacy.

Carrie snuggled into the covers again and closed her eyes. She didn't want to think about that other time, the time her father had been right. The time another male voice had whispered urgently in her ear, "I'm not going to hurt you, Carrie."

*Thirteen years earlier...*

*"Come on, Carrie, it'll be fun."*

*The boy who clasped her arm with a proprietary authority was her dream date. In fact, he was everyone's dream date, and he'd picked her, a lowly sophomore, to take to the movies one fateful night. Mark Adelson would soon be leaving for Ohio State and he wanted to get to know her—Carrie*

Foster—before he left town. Besides being incredibly handsome and funny and everything she'd ever admired in a guy, he was the son of one of the most renowned defense attorneys in Cleveland and therefore would probably be viewed by her parents as an ideal boyfriend.

They'd attended the movie where Mark hadn't done more than hold her hand. But afterward he'd stopped at a friend's house where an unsupervised party was going on.

He tugged her gently to the top of the stairs in his friend's Colonial mini-mansion in Fox Creek. When they'd first arrived at the party, she'd looked around for the parents, knowing her own parents would have insisted on chaperones, but they'd been nowhere in sight. Now she realized she was alone with about fifty partying seniors.

Mark took another pull from his second beer. "Let me show you the house," he said. "It's got six bedrooms." He gave her a sly, suggestive smile. She tried to smile back but instead bit her bottom lip.

Mark knocked lightly on the first door with his knuckles. A masculine voice called out, "Occupied." Mark continued down the *hall to the next bedroom. The door was partially opened, and he slipped inside, pulling Carrie behind him. She supposed the room was tastefully decorated like the rest of the house, but truly she didn't see much beyond the full-size bed in the center of the room.*

*Mark shut the door. He didn't bother flicking on the light switch, instead he guided her into the room by scant moonlight coming in the pair of windows.*

*"Isn't this great?" he said. "I can finally be alone with you. It's all I've been thinking about since I picked you up."*

*All she could think about was that his strong grip had dropped from her arm. She took a step away from him. "Did you like the movie?" she asked. That seemed a safe topic.*

*He quickly erased the distance she'd put between them. "Sure, but this is better, don't you think?" His finger slipped under her spaghetti strap and lowered the dainty material to her upper arm. She felt exposed, vulnerable, though she was still covered in the beautiful light green dress she and her mom had picked out for this special first date.*

*"I don't think so, Maggie," her father had said two weeks before when she told her parents about Mark asking her out. "She's not old enough. Besides, what do we really know about this Adelson boy?"*

*Carrie had been surprised and she said so. "What do you mean, Daddy? You know all about his father," she'd said. "They're a good family."*

*"That may be so, but I'm worried about you, at your age, going with a boy two years older. There can be a world of difference between a sixteen-year-old and a high school graduate."*

*Carrie had pleaded with her mother. "Talk to him, Mom. I'll be absolutely mortified if I have to tell him my parents wouldn't let me go. And I want to go more than anything I've ever wanted in my life. Mark is the most popular boy in the senior class and he picked me!"*

*Maggie Foster, always the calm, sensible one, said, "Give us some details, Carrie. What movie theater are you going to? What time will you be home?"*

*"It's the Twenty-four Plex," Carrie said.*

*"The movie is over at eleven. But Mark said we might go out for something to eat after."*

*"Which means you won't be home until very late,"* Martin had said.

*"I think it will be all right, Martin,"* Maggie said. *"Carrie is a smart, responsible girl..."*

*"I'm not worried about Carrie being responsible! What about her asthma? What if she has an attack?"*

*"I'll have my inhaler, Daddy! I'll be fine."*

*He'd looked from his wife to his daughter and back again, apparently knowing he was going to lose this argument. "I want you home at midnight,"* he said.

*"Midnight? Daddy, no."* Carrie got down on one knee in front of Martin's chair. *"One o'clock at least. We'll just get to the restaurant and have to leave. That's not enough time to even order food."*

*He sighed. "No drinking."*

*"No way. I'm sure Mark doesn't drink. He's all about sports."*

*Maggie had smiled, placed her hand on her husband's shoulder. Looking at her daughter, she said, "Just be home by one,*

Carrie, and if this date is so important, maybe we can get you a new dress."

And now Carrie had the most unsettling feeling that her precious dress was going to be removed. She shivered, though it wasn't cold.

Carrie cupped the front of the dress to her chest to keep it from falling away, and then it happened. Her lungs felt like they were slamming shut. She couldn't breathe. Horrible, scratchy noises came from her throat.

"My inhaler..." she managed to say.

She found her purse on the floor, rescued the inhaler and administered the medication. "I have to go," she said when she could breathe again. "I'll find my own way home."

While yanking her zipper halfway up her back, she ran out of the house to the curb by the road. She ignored the shouts from the kids in the yard, dug in her purse for her cell phone and called home.

"Carrie, where are you? Are you all right?"

Her father's voice had never sounded better, like a light in the darkness. "Daddy, can you come and get me?"

"Give me an address. I'm leaving now."

*The rest of the night was a nightmare of trying to convince Martin not to call both the police and Mr. Adelson, not to report Mark to the principal of the high school. Carrie couldn't bear that. She didn't want to think about the kids in her class hearing this story, maybe even making fun of her. When she stumbled upstairs at nearly three in the morning, she knew she wasn't ready for some of life's tests. She'd been so stupid and naive and she'd vowed that night that her father would never see the bruises on her arm, or the emotional ones on the inside. And she wouldn't rush growing up...*

Dressed in her sweatpants and a clean T-shirt, Carrie padded into Keegan's kitchen a few minutes later. Wearing flannel pants and a gray Henley, Keegan looked relaxed. He brought a steaming bowl of oatmeal to the table and a plate stacked with buttered toast. How different this older, kinder man seemed. Keegan truly wanted to take care of her. He didn't appear to have an agenda.

"Hope this will fill you up," he said, holding the chair for her.

She added milk and sugar to the oatmeal and took a bite. "It's delicious."

Keegan devoured his cereal in a few minutes while his gaze remained transfixed on the television.

"What's new in the world today?" she asked him.

"What else? Strife, hatred, earthquakes, people running for their lives. It's the world we live in these days."

Wow, didn't he ever look for the good? She knew of a few news stations that actually counteracted the horrible pieces with tales of redemption and brotherly love. Apparently Keegan didn't watch those stories. But he did watch the news, almost obsessively, she thought.

She decided to distract him with conversation, but she knew so little about him that an appropriate topic didn't come to mind. So she said, "Why don't you see your son more often?"

He stared at her a moment, as if the words "None of your business" sat on the tip of his tongue. But he said, "Because I don't live with his mother, and Taylor does."

"How long were you married to his mother?"

He raised his coffee mug to his lips and

took a long swallow. "Ten years. We divorced nine years ago when Taylor was only four."

"I'm sorry. That must have been hard on everyone."

"Maybe, for a while. But it was the right decision. My ex-wife was all about the kid, you know. And I… Well, I had stuff going on in my life." He stood and carried his bowl to the sink. When his back was toward her, he added, "I don't blame my ex for any of it. Like I told you last night, I wouldn't have won any mugs with *World's Best Dad* printed on them."

And yet he'd admitted to calling the teenager twice a week. Obviously there was a strong connection.

"How often do you see Taylor?" she asked.

He looked over his shoulder. His face was grim as if he wasn't sure he would answer. But then he did. "Last time was right before I moved here to the campground, over a year ago. I flew to Seattle for Taylor's twelfth birthday." Keegan picked up Carrie's bowl. "I was glad I went, but it was awkward with the grandparents, aunts and uncles and all. Taylor has a lot of family there."

"And you? What about your family?"

"My dad is...somewhere, I suppose. My mom died. I was an only child, something I'd always said I wouldn't do to my own kid. Guess I failed on that promise."

She'd gone this far with the conversation and was actually pleased that Keegan had opened up this much. So she said, "But you'd like to see more of your son, right?"

His brow furrowed. "Of course. He's my kid, but he lives three thousand miles away. I'm pretty sure his mother chose Seattle because it was on the other side of the country from me."

"That's rough." She wanted to ask him why his ex-wife resented him so much. Had he been a poor provider? Carrie didn't think so. Had he cheated on her? None of the standard reasons for divorce seemed to fit Keegan's MO of basically being antisocial but not mean or vindictive.

He shrugged, returned to the sink and ran the hot water. "You get used to it. A person can get used to almost anything if enough time passes. And I stay in touch with the phone."

She sighed heavily, drummed her fingers on the tabletop.

He whirled around to face her. "Look, don't waste any sympathy on me. I was a horrible father. Never around, always off to corners of the world where I couldn't be reached. As far as parenting goes, you know the old saying, 'You reap what you sow.'"

"You abandoned them?"

"Not the way you're thinking." He began scrubbing the dishes as if they had a week's worth of grime on them. "I had a job that kept me on the road. I supported them, called nearly every day when I stayed put long enough. But as far as being a good husband and father, truthfully, I lacked a few merit points in my record book. Luckily Taylor had a great mom."

"You were in the corporate world?"

He seemed amused. "Not exactly. And anyway, we're done talking about this, okay?"

"Okay." Why wouldn't he tell her what he'd done for a living? Carrie stood, supporting herself on the edge of the table. "It's a nice day, isn't it?"

"Good enough. Warmer. Snow melted a bit."

"I'd like to go outside then."

"I guess that would be okay, though you

can see pretty much all of what's here by just looking out the window."

"That's where you're wrong," she said. "In every natural environment, what's important lies beyond what the eye can see—in the dirt and roots of growing things. Same can be said for people, too."

He paused, considering her words. "But sometimes people don't want you examining their roots."

She understood that no further questions would be allowed at this point.

"I'll get you a chair and set you up."

"And some paper and pencils, too, if you don't mind. I want to sketch."

"You've got a cell phone. Why don't you take a picture?"

She smiled at him. "I might do that, too."

Keegan took a folding chair from a closet. "If you don't mind my asking, what do you expect you'll find to sketch out there? It's winter. Most of the plants, at least what's left of them, are hibernating. There are no leaves on the trees."

"There aren't even many trees," she added.

"That's true. This lot used to be shady and nice. A couple of years ago, Dutch elm disease got a bunch of the trees. My grand-father was upset."

"I can imagine."

"Anyway, my point is that for a natural-ist like yourself, it must be pretty boring."

She stared at him as he slipped his jacket on. "I wonder if you even know what's outside your door," she said.

"I know what isn't. We've just discussed it."

She smiled at him, but it was a smile of indulgence, not pleasure. "I believe that every living thing has potential," she said. "As long as cells keep multiplying, there is always a chance of renewal for everything in nature."

"I suppose you believe that about people, too?"

"Well, I did." She shrugged and gave him a genuine grin this time. "Now, maybe I'm not so sure."

He held up one finger. "Now you're learn-ing. Those spindly old plants out there, and maybe even other breathing entities on this property, are just lost causes."

She stood, grabbed her crutches. "You never know."

# CHAPTER SIX

KEEGAN LEFT HER sitting in the lawn chair. She was bundled up in her designer jacket, a pair of leather gloves and a stocking cap. For extra measure, he'd draped an old quilt over her shoulders. The temperature had crept up to the thirties, so he figured she wouldn't freeze to death.

After an hour, he went to check on her. He'd opened the back door just a crack when he heard her cell phone ring. He considered latching the door and giving her some privacy, but that kind of considerate behavior hadn't gotten him where he was today. Not that his position at the moment was anything to brag about. But not too long ago, he'd been a fairly well-respected journalist, and you didn't get that kind of notoriety without being nosy, or curious, as he liked to call it, if not outright dogged in his pursuit of the facts.

Besides, he still knew very little about his

houseguest, and not knowing things pretty much drove Keegan up a wall. He needed to know all the facts, the good, the bad and especially the ones about Carrie Foster. Who was this delicate creature with the cheerful attitude, the sweet face and the urge to live like a Keebler elf in a hollow tree?

So as he'd done many times from behind rocky outcroppings, through dusty ventilation systems and with his ear pressed up against crumbling tunnel walls, he tuned in and listened.

"Jude, hi! How's my favorite big sister?"

She sounded positively chipper. Whoever Jude was, she'd never know her sister had a busted up car and leg.

Carrie laughed. "You're right. I'd have said the same thing to Alex if she had called. Someone's got to keep peace in this family. So tell me about you and Liam. Is he out of the hospital yet?"

This pause went on for several minutes. Carrie uttered a few *aahs* and *wows* to let her sister know she was engaged and involved. She finally ended with, "I don't want to say I told you so, but…" She sighed. "And I couldn't be happier if I was getting a ring on New Year's Eve. You deserve this, Jude. Liam sounds like a wonderful guy."

Carrie went on to ask about other family members, he supposed, including several of the four-legged variety, horses, goats and a dog or two, which he was certain Carrie's asthma kept her from enjoying. Wherever these Fosters lived, Keegan bet they never enjoyed a peaceful moment. He could relate to that, with the exception of the last year.

"I'm fine," Carrie said. "Michigan is beautiful. I'm working on plans to reforest some of the neighborhoods north of Ann Arbor. Every day is busy, busy, busy!"

Keegan shook his head at the series of lies. If Carrie truly was talking to her favorite big sister, why didn't she tell her that she'd had an accident and was living with a hermit in a godforsaken campground?

"Tell Daddy everything is great, couldn't be better. And, Jude, tell him I love him. Kiss Mama and Wesley for me."

The conversation obviously over, Carrie slipped her phone into her jacket pocket. She stared long and hard at some nondescript spot along the tree line behind Delores's camper. Then she picked up her pencil and began to sketch. And Keegan went back to work at his computer, his head still filled with more questions than answers. But he was soon firmly embedded with the 104th armored brigade in the Middle East.

The Humvee just ahead of us was hit hard. The explosion battered the undercarriage, and somehow smoke and flames found their way into the heavily armored vehicle. The doors flew off and skidded along the ground into the nearby desert. Two soldiers crawled out of the smoky plumes. There had been a total of six passengers inside the Hummer when we left the base camp. Our driver swerved to avoid a piece of windshield jettisoning toward us. I covered my head and ducked onto the floor of the backseat. Our vehicle shuddered to a halt, and we all poured out—soldiers and reporters alike. We had four men to find, and we hoped it wasn't too late.

Keegan took a gulp of bitter, lukewarm coffee and wished he had laced it with whiskey. But, no, those days were over. He no longer deadened the pain with alcohol. Now he tried to do it with a computer keyboard… *tried* being the operative word. He told himself every day, as he recounted the experiences of his career, that getting the words on a screen would alleviate some of the ache. Some days it actually worked.

CARRIE'S SKETCHING HAND seemed to have a mind of its own, and she let it, along with her keen bespectacled eyes, determine her strokes. Never before had she enjoyed such a blank canvas as provided by Keegan's potential paradise. In two hours she had designed six distinct areas of the campground—a pond for fishing, a playground, renovated showers and lavatories, a pool, a picnic area and a small, rustic amphitheater where campers could learn about native foliage and the history of Lake Erie. If this project were hers to build, she would utilize native trees and plants to add shade, variety and nesting places for nature's tiniest creatures.

She left the old trailers belonging to Duke and Delores in her sketches with thoughts of repainting and repairing them. The streamlined campers would add a touch of vintage charm to the reforested landscape. She would paint one yellow with aqua trim and the other green with tan trim.

She had just started her seventh sketch when Keegan came outside. "How are you doing?" he asked. "You ready to come in?"

"Not just yet. Come here. I want to show you something." Did she think he would be interested in her sketches? No, but a girl could hope.

He pulled up an old crockery pot, turned it over and sat. "I hope the dog hasn't been around."

"No, I've seen his face in Duke's window, so I guess they are both inside until it warms up a bit more."

Keegan leaned close to her. "What do you want me to see?"

She flipped the pages in her pad until she could show him the first sketch. "Do you know what this is?"

"Nope. Haven't the faintest idea. But if you drew this, I'd say you have some talent at natural scenes."

"Well, yes, I do, but I didn't ask you to look at this so I would get compliments on my artistic ability. I was hoping you'd recognize the space I've drawn."

He studied the drawing a moment before pointing to a particular area. "Wait a minute… is that the tree line that marks the end of my property?"

"Exactly. It's the area just to the left of Duke's trailer, and it could look like this. All these plants and landscaped patches are my ideas for beautifying this whole campground. And the trees, too, of course. We'd need lots of trees, and I could get some that already have a few year's growth on them."

He frowned. "We? What does that mean?"

She hadn't intended to use that word. Of course she knew that the campground was Keegan's, and there was no "we."

"Nothing," she said. "Just an expression."

"Interesting. Like I said, you have a talent for drawing, and I suppose all this imagination would matter to someone who wanted to keep this sorry lot as a campground."

She stared into his eyes, hoping he would see what she envisioned. "Hasn't the idea even occurred to you?"

"Of course it has, and since this is the second winter I've spent here, I've finally learned my lesson. And what I learned is to get out while I can. Besides, I'm not much of a manager type. If I tried to run this campground by applying my limited skills at maintenance, I'd watch it go belly-up in a matter of months."

"But you already own the property. Couldn't you hire a manager? A groundskeeper?"

"Carrie..." His voice held the hint of a warning.

She quickly turned another page, showing several concrete pads for campers and Delores's unit in the background. "There is so much potential for this property," she said. "The pads are already in, along with the electrical and sewer hookups. It's practically begging for someone to take an interest in it."

"Yeah, and it would cost a fortune to bring it all up to code." He started to stand up. "Nice work, Carrie, but even if I wanted to do something with this property again, I don't have the cash to turn this seven acres of scrub into a place people would pay me to visit. It could be tens of thousands of dollars to accomplish even some of what you visualize."

She wrapped her hand around his wrist and tugged, hoping to persuade him to sit on the crock again. His eyes narrowed on the two inches of skin under her palm.

"Yes, that's true," she admitted when he'd taken his seat. "But you're not aware of the help you can get from the government in the form of grants and loans."

"Right. The government is going to pay me to plant some hedges and trees on the same property that, just two days ago, you said was neglected." He shook his head. "I don't think so."

"When I said that, I wasn't fully aware of the true potential of this land. And don't forget, I work for that branch of the government. My recommendation would make a big difference in a decision to allocate the money. You do know, don't you, that the Lake Erie cleanup campaign has been on-going for years now?"

He nodded. "Yes, I know that."

"The Forest Service is quite pleased about the improvements. They are hoping to turn this part of Ohio into a major recreation area. And this campground, situated right across the road from the reclaimed beach, is perfect."

"Which is why I've already made a decision about it," he said.

"You have?" Could she allow herself to be hopeful? "What are you going to do with this land?"

He stood. "You probably won't like the answer, you being a card-carrying tree hugger and all, but I plan to sell this land to a hotel chain, pocket the cash and be on my way."

Her jaw dropped. "No! You can't."

A hard scowl settled over his features. "I believe I can. I have the deed."

"But another hotel? We don't need another hotel! We need grass and trees and places for families to play and squirrels to gather nuts and birds to build nests." She grabbed his hand. "I can help you. This is what I do. Won't you at least consider…"

"Look, Carrie, you want this to be a recreation area. What's more recreational than a hotel with all the amenities?"

"That's not what I meant."

"Nobody's keeping you from doing what you do, Carrie. There are lots of defunct campgrounds in this area. I'm sure you can find another one you can retrofit to your liking." He disengaged his hand. "But it won't be this one."

He went into the house and closed the door. Carrie studied all her sketches again but had lost the incentive to produce another drawing. It was all such a shame. But then she looked at the horizon and smiled. Perhaps Keegan's decision wasn't irreversible. Her car wasn't fixed yet. She had nowhere else to go. In the time she had left, if he didn't kick her out, who knew what she could accomplish in the way of persuading one stubborn man to value the land his grandfather left him. Her mother once said, "Carrie could talk a rattlesnake into tying her shoes." All at once Carrie believed it might be true.

She came inside for lunch, and after eating the sandwich Keegan had prepared for her, she chose a book from his small library and settled on the sofa. A few snow flurries drifted by the windows. A fire in the old stone fireplace made the cabin feel warm and cozy, and since the house was well ventilated, she wasn't bothered by the wood smoke. Keegan worked at his computer, went outside once to throw a stick for Flo and eventually related the choices he had in the fridge for dinner.

"I'm going to the market tomorrow," he said. "So if there's anything you want, let me know."

Carrie's mood brightened considerably. "Do you think I could go with you? I could ride in one of the motorized chairs that all supermarkets have."

"I'm not going all the way to the supermarket, and the local grocer doesn't have those chairs. But you can ride along with me if you want to."

"I definitely do."

"Okay, then."

"And Keegan? I really want you to sleep in your bed tonight. I will be fine on the couch."

"I know you say that, but I've discovered a few lumps in that sofa I didn't know were there. I've made them fit to the crannies of my body so I'm used to them."

"One more night, if I'm still here, and then we make the switch." She stated her ultimatum more as a test to find out if Keegan planned on her being with him for the fore-seeable future.

He nodded. "Since we didn't hear from Grady, and since you can't drive anyway, I'm thinking you'll still be here. But, okay. Tomorrow night we'll switch. If you change your mind, it's not a problem."

Carrie smiled to herself. So far, she was staying. And liking it. Not the part where he was waiting on her. Carrie really hated that. But just the comfort of being around some-one she could trust. Keegan allowed her to be herself. If he didn't particularly care for the person she was, at least he didn't show it.

DURING THE DRIVE to the local grocery mart the next day, Carrie made out her list of items she'd like Keegan to purchase. She gave him a twenty-dollar bill to cover the cost. He slipped the bill and the list into his pocket. "I included a couple of items that no man wants to buy," she said with a grin. "I hope you won't mind picking them up. Otherwise I'll have to go in with my crutches."

He smiled. "I think I'm secure enough in my manhood to handle it, Carrie."

He left the motor running in the SUV,

and Carrie settled back, closed her eyes and listened to the radio. Soon her thoughts wandered to this new roommate situation and her own strange behavior with regard to Keegan Breen. What was it about him? On one hand, he complained about his bothersome neighbors. Yet he allowed them to stay on his property for free. Was he truly a grouch who disliked being around people, or deep down, was he a caring man?

At first he'd been less than enthusiastic about having a houseguest, but he'd shown remarkable gentleness and care when he changed her bandage or fixed her meals. His words came back to her now. *"You can't stay here. You need to call someone to come get you."*

His no-nonsense instructions were those of a man who didn't have company, didn't want company and had no use for visitors. But still, from the first day, she'd felt protected and even welcome, maybe not in the way the Fosters welcomed people, with boisterous backslapping and hearty hellos; but for a man like Keegan, a brooder with a mysterious past, he'd been a kind host.

And once he'd shaved off that several

days' worth of stubble from his face and combed his hair, Carrie had determined that he was unexpectedly handsome. There was nothing boyish about him, making him very different from the guys Carrie had dated in the past. But she was attracted to him, more than she wanted to admit.

In her lifetime, she'd only dated boys and young men. Younger fellows were easy to flirt with, and they generally responded to Carrie's teasing. But those relationships had left her feeling hollow and disappointed. She didn't have a need to flirt with Keegan as if his adoration would somehow prove her worth. She was comfortable just being herself.

She'd never discovered why her heart seemed to require so much from a romantic relationship with someone her own age. She enjoyed dating. She liked having a steady boyfriend, being able to count on a Saturday-night date. But when the guys got too close and appeared to be staking a claim to bragging rights, she always backed off. She pondered the possibility that Keegan's lack of youthful qualities made him more appealing. He didn't constantly behave as if he had something to prove.

Keegan was a different breed altogether. He was honest to a fault, plainspoken though obviously intelligent, slightly gruff and more than a little marked with age. The fine lines on his face only added character to the scar she'd noticed on his cheek, and the faint limp when he favored his right side on cold mornings. And Carrie found herself staring at him for long minutes at a time—and fantasizing about what he thought of her.

Thank goodness he'd stopped calling her a princess, but she knew he was aware of the difference in their ages. He'd told her he was forty-one. That was only an eleven-year difference. Not a big deal to her, but it was obviously a factor to Keegan. Though he hadn't argued when she wanted to go outside, he still basically treated her as he might a younger sister, setting up the chair for her, throwing a blanket over her shoulders. Carrie already was the younger sister to two siblings, and that relationship was not what she wanted from Keegan.

But what did she want from him? Goodness, the question made her face heat. Her father would say that Keegan was a totally inappropriate match for his baby girl. In a way, that was true. Keegan had obviously lived a varied and full life. He'd been married, had a child, suffered injuries for reasons she still didn't know. Carrie was innocent in the ways of love. Her sisters always told her she could have any guy she wanted, and truly she could flirt at the drop of a pin, but the truth was, she'd never felt right about making the jump from innocent flirting to an intimate connection.

Since the night of the fateful date with Mark, she'd never been comfortable with forceful and demanding males. She could tease the quiet ones, encourage the uncertain ones, but a strong, dominant male made her run for the forest—literally.

Yet—and this was perhaps the most puzzling aspect of all—never once had she been worried with Keegan—older, noncommunicative, secretive, a complete stranger. From the moment he'd picked her up out of her stranded automobile, she'd felt secure and connected to him.

So again she wondered…what did he think of her? If she analyzed his behavior so far, she'd have to admit that he regarded her as no more than a bothersome victim who'd stumbled into his path, a responsibility he was willing to accept for the time being anyway.

If she could get him to at least consider her plans for the campground, then maybe he would begin to see her as an equal, a bright, accomplished woman who only wanted to leave the planet a better place for everyone. Could she earn his respect? As she watched him approach the car, several grocery bags in hand, she realized that she very much wanted to. A pleasant tingle crept across her shoulders, a feeling that was alien to Carrie's emotional storehouse, but one that hinted that perhaps respect was not all she wanted.

"We're not going to starve," he said, sliding into the driver's seat. "And, yes, I picked up your girlie things."

"Thank you."

They'd gone about halfway back to the cabin when Carrie decided to open a conversation again. "About those drawings I made yesterday…" she said. "I've added another few details…"

He glared at her from across the couple of feet that separated them in the car. "Don't start again, Carrie. I told you what was going to happen with the property. I'm not going to change my mind."

She clamped her lips together and stared out the side window at the snow-covered pastures. If she were keeping score, so far Keegan's stubbornness had earned a point. And Carrie's quest for respect was a fat zero.

They drove the rest of the way in silence. When Keegan pulled up in front of the cabin, Carrie said, "I like it here, but if you want me to go to a motel, I will. You'll have to pick the closest one and take me, of course."

His brow furrowed, and he gave her a questioning stare. "Where did that come from? Have I asked you to go to a motel?"

"No, but you should know that I would be willing. I can probably take care of myself at this point."

The corner of his mouth twisted into something resembling a grin. "Take care of yourself? You wouldn't eat right, you wouldn't remember to change the bandage on your forehead and you'd probably drive that dang car halfway across the country once you got the keys back."

That was exactly what she would do— drive right back to Michigan, broken leg on the accelerator.

"Well, then," she said. "Since you, in your own charming way, are hinting that I should stay, I guess I will."

He laughed out loud. The sound was full-bodied and unexpected in its spontaneity, so much so that Carrie laughed along with him.

He put the truck in Park and opened his car door. "I'm glad we got that settled."

## CHAPTER SEVEN

LATER THAT EVENING, after dinner and visits from both Duke and Delores that had left Keegan less than cheerful, Carrie sat on the sofa reading her book.

"I don't know what Delores thinks is going on in here," Keegan said. "She was clucking over you like a mother hen and staring at me like she was a bull and I was wearing red."

"She's just a caring person," Carrie said.

"No. She's a suspicious, nosy old trouble-maker, and I hope you're not giving her a false impression."

"I'm not giving her any impression. I'm sure if she's drawing any conclusions at all, it's because she already knows you so well."

Keegan harrumphed, picked up the remote and said, "Mind if I watch the news channel?"

How could she mind? This was his house, and watching the news was what he did.

"Of course not. Anything special we should know about in the world today?"

"No, but there's a broadcast leading up to the New Year. The station is showing the biggest stories from the new millennium."

"That should be interesting," Carrie said, turning a page in her book. "I can put in my earbuds."

He gave her a quirky smile.

"What's so funny?"

He chuckled. "You just said the program would be interesting, and then you figured out a way to avoid hearing any of it."

"You'll let me know when the good parts come up, right?" She plunged a soft plastic bud into each ear.

After about thirty minutes, during which time Keegan had been glued to the screen with a cup of coffee in his hand, Carrie glanced at the television. She recognized the distressing scenes of New Orleans during Hurricane Katrina. She'd been in her last year of high school when the storm occurred, and felt so sorry for all the misplaced people. Jude had been terribly upset about the animals that no longer had homes. Between the two of them, they'd managed to badger friends and neighbors for donations which they sent to the Red Cross.

Carrie pulled the buds from her ears and laid them on her lap. "I remember this so well," she said. "How horrible that must have been. I understand parts of the city are still suffering from the effects."

Keegan's face was grim. "It was horrible, all right."

Surprised by the depth of emotion in his voice, she wondered if he had done more than watch the disaster on television like she had.

And then the file footage shifted to the New Orleans Superdome which had gained an infamous reputation as a last-resort shelter for residents with nowhere else to go. A camera scanned the interior of the arena, capturing bedrolls and cots side-by-side taking up the entire space normally reserved for sports games. Reporters interviewed folks who protested conditions in the Dome but had no alternative since city officials had locked them inside.

All at once, a voice, deep, controlled, impassioned and, of all things, *familiar*, caught her attention. She slipped off her reading glasses and stared at the TV as a reporter asked a question. The camera was focused on the protester, and only showed the back of the reporter's head and his dark, collar-length mussed hair.

"Well, enough of this," Keegan said, reaching for the remote.

"Don't you dare turn that off," Carrie said. "That reporter…" The camera swiveled around to show the man's face, younger, wrinkle-free, and oh, so handsome. "That's you! You were in the Superdome!"

"I got caught same as everybody," he said. "Thought I'd do some amateur storytelling as long as I was there."

"Nonsense. Your questions are rehearsed, well thought-out. And you're on a national news broadcast. Amateur, my great-aunt Fanny!"

"'Great-aunt Fanny!'" He pretended shock. "Such language."

"Never mind. Who are you?"

A line appeared at the bottom of the screen indicating the source of the interview, the name of the reporter, and his position as "special correspondent."

Forgetting her leg, Carrie pushed herself

off the sofa and winced in pain. "You're Patrick Breen! I thought I recognized something about you, your voice. I've seen you lots of times. You're famous."

He frowned. "I thought you didn't watch much news."

"I've watched enough to recognize you!"

He lowered the volume. "Okay. I *used to be* Patrick Breen," he admitted. "Now I'm just Keegan."

"But...but..." She couldn't come up with the words. "You had a fabulous career. You went everywhere, the Middle East, China, Israel, even New Orleans as it turns out." She took a deep breath, keeping her eyes glued on her target as if he might fade from sight as an apparition would. "Weren't you the subject of a special a couple of years ago?"

"That?" He tried to minimize his importance. "It was just a small segment."

"—about a reporter who took any assignment, no matter the danger to himself. I saw part of that documentary." She shook her head in disbelief. "And now you're here in Ohio, on a campground in the middle of nowhere."

He shrugged. "Looks like it. And don't get excited. This isn't my first rodeo to places in the middle of nowhere."

"For heaven's sake," she said. "This explains a lot."

"I don't know why it should," he said.

"For one thing, it explains your interest in the news. I'm thinking it also explains your obsession with the computer. You're still writing." She tapped her fingernail on her upper lip. "What it doesn't explain is why you're living here."

He smirked. "A lot of people retire from their jobs just like I did."

"No, not just like you did. Most people get their gold watch and buy a set of golf clubs. You disappeared. You went off the grid." She suddenly remembered references Keegan had made to his past and all the pieces fell into place. "All that talk about injuries you mysteriously sustained that didn't make sense until now. And you live like a hermit because you don't want anyone to find you."

He narrowed his eyes. "Carrie, isn't that why anyone lives like a hermit?"

"Quit making this sound like you're

just one of many people. You're not." She paused. "And it explains…" She suddenly cut off her words. She was going too far.

"Explains what?" he said. "Go ahead, say it."

"No."

"Then I'll say it for you. It explains why I was such a crappy father and husband."

She slowly nodded her head. "Yes, it does. You were always off somewhere, not knowing if you'd make it back or not." She sat down and tapped her foot on his floor. "I think you craved the excitement above all else. You're a danger junkie."

"I *was* a danger junkie. Now I'm a quiet, respectable, law-abiding hermit."

"Whose only excitement these days is rescuing people from snowbanks. Quite a comedown, I'd say."

Again the shrug. "I'm not complaining. I've come to appreciate the quiet life."

"Have you? Have you really? How does someone like you give it all up and settle in a defunct campground?"

Her eyes widened as she realized her heart was beating rapidly. "Keegan, tell me this isn't another story. You're not hanging out here because there's some escaped madman on the loose? Should I be watching for danger around every corner of this cabin?"

He chuckled. "I wouldn't be here if there were danger, Carrie. I'm done with all that. I'm leaving all the madmen and the war-torn corners of the world to the younger reporters."

"Well, you're not really old, but okay. And what about this property... Is it really yours?"

"Yes. I'm not a squatter. This land belonged to Robert Sean Breen, the Irish immigrant who settled right here when he got off the boat at Ellis Island in the late thirties. And he left his empire to me, his only grandson."

"And this grandfather...you knew him well?"

Keegan's voice lowered. "Very well. You might say he was my best friend growing up."

"And you're going to repay him for his kindness by selling out to a hotel chain?"

He scowled. "We're not getting into this again, Carrie."

"But my guess is, you don't even need the money. It's none of my business, but you must have put away a nice retirement amount by accepting the most dangerous assignments and going to the most hazardous places on earth."

He shook his head, and she worried that he would shut her out now. Her last comment had been rather personal. "It is none of your business, but overall, I got paid well enough, especially for a freelance reporter," he said.

"So why did you even come here? Why not hire a Realtor and sell the land through a third party? If you have no interest in your inheritance..."

He held up a finger. "I never said I had no interest. When I had the opportunity to come here, I took it. I'd spent many happy weeks here as a kid, and I wanted to come back. I was pretty much a loner when I was growing up. My mom worked crazy hours. My dad was gone. But I'm not a kid anymore, and now my reason for staying here for the last year has been a desire to, as you put it, stay off the grid. Peace and quiet, Carrie, just like you must experience around your beloved trees. I needed it. I found it. Here."

Finally he'd said something she could relate to. She valued every quiet moment she spent in a forest. She relished the feel of her hands in damp soil when she planted a sapling on a street undergoing renovation. She could almost convince herself the trees cared as much as she did. Maybe she and this embattled man had something lasting in common after all. Except he didn't seem to have any regrets about leaving his legacy and walking away.

"Those injuries you've talked about—why do you limp in the mornings?"

"Gunshot, but not serious. Just grazed. Wrong place, wrong time."

Recalling his activity the last couple of days, she said, "If you're no longer reporting, do you mind if I ask what you're doing on your computer all these hours?"

He scratched the back of his neck while nearly a full minute went by. "I'm no longer reporting, but, like you said, I am still writing. I'm working on my memoir."

"Your *memoir*?" The word made him sound much older than his years. But many famous people wrote autobiographies. Why should he be any different?

"Yeah, but I don't flatter myself into thinking that anyone will want to read it.

I'm mostly getting my experiences down on paper as a sort of catharsis, if you know what I mean." He paused, frowned. "Sometimes my experiences get muddled in my brain. Writing about them brings a certain clarity to what I experienced."

And from what she knew of him, he'd experienced a lifetime of living in just a few years. So if he truly didn't think anyone would read his words, then his writing wasn't a means of earning additional money. The autobiography was a way of bringing clarity to his life, but also, possibly, a sort of soul cleansing of the terrible things he'd seen. At this point, seeing the dark shadows cross his eyes, she could only assume that the latter explanation held a lot of truth.

Who could say for sure? What did Carrie know of danger junkies anyway? The most dangerous activity Carrie pursued was breathing the open air through her troubled lungs. Even Jude's fiancé, who once a year took off on an adventure somewhere with his friends, always planned and prepared. She assumed a reporter in a war zone didn't have the luxury of even planning his next meal.

"What about Duke and Delores?" she asked. "Do they know who you are?"

"Duke does. He has nothing to do but watch television, so he recognized me right off. Delores just thinks I'm a crackpot who never remembers to badger her about her rent. She's happy believing that…and providing me with scones masquerading as rocks."

Carrie smiled. "So what now? What are your plans for the future?"

"Oh, I've got some," he said. "Like for instance, right now I'm going to bed."

Carrie glanced at her watch. Nearly two hours had gone by since she'd read a word in her book. And she was no longer interested in the story. The novel couldn't compete with the real-life journey she'd just heard. "Take the bedroom, Keegan."

He started to protest, and she waved off his argument. "I insist. You need a good night's sleep, and I've done nothing but sleep, so the bed is yours." Patting the sofa cushion, she said, "I'll be fine right here. And besides, I'm not ready for bed yet."

"Okay." He stood and ambled toward the bedroom. "Call me if you need anything. Otherwise I'll see you in the morning."

"We can give Grady a call then," she said. "See if he's had any luck with the car part."

He smiled. "Sure, we'll call him, but I'm getting kind of used to having you around, so if you're stuck here awhile longer, don't worry about it."

"You don't mind my constant questions?"

"I wouldn't say that, but as a former reporter, I can hardly blame you for probing into my past life and being generally nosy, now can I?" He stopped at the door. "But maybe soon we'll turn the tables and I can ask you a few questions."

He shut the door and she turned up the volume on the TV so she could hear the next day's weather forecast. If it was going to be a nice day, she'd spend it outside and possibly avoid any questions he might ask.

KEEGAN HAD TO admit his bed felt pretty wonderful. Maybe it was the expensive mattress he'd invested in. Or maybe it was the lingering scent of lavender left by the previous occupant. Carrie did smell good. The subtle, breathe-deep kind of floral headiness that made a man's mind wander—to where it probably shouldn't.

He was beginning to enjoy having company in his lonely cabin, not just any company, but this cheery save-a-tree, save-the-planet optimist who would like nothing more than to change his mind about his future plans. He grinned to himself. Carrie Foster wouldn't succeed in getting him to cancel the sale of his property, but it was miracle enough that he was willing to listen to, and even enjoy, her low, seductive voice trying to get him to.

Wow, where did that come from? Seductive? He didn't fool himself into thinking she was in any way a female he should be interested in. No. She was his opposite, a nature-loving, peace-seeking woman-child inexperienced in the kind of world that had shaped his personality. He'd seen the worst of people. She probably refused to admit there was a worst.

He hadn't always been like this, though he couldn't remember a time when his glasses were rose-colored. During his childhood he'd been on his own, scraping coins from the sofa to buy a soda. The experience had made him a curious realist most of his life. Unfortunately his years as a correspondent had changed him from a realist to a pessimist and taught him that evil existed and couldn't hide its ugly underbelly from inquiring minds determined to expose it.

Still, there was Carrie, and he couldn't deny the influence she'd had on him in just a few days. He had to admit that she was the one person in years who had half a chance of changing him back into the person he used to be, the less jaded, less wounded Patrick Breen who enjoyed his summers at his grandfather's campground.

"Don't even think about it, Breen," he said into his pillow. "You've left too much heartache in your wake to risk spoiling something so good." But he could dream, couldn't he? He could imagine that he was worthy of someone like Carrie. He wondered if she'd had many relationships. Somehow he doubted she had. Despite the fact that she had a killer smile and bottomless blue eyes that didn't let a guy turn away, she wasn't the type to sacrifice principles for casual fun. For some reason, while she appeared to enjoy the company of men, she seemed above the fray of mortal males who took without fully giving back.

He rolled onto his side, stuffed a pillow between his knees to ease the ache of an old surgery which had removed a piece of shrapnel from his hip. He should be dog tired. He wanted to sleep. He needed to, but he didn't want to sleep so soundly that the nightmares would come back.

Some nights, when the past haunted him beyond what was rational, he stayed up all night so the ugliness of what he'd witnessed wouldn't cause him to wake in a sweat, with the moans of a suffering populace coming from his own lips. No, that was not the experience he would want to expose to someone as sweet as Carrie. That was the part of living like a hermit he hadn't confessed to.

## CHAPTER EIGHT

SOMETIME IN THE middle of the night, Carrie woke to sounds of intense anguish. Except for a small night-light, the cabin was dark. Her eyes popped open in alarm. She jerked upright and raised up on her elbow to listen. The groans came from the bedroom, and they were sorrowful and tortured and caused the skin on her arms to tingle in a shared terror. What was wrong? Had someone broken into the cabin? What would she do? She couldn't run.

One goal, to get to Keegan if he was suffering, guided her actions. She rose from the sofa, grabbed her crutches and went as quickly as the awkward sticks allowed to the bedroom door.

"Keegan?" She kept her voice low and soothing as she peered through a crack in the door. The moonlight coming in an open window was bright, and she quickly determined there was no one else in the room.

Keegan didn't answer and instead released another long painful sound from his throat and what seemed the depths of his soul.

She went inside and approached the bed. He was asleep, yet his body responded to some personal suffering that she could only imagine. Under the covers his legs moved frantically as if he were trying to run. He spoke in guttural sounds she couldn't make out. His hands clawed at the covers, tried to push them away as if they were restraints.

Carrie gently laid her hand on his bare arm. "Keegan, shhh now. It's all right."

He turned toward her. His eyes opened to give her a glassy stare. He wrapped his hand around hers and jerked with a sudden pull that sent her sprawling onto the bed. He yanked her to him, engulfing her in powerful arms that had once felt protective and comforting, but now frightened her with extraordinary desperation.

Her own insecurities flooded her mind. "Keegan, wake up. You're still asleep. What's wrong?"

He only increased his hold over her, bringing her close to his chest, burying his face in her hair. When she felt his hot breath on her neck, she panicked, gulping air, trying to ease the pain in her chest. "I can't breathe," she ground out. She pushed against him. He released her and groaned once more as he fully awakened.

"Carrie…" His voice, trembling and uncertain, seemed to come from a faraway place. "What are you…? How did you…?" His eyes glittered gold in the darkness as he struggled to find his way back from wherever his dreams had taken him.

Carrie scrambled out of the bed, balanced against the side of the mattress on her one good leg. "Keegan? You were dreaming," she said between insufficient draws of air.

He crawled out of bed on the other side. "Where is your inhaler?"

"In my purse, on the floor next to the sofa."

He rushed from the room and returned seconds later, the device in his hand. "Here, use it."

She sat back down on the bed and pulled in two complete soothing breaths. "I'm okay now. I don't think I need it. You startled me, that's all."

"I scared the wits out of you is more like it," he said, rubbing the back of his neck. "I'm sorry, Carrie. I have these dreams…"

"It's all right," she said, and patted the mattress next to where she sat. "You're winded yourself. Here, sit."

He gave her an intense stare. "Are you sure? I don't want you to fear me."

"I don't." She smiled. "Not now anyway. When I heard you in your sleep I only wanted to help."

After a pause, he sat next to her, sweat glistening on his face and staining his T-shirt. "You can't help me, Carrie. Why do you think people choose to live as I do? It's not always because they have a problem with society. Often they make the decision to be alone because they know they can't be helped, and they've elected not to inflict their pain on others."

"I don't believe that," she said. "I don't know what your dream was about, but I believe that no one is beyond help." She wanted to touch the smooth, muscled skin of his thigh at the hem of his boxer shorts. She wanted to show him a sample of human kindness that might break down his wall of hopelessness. But instead she clasped her hands in her lap. "I'm a good listener, Keegan. Tell me about the dreams."

"They're not for you to hear, Carrie, but thanks. Someone like you...you can't imagine."

"Try me," she said. "How do you know I can't relate?"

He stared at a spot on the wall, refusing to look into her eyes. "Go back to sleep. This won't happen again tonight. It's over."

"I'm not leaving you alone."

He looked at her now, a gentle smile curving his lips. "I doubt either one of us will sleep any more tonight," he said. "You're really not leaving the room?"

She shook her head. "Nope."

"Then, would you lie next to me for a few minutes? It would be nice to feel someone I can trust. I promise I won't..."

"I know. Yes, I will."

He settled into the bed and raised the covers to accommodate her. She crawled into their warmth, and he pulled the comforter to her shoulders. His arm rested across hers, and he gently tugged her back to his chest. "Are you okay?" he asked. "Your leg?"

"It's fine." She expected to feel the first skitter of panic up her spine, the one she'd tried to overcome all her adult life.

"Are you cold?" he asked. "I can close the window."

"No, it's okay." And then, quite by accident, she relaxed in his arms, almost snuggling next to him in a familiar, comforting way. Keegan's breathing was normal, deep and rhythmic. Yet she knew he wasn't sleeping. His fingers flexed against her rib cage, and she instinctively nestled closer. *This must be what security feels like*, she thought. Encompassing and warm. Keegan had no ulterior motive to hold her except to make them both feel safe. Images of the last few minutes vanished as she gave into the sweet abandonment of fear and reluctance.

She knew she couldn't stay like this the rest of the night. When she sensed Keegan was asleep, she would go back to the sofa. Lying next to him, though amazingly nice, was a level of intimacy she wasn't ready for, and she didn't know when or even *if* she ever would be ready. But not tonight. Definitely not tonight. Until she heard the steady breaths of a man in deep sleep, though, she would stay with him and recall her own haunting dream.

*Five years earlier...*

*"I love you, Carrie. I want to be close to you. I want to make love to you."*

*Jeff was a good man. Carrie had met him in college. She'd flirted with him until he'd practically fallen into her lap, and they'd dated for three years. He talked marriage and children and a home. She'd thought he might be the one to change the timid qualities she hated about herself. She allowed him to touch her, kiss her, always drawing away when the intimacy became too much. But this night was different, and she had agreed to it.*

*"I've booked a room for us at the university inn," he said. "It will be perfect, like a mini vacation. We'll be alone and together. No pressure from phones or people showing up unexpectedly. The time seems right, Carrie."*

*"Sure, Jeff," she'd said. How could she argue with him? All of her friends talked about their sexual adventures, and at the age of twenty-five, Carrie had nothing to*

*add to the conversation. "You'll take care of everything... You know, birth control..."*

*"Absolutely. I'll pick you up at eight."*

*He'd taken her to dinner and for a short walk afterwards. He'd been a gentleman, and yet there had been a continuing undercurrent of expectation. She could feel it in his urgent touches, his whispers of what was to come. Other women must delight in such attention, she thought. What was wrong with her? Why couldn't she abandon the fear, the thought that she was taking a risk far greater than she could handle? Committing to a forever she wasn't sure she wanted? What if she allowed Jeff to make love to her and she didn't like it? What about all their plans then?*

*They'd gone to the inn. The room was warm and cozy. A fire had been lit on the hearth. Champagne rested in a silver bucket next to a vase of roses. He'd thought of everything. Jeff was the perfect man. He could be the perfect lover.*

*He fumbled with the buttons on her sweater, unzipped her jeans. "I...I have to use the bathroom," she'd said.*

*After a few minutes he'd called to her.*

*"What are you doing, Carrie? Is everything okay in there?"*

*"Yes. Fine." She'd come out wearing a nightie that she had just purchased that day. Jeff was lying on top of the bed, naked from the waist up. Smiling, he pulled her down next to him. She was suddenly trembling.*

*"Listen, honey," he'd said. "This is the next step for us." His kisses, wet and slightly slick, covered her face. His hands seemed almost frantic, as if he needed to feel every part of her at once. He seemed invasive, in-sisting, not like her Jeff.*

*Every instinct screamed that this was not what she wanted. "I can't do this," she'd said at last. "I'm sorry, but I'm just not ready."*

*He flopped back on the mattress, and muttered a few words she'd never heard him use before.*

*His voice was harsh. "When will you be ready, Carrie? When my hair is gray and I'm still waiting for our first child? What is wrong with you? Are you frigid? Do you hate the thought of making love with any-one? Or is it just me?"*

*She struggled with her clothes while he asked the questions.*

*"You need to take me home," she said. "I'm sorry. What else can I say?"*

*"I can't do this any longer, Carrie. I can't be the Prince Charming to the Ice Queen."*

*"I can get back to my apartment on my own." She put on her coat.*

*"I feel sorry for you, Carrie. I really believe that you'll never know..." He slid off the bed, dressed quickly and walked her to his car. Without speaking another word, he dropped her at her sidewalk and sped away. He moved soon after, and she never saw him again. But for years she remembered what he'd said. "I really believe that you'll never know..."*

Once the memory faded, Carrie continued convincing herself that she wouldn't stay the night with Keegan. She would go back to the sofa. It's where she felt safest. She wasn't ready to be with a man this way... Those were her last thoughts as she drifted into a sound sleep next to the most unlikely man who was now keeping her feet warm.

## CHAPTER NINE

MARTIN LEANED OVER the bed and kissed his wife's forehead. "Good job, Maggie Mine," he said. "You ate some toast and drank some tea, but you should be hungry again by lunchtime."

In truth, Maggie's appetite was fading, and Martin knew it. He would have noticed the changes in her even if he weren't a doctor. But as a doctor, her decline baffled and frustrated him. As a husband, it broke his heart. She ate enough to stay alive, but not enough to thrive. Although what that meant in terms of her general condition, even Martin didn't know. Thriving, for Maggie, had stopped being an option two years ago. Still, her heartbeat was strong, her limbs flexible, her skin healthy. Her face, her beautiful face, still made his heart ache for what had been.

"I have a light day, darling," he told her. "I'm consulting on a couple of cases this morning and seeing a handful of patients. I should be home early, and then we'll call Carrie and make sure she's behaving herself. She told me she was making plans to move to Tennessee." He smiled. "I suppose that's preferable to Michigan. Our youngest is like a migrating bird, always fluttering off to more temperate climes."

His daughter's lovely face came to mind as clearly as if she were in the room. "I guess I don't give her enough credit for common sense," he admitted with a shrug. "But you can't take the doctor out of the father."

Martin was on his way down the stairs when Rosie, his housekeeper, called up to him. "Miss Aurora is on the phone, Martin. Do you want to talk to her?"

"Yes, of course." He went into his study to speak on the house phone. He always liked hearing from Aurora, though he seldom knew what to expect. "Hello, Aurora. How are you?"

"I've had some bad news, Marty. I'm going away today."

"What's happened? Where are you going?"

"I'm going to Parkersburg, West Virginia.

I just received a call from a police officer there."

He knew. If the quaking in Aurora's voice hadn't told him, he would have suspected. A police officer from out of state phoning.

"Please, Aurora. You can tell me. What's going on?"

"It's William." Her voice caught on a sob. Martin knew it was bad.

Her son had arrived in mid-December, which was the first time Martin had ever seen him. The thirty-year-old had looked scraggly, down on his luck. He drove an old rattletrap automobile. Aurora had seemed less than pleased when he arrived. She'd been secretive about William's problems, but had finally admitted to his drug problem and numerous stays in rehab facilities.

William had stayed about a week, doing odd jobs at the bed-and-breakfast under Aurora's watchful eye. No one could ever say that she viewed her situation as fixable. She was too realistic, and she knew William couldn't be trusted. She'd been about to tell him to move on when he discovered money in Aurora's dresser. He'd taken that and some jewelry and left early one morning. Aurora had been sad but not surprised.

Martin cleared his throat, tried to be delicate. "Has he been arrested, Aurora? Does he want you to bail him out?"

"Not this time," she said. She took a deep breath which seemed to stick in her throat. "He's dead, Marty..." She couldn't go on and sobbed into the phone.

"What do the authorities want you to do, Aurora?"

"I'm going to identify the body, but I know... I just know in my heart that it's William." He pictured her straightening her strong back, finding solace from the well of her spirit. "A mother knows these things.

"I just wanted you to know, Marty, in case you noticed my car gone, the house dark. I didn't want you to worry."

"You'll never stop me from worrying about you, Aurora, and especially not now. Parkersburg isn't such a long drive, only three to four hours. Give me a few minutes to make some calls, and I'll drive you."

"No, Marty. I couldn't possibly..."

"You can't possibly keep me from going

with you. Maggie is stable, my work calendar is light. I'm going and that's final."

He could almost see her shoulders sag with her long sigh. "Thank you, my dear friend. Thank you."

Thirty minutes later, Martin was on his way to Aurora's Attic. He wondered if Aurora had ever seen a dead body. Of course he had, but even for him, it was not easy to contend visibly with the irreversible nature of death. And this was her son. She'd loved him, still did, he imagined. Like him, she was a parent, and a parent's love never ended.

They arrived at the police station three and a half hours later and went directly to the morgue, which was located in the building's basement. Martin held Aurora's elbow. He'd never thought of her as a frail woman, but today her arm seemed thin, her body almost breakable. He was glad he was with her, not only as a friend, but as a doctor. No parent should ever have to face this challenge.

A technician uncovered the body. Martin recognized the young man he'd seen on Aurora's porch. She reached out one trembling hand and lightly touched her son's still face. Martin silently uttered two prayers, one for Aurora asking for strength and peace, and one for himself, that he would never be forced to view any of his children this way.

Upon receiving a verbal identification, the technician had Aurora sign a statement. Then he handed her an envelope with William's effects. They opened the envelope in a café a few blocks from the police station where Martin had insisted they go for some lunch, and to gather their thoughts. Included with William's worldly possessions was a wallet with twenty-five dollars in cash as well as the jewelry he'd stolen from her.

"You see, Marty," she said. "It's just costume, not really worth much." After managing to eat a few bites of an omelet, Aurora said, "I'm ready to go home now."

As they walked out of the restaurant, Aurora bundled the jewelry into her fist, stopped along the sidewalk and dropped every piece into the nearest trash can.

CARRIE TRIED TO hide the smile on her face when she hung up the phone after her conversation with Grady the mechanic.

"What did he say?" Keegan asked from the desk where he was working on his memoir.

"The part isn't in yet," Carrie said. "Apparently this type of steering box has to be ordered from the factory in France. Grady doesn't know when he'll get it."

Keegan nodded. "Cars like those are fun, but not too practical."

"I've learned my lesson, believe me," she said, hobbling into the kitchen. "What would you like for lunch? I'll fix it today."

Not counting the first awkward moments upon awakening this morning, Carrie and Keegan had been comfortable in each other's company. The relationship was moving toward being easy, as if they'd known each other more than just four days. Not so at eight this morning when both had opened their eyes within seconds of each other.

Realizing she was still pressed up against Keegan's side, Carrie had squirmed to put a few inches between them. The movement had allowed Keegan to roll over with a satisfied yawn while he threw his arm over the mattress on his side of the bed. Carrie had tried to exit the situation without fully waking him, but when her feet had left the warmth of the blankets, a shiver had alerted him to her presence.

"How'd you sleep?" he'd asked through another yawn.

"Fine. I…ah…I intended to go back to the sofa so you could catch up on your sleep without fussing over me, but obviously I never made it. Sorry."

"Don't be sorry," he'd said. "I slept like a log. If I thought I could conk out like that every night, I wouldn't care if that danged car part ever arrived."

Carrie knew he was kidding. And he was just being nice, considering the solace she hoped she'd brought to him in the middle of the night. Keegan was definitely fighting some personal demons. She wished he would open up to her and tell her about the dreams, although maybe he was getting the therapy he needed through his writing.

She concentrated on the items in Keegan's pantry. "So," she said. "Lunch?"

"I'm thinking a thick cheeseburger, some fries and a cold beer."

She laughed. "Well, sure, but we don't have any of that stuff."

"Rocky's Diner does. Only about ten miles down the road. Let's go out to lunch."

"That's a great idea," she said.

"I'll go with you!" Duke's voice carried through the narrow opening in the window of the front door. "Wait just a minute, and I'll get Delores," he added. "I need to stop at the drugstore, too, Keegan, and pick up a few groceries. That's no problem, is it?"

Keegan grimaced.

"We'll pass those stores, won't we?" Carrie asked.

Keegan hitched one obstinate shoulder. "I suppose."

"Sure thing, Duke," Carrie said. "Tell Delores we're leaving in a few minutes."

Fifteen minutes later, the lone residents of the Cedar Woods Campground bundled into the sturdy Chevy Tahoe and headed down the road. Keegan turned up the heater when Delores complained of being too cold, and turned it down again when Duke swore he was going to burn up. Carrie sang along to the radio and passed furtive glances at Keegan to determine if he was enjoying any part of the outing. He didn't seem to be.

Rocky's Diner was crowded with a variety

of local folks—workmen, housewives, a few professional types. It seemed a friendly, welcoming place. A few patrons even commented sympathetically on Carrie's awkward journey with her crutches. Hardly anyone spoke to Keegan.

"Don't you know any of your neighbors?" she asked him.

"I'm a hermit, remember? Not knowing neighbors is the first statute of our bylaws."

"Still, you've been here over a year. You must know someone!"

And he did. An attractive, thirtysomething lady came into the diner and caught Keegan's attention immediately. Her bobbed black hair swung with silky grace at her jawline. Her lithe body moved with precision and finesse as if she were making it her priority to be noticed by everyone in the café. She spoke to a few patrons before heading over to Keegan's table.

"Hello, darlin'," she said to him. "What a surprise seeing you in here. I don't think I've ever seen you at a table before."

"That's because I'm a takeout kind of guy," he said.

She spoke briefly to Delores and Duke

and waited patiently with one eye on Carrie. "Aren't you going to introduce us, Kee?" she said.

"Sure." He mumbled his introduction. "Carrie, this is Jeanette. This is Carrie."

A silence awkward with unfulfilled details permeated the area around their table until Jeanette pulled up a chair and settled between Carrie and Keegan at a small four-top clearly not intended for more. "And where did you come from, honey?" Jeanette said to Carrie. "Are you a relative of Kee's?"

"Ah, no. I'm sort of his current charity case," Carrie said. "He got stuck with me the day of the blizzard."

Jeanette flashed wide eyes at Keegan. "What's she talking about, Keegan? Is she staying with you?"

Keegan explained about the accident, the car repairs and the injuries Carrie sustained.

"How long until you're off those crutches, darlin'?" Jeanette asked.

"About three more weeks I'd say," Carrie told her.

"Three weeks? Oh, my." Jeanette stared at Keegan. "She's going to stay with you all that time?"

Carrie waited anxiously for Keegan's answer. When he didn't give one, she said, "I don't want to wear out my welcome. Keegan knows I'll leave just as soon as I can."

Jeanette gave Keegan a coy smile. "Looks like a leopard really can change his spots, doesn't it? Keegan the Good Samaritan."

"I expect to be on my way long before three weeks," Carrie said, and noticed the stiff smile on Jeanette's lips gentle into something more natural.

Jeanette stood when someone called her name from across the room. "That's Suzie. I've got to run," she said. "You call me if you need anything, Carrie." With a pointed stare at Keegan she said, "I'll be glad to run supplies out to the cabin." With a hand on Keegan's shoulder, she added, "She's a cute little thing, Kee. I thought maybe she was your little sister. You take good care of her."

Keegan grunted and took a long draw from his beer.

Silence settled over the table until Delores spoke up. "It's the darndest thing. I've had a half glass of water and already I've got to go to the ladies' room. Will you come with me, Carrie?"

Glancing forlornly at her crutches, Carrie said, "I will if you really need me to, but…"

"Good. I do. Don't know why I hate going by myself. Afraid someone will open the wrong door on me. Modesty is the curse of the Midwestern woman. We'll walk slow."

Once inside the restroom, Carrie indicated an empty stall and immediately realized that Delores did not need to use the facilities. "What are we doing in here, Delores?" she asked.

"That cheeky hussy!"

"Who? Jeanette?"

"Of course, Jeanette. She's no good for Keegan. She's head and shoulders above him in wiles and traps and chasing after a man. You know Keegan… He's just a simple country boy." Delores pointed to her head. "I love him like a son, but there's not much up here if you know what I mean."

Carrie had to swallow to keep a belly laugh from escaping. Keegan a simple country boy? She remembered Keegan telling her that Delores had no idea who he really was. "What makes you think Jeanette is after Keegan?" she finally said.

"You saw the way she was looking at him,

all sparkly eyed and mouth watery. You'd have thought he was the best thing on the menu." Delores leaned close to Carrie's ear. "She's a fox, that one, and poor Keegan is the henhouse."

Carrie didn't know how to respond. Truthfully, she'd be surprised to learn that Keegan hadn't had a female visitor stay overnight at some point. And why shouldn't he? He wasn't married. He was living alone with no responsibilities. He was ruggedly handsome in a way that most women would find very attractive. And he was certainly mysterious. She wondered if Jeanette knew about his past, or cared.

Her mind lingered on the assorted descriptions Delores had used about Jeanette. This was none of Carrie's business, and Keegan was certainly experienced enough to handle his own love life. But still… He was a man, and Delores might be right. He was certainly no simple country boy, but did he even realize that Jeanette was trying to trap him?

BESIDES BEING ALL mouth-watery as well, lunch was a delightful taste of freedom for

Carrie. In fact, she enjoyed hearing that Keegan had never sat at a table before in the diner. That meant he'd been willing to break his rules for her. Besides that, her perfect farsighted vision had kept tabs on Keegan and Jeanette, and Carrie was gratified that, once Jeanette left their table, he never once looked in her direction.

Why should that make Carrie happy? She certainly didn't have designs on Keegan, and even if she did, Carrie was only good at innocent flirting. She didn't have the arsenal of a woman like Jeanette—that sass and swing and overall confidence. Yes, Carrie was attractive in a youthful, don't-wanna-grow-up way, but Jeanette—she was fully grown in all the right places. And she'd probably already had her hands on Keegan, literally and figuratively.

After the required stops at the drugstore and market, Keegan drove his entourage back to the campground.

"I need a nap," Duke announced, and hobbled his way to his trailer.

"I'll make some scones to thank you for today, Keegan," Delores said, and despite his protestations that payback wasn't necessary, she headed off to her kitchen.

That left Keegan and Carrie with lazy full bellies and an afternoon ahead of them. Carrie decided she could use a nap, or at least a time to unwind, but she figured that was because the memory of a night snuggled next to Keegan was still fresh on her mind. *That was a one-time thing, Carrie*, she told herself. As surprisingly pleasant as it was.

Keegan turned on the TV and watched a few minutes of the news. Apparently satisfied that the world wasn't coming to an end today, he picked up the remote. "I get a lot of movies," he said. "Do you want to watch one?"

"I don't know. How about if we just talk?" *What's wrong with you, Carrie? You just can't leave well enough alone, can you?* Just hours ago she'd been trying to think of a way to avoid answering questions about herself.

"Talk?" Keegan stared at her as if she were an alien being. "We talk all the time, don't we?"

She smiled. "Well, there's meal planning and answering a couple of simple questions with as few words as possible… And then there's actually talking. That requires eye contact, a selected vocabulary, an orchestrated thought process…"

He waved the remote in front of her face. "Sounds like work, doesn't it? I mean, that's what I do when I write."

She gave him her best you're-so-clueless look and he chuckled. "What do you want to talk about, Carrie?"

She moved over on the sofa and patted the seat next to her. "Oh, you know, your life here in the boonies, what you do all day, your hobbies…"

"Life is quiet, I write, watch TV. I don't have any. Okay, what's next?"

"Your friends and acquaintances. There must be people you enjoy spending time with."

"Nope. And not to flatter you overmuch, but you are the first person I've been able to stand in a long time."

"My, you do risk swelling my head with that compliment." She paused a moment before saying, "What about the lady at the diner, Jeanette? She's a friend, isn't she?"

He waited a few seconds before nodding

slowly. "Delores. The trip to the ladies' room. She filled your head with all sorts of gory details."

"Are any of them true?"

"Ha! I've admitted to being a hermit, but I never said I was a monk. Now, if you want to play truth or dare, I guarantee I can make you blush, but you'll have to answer, too."

She frowned. "You won't make me blush," she said rather haughtily. "I don't have anything to hide."

His jaw dropped, but she knew he was only pretending to be surprised. "Honey, you've been hiding everything since you got here."

That was true, but as far as her past experiences with men, she didn't have many secrets. Did she regret that fact? Too many ways to mention. "I'm not going to play truth or dare with you," she said. "If we did play, I would just be shocked, and you would just be disappointed."

His arm settled on the back of the sofa, his fingers lightly touching her shoulder. He smiled. "Are you saying that as far as boyfriends and lovers are concerned, you have a pristine past?"

"No… I'm not saying that. Just that compared to you, I imagine my exploits are not very…"

"I believe I made a promise to you that you would have to answer some questions for a change."

So he hadn't forgotten. His hand slipped up to cup her nape under her hair. "Let's assume Delores is looking in the window right now. After all, I wouldn't put it past her."

"And what would be the point?" His fingers pressed gently on her skin, sending pleasurable waves to her shoulders. If he did tell her the point, she didn't think she'd remember.

"Let's give her something to think about." He leaned closer. Carrie's heartbeat accelerated. "If I kissed you right now, she'd have a juicy morsel to chew on for days, and you'd have a story to use the next time you played truth or dare."

He pulled her face to his. She swallowed. "You're not going to kiss me, though."

"Yes, I think I am, but purely for the entertainment value."

His lips were practically touching hers.

Carrie's mind spun in a crazy wonderful arc. "For Delores's entertainment, you mean?"

"Not entirely, Carrie," he whispered. "Not even partly." His lips brushed hers, soft, gentle and moist. "I should have done that last night, but I sort of promised I wouldn't."

"And you always keep your promises." Her tongue peeked out to trace her lips with hope that he would take the hint.

"Not always. If I promised you right now that I wouldn't kiss you again, it would be a lie."

His mouth came down hard and hungrier this time. He leaned her back against the sofa. His hands cradled her face. His tongue pressed on her lips, invaded her mouth. The kiss was hot and sweet, a dizzying contradiction that left her breathless, but this time in a good way. Oh, so good.

He ended the kiss with a few blissful nibbles on her cheeks, her ears. His mouth was like velvet and sandpaper, the softness of an experienced lover combined with the ravages of a bitter winter wind. She melted with the tenderness while she gasped at the raw pleasure tingling in her nerve endings.

He drew back. "That was nice," he said. "Wouldn't mind doing it again."

"I can't believe we did it that time." She might have said more, but she could hardly breathe—this time for all the best reasons.

He picked up the remote. "Well, a man would be a fool not to take advantage of a situation like this. I mean, a cold day, a warm fire and a lady who can't run away."

She smiled but kept her gaze on her lap. In a voice so soft she didn't know if he even heard, she said, "I wasn't thinking of running."

# CHAPTER TEN

FOR THE REST of the day Carrie had trouble concentrating on anything that wasn't directly or indirectly about Keegan. The way he didn't bother to comb his hair when he came out of the bathroom after a shower. The way he held one long finger against his chin when he contemplated dinner choices in his cupboard. The straightness of his back and his keen focus as he sat at his computer.

Was he thinking about her, about the kiss? He glanced over at her a few times and smiled. She hoped that meant he was remembering the kiss with appreciation.

Was she as good a kisser as Keegan was? He held his own very well in that category. She'd been wrapped in his arms. He'd ministered to her cut with gentleness, but that kiss overshadowed everything else and made her certain that if it happened again, she wouldn't mind at all. And she began to think that if his interest went beyond kissing…well, no use wondering about what might never happen.

After dinner, Keegan sat in his favorite easy chair and pulled his phone from his pocket. When he looked over at Carrie and caught her staring, he smiled. "Calling Taylor," he said. "Just so you know."

"Of course." She shrugged. "It's none of my business."

He laughed softly. "You know what they say, 'If I had a nickel for every time…'"

She pushed her reading glasses up to the bridge of her nose and concentrated on her book. "Very funny."

The conversation went about as it had several nights ago. Keegan spoke to his son as if he were a distant, concerned uncle, asking about school, sports, his friends. Keegan was polite and encouraging, and she assumed the same manners were on display from his son. Not once did Keegan laugh, tease or cajole as the Fosters regularly did with each other. He could have been an executive speaking to a coworker in an office environment. Carrie reminded herself that it had been more than a year since the two had physically been together. Distance is difficult, a potential bond killer.

When he disconnected, Carrie said, "How is Taylor?"

"He's fine," was the succinct answer. "Nothing much new."

She remembered when she was thirteen years old. There was always something new that she couldn't wait to share with her parents.

"I'll bet you wish you could see him."

"Well, sure, and I will. I'm planning on flying out to Seattle this summer."

"That's a long way off. Have you ever thought of bringing Taylor here?"

"To the campground?" Keegan stifled a laugh. "Yeah, any kid would be thrilled to spend a few cold, bitter days in this rockin' environment."

"You enjoyed it when you were his age, didn't you?"

"Well, yeah, but that was when my grandfather was alive. And I wasn't around much in the winter. There was always a lot to do in the good months. I helped around the campground, we went fishing and boating. Back then it was fun."

"Have you thought about ways to make it fun in the winter, as well? Taylor might surprise you and really enjoy himself here."

"Carrie, kids are different today. They're not like I was. Taylor's into electronics, movies, probably girls."

She smiled. "My, you are old! There were no movies or girls when you were growing up?"

He scowled. "All I'm saying is that Taylor would be bored stiff here. I was never bored. There was always land to explore and creatures to catch. And my grandfather kept me busy sweeping the concrete pads and gathering wood."

She wanted to remind him that there could be lots to do again on these seven acres, if she had her way, but now wasn't the time to bring up her sketches again.

"Besides," he said, "I won't be here much longer. Just waiting out the winter until I can spruce the grounds up a bit to make the property more saleable. And urge Duke and Delores to hook up their trailers to the nearest pickup and find greener pastures."

"What do you suppose will happen to the two of them?" she asked.

"I don't know. I've let them live here rent-free for a year. I figure my responsibility is over." He took his jacket from a hook by the door. "I'm going outside to move the trash cans to the curb. I'll be a few minutes because I have to get Delores's and Duke's, as well. If you need anything just holler. I'll hear you."

Carrie didn't believe for a moment that Keegan hadn't considered his neighbors. She figured he'd spend his last days at Cedar Woods finding Delores and Duke a new place to park their trailers. Keegan was a much more caring guy than he let on.

She thought about missed opportunities between this father and his son, ones that Keegan would regret. He shouldn't let such valuable time slip away. Soon his son would be grown, and if the two didn't build a base of friendship and respect now, maybe they never would. Even a few months could result in a big difference when a kid was only thirteen.

She picked up her book but didn't open it. Instead she glanced across the room to Keegan's chair. On the end table sat his cell phone, and an idea struck Carrie with such force that she couldn't ignore her excitement. Could she do this? She made her way to the chair, picked up a pencil and paper, and opened the antiquated cell phone to the last screen, showing most recent calls.

There it was, a call of five minutes duration with an out-of-state area code. Taylor's number. She scribbled it on the paper. Of course, the number could belong to the household or Keegan's ex-wife, but Taylor was thirteen. Carrie figured most kids his age had their own phones.

She should have a few minutes before Keegan came back, but just in case, she went into the bathroom and closed the door. Sitting on the commode, she brought up the dialing screen on her own smartphone and input the number. A young, husky voice answered. "Hello."

"Taylor Breen?"

"Yes. Who's this?"

"My name is Carrie Foster. I'm a friend of your father's."

Taylor inhaled a quick breath. "Is he okay? I just talked to him."

"Yes, he's fine. But I know he misses you, and I'd like to surprise him. Your dad has done a number of favors for me, and this would be my way of repaying him."

"What do you want to do?"

"I'd like to bring you here to where your

father is staying. I'll pay for the plane ticket of course, round-trip. The best route should be Seattle to Cleveland."

"But Dad's in that campground in the middle of nowhere, isn't he?"

Taylor sounded less than enthusiastic. Perhaps he wouldn't want to give up his life in Seattle for a few days in the wintry country-side.

"Yes, he lives in the campground, but he has a charming cabin. It's cold now, but the snow is beautiful. Just a long weekend to start, and you two will find plenty to do. He has some cross-country skis here. Maybe you'd like to try that."

"This would be a surprise?"

"Yes."

"I don't think my dad likes surprises," Taylor said.

Ordinarily, Carrie would agree with him, but she hoped this time would be different. "I bet he'll like this one."

"I'll have to ask my mom. She'll probably want to talk to you, too."

"That's fine. I'm happy to speak with her. Tell her your dad will pick you up at the air-port."

"Okay. I'd kind of like to come."

"Great. When do you suppose you can get away?"

"Maybe Saturday. It's still Christmas break from school. We don't go back until next Wednesday. I could fly back to Seattle on Tuesday."

Two days! Carrie could pull this off. She doubted many people were filling seats from Seattle to Cleveland this time of year. "Put your mother on the phone, Taylor, and let me explain everything. And then I'll call the airline. I'll text you the details."

Convincing Taylor proved much easier than convincing his mother. But Carrie coaxed and cajoled Marta Breen into accepting that Carrie didn't have an ulterior motive. She explained about her accident and Keegan's kindness in helping her. She used her own connection with the Forest Service and told Marta how to look up her credentials. And mostly, she told the mother that Keegan missed his son and wanted to see him.

"I want this to be a surprise, Marta," she said. "I owe Keegan so much."

Taylor's voice in the background was insistent and pleading, and finally, Marta said,

"I guess it would be okay. Taylor does want to see his dad."

Carrie heard the front door of the cabin open just as she ended the call. "Please, let's keep this a secret. I want it to be a true surprise for Keegan."

"All right," Marta said. "Let Taylor know if you get the tickets. And Carrie…?"

"Yes?"

"How is Patrick?"

Naturally, Marta would still refer to her husband by his other name. "He's fine. Healthy, making plans for the future. He misses his son terribly."

"He's a good man," Marta said. "Difficult to live with, or live without, as in our case. But he's still a decent guy. Take care of my son, Carrie. I'm counting on you."

"I will." She disconnected, made a quick call to an airline to reserve the seat, and left the bathroom. She hoped the grin on her face wouldn't give away the fact that a secret was brewing.

"WHAT'S GOING ON with you?" Keegan asked. Carrie was usually cheerful, but tonight she looked positively euphoric. She tried to read her book but seemed unable to be still. She kept looking over at him as he worked. Well, he understood that part. He kept looking over at her, too.

"Nothing," she insisted. "It's been a nice day. Lunch out, meeting new people."

"You mean Jeanette?"

"Of course I mean Jeanette. Who else would I mean?"

He narrowed his eyes, trying to read what was going on in her mind. Sometimes his reporter's instincts did not allow him to let a pleasant moment be just that—pleasant. "I'm glad to know that meeting Jeanette was such a high point for you."

She rested her book on her lap. "Actually it wasn't her so much. I was gratified to see that you have friends."

"I have friends," he protested weakly. "As many as I want, anyway."

"Well, sure, but living here in isolation, don't you find that you need variety in your life, something to keep you occupied, hold your attention?"

He smiled, thinking back to the afternoon. "I had someone's lips keeping me occupied earlier," he said. "How about you?"

She grinned, a coy upturning of her lips that seemed as much an invitation as an agreement. "I'm not talking about that kind of stimulation. I meant…"

"I know what you meant." He opened a drawer in his desk and took out a deck of cards. "Tell you what… Let's go for some variety right now. Do you play gin rummy?"

"I happen to be a master at gin rummy," she said.

He cocked an eyebrow at her. "The lady has skills, eh? That sounded like a challenge to me." He moved a pillow to the coffee table so she could rest her leg there. Then he sat next to her on the sofa and started dealing.

"What are we playing for?" she asked, giving him just the opening he'd been waiting for.

"Winner gets to decide how to say goodnight." He cleared his throat and glanced sideways at her. "That's assuming you're not sleeping with me again tonight, which would definitely be my choice."

"You assume correctly," she said in a haughty voice he was beginning to quite like.

"Okay, then. Whoever gets five hundred

points first wins. But I should tell you, Carrie…"

"What?"

"I'm going to try my hardest, but whoever scores highest, I'm hoping we will both end up winners."

She licked her soft pink lips, the ones he had been thinking about most of the day, and raked her fingers through strands of blond hair falling over her shoulder. Cute, tempting and yet somehow innocent. He'd never met anyone quite like her, and he was enjoying every minute of trying to figure her out. *Enjoy*… That was a word he didn't find in his vocabulary too often these days, either.

She picked up her cards and fanned them out in her hand. "Both winners?" she said. "I rather like that idea."

# CHAPTER ELEVEN

THE NEXT DAY was a period of expectation for Carrie. She'd decided not to tell Keegan anything about his son's visit until they were in his car on the way to the airport the following morning. That was about as much of a surprise as she could pull off with a man like Keegan, a man who craved answers to life's most perplexing questions. There was no chance she'd get him to drive the whole distance to the airport without knowing exactly why.

Carrie was happy. Her nerves were on edge, but the anticipation felt good. She didn't think she'd sleep a wink the night before.

And almost as if he knew she'd planned something pretty spectacular for him, Keegan had been caring and kind and affectionate without being pushy. She enjoyed the occasional peck on her cheek, the touch to her shoulders and arms as he passed by. Without talking about the changes, they had definitely become more than accident victim and Good Samaritan. He'd done no more than kiss her, yet he had made her feel secure and comfortable in his presence ever since she'd first met him.

She didn't know what they had become to each other, but their time in the cabin was relaxed and natural, and Carrie didn't want to think about the day her leg would be healed and she would have to leave. She didn't love Keegan, but she liked him more and more. When she opened her eyes in the morning, she liked knowing he would be the first person she'd see. When she ate across the table from him, she liked being the one he talked to. When they watched a movie together, she liked when he paused the film so they could talk about what was going on in the plot. But love him? No, all these things weren't love, were they?

On the other hand, in one week, her feelings for him had grown to be as deep and profound as she'd experienced with any of her other boyfriends. She was beginning to believe that love, even an intimate relationship with a man, wasn't an emotional impossibility for her.

Late Friday afternoon, he came and sat beside her on the sofa. "Tomorrow is New Year's Eve," he said. "You probably make a big deal out of that holiday. Party dress, dancing, kissing at midnight."

"Last year, I pruned trees in a greenhouse until the ball dropped in Times Square," she said. "For real excitement I kissed a rose petal."

He squeezed her shoulder. "You'll do better than that this year. Sorry I can't take you out for a fancy dinner, but we can go to the diner if you like. I'm not much for dressing up these days, and you aren't getting around so well anyway."

She smiled at him. "Why don't we just let New Year's Eve take care of itself? And as far as my leg is concerned, I practiced walking without the crutches, just using the boot, and I did quite well."

"Good for you. A real step forward, pardon the pun." He waited a few minutes before saying, "Did you call your office in Michigan?"

"I did. Told my supervisor I had been in

an accident and I would need a bit more time to heal before I could come back to work."

"Wow." Keegan grinned. "The whole truth and nothing but the truth. How did he take the news?"

"Actually he offered to come pick me up, but I told him I wanted to wait awhile longer on my car. He understood all that foreign car, steering box jargon. But, Keegan…?"

"Yeah?"

"He'll come whenever I ask him to. You don't have to keep me here until I start to smell like week-old trout."

"So far I don't have a problem with your smell." He paused as if he wanted to say more.

"But you do have a problem?"

"A small one. I'd like to ask you some questions, get to know you better. Is that okay?"

She'd thought she would dread this time in their relationship, but instead, she figured it was right for Keegan to want to know more. "Sure, ask away."

He put a hand on each of her shoulders and turned her gently to face him. "I don't know what's going on here exactly, Carrie.

When I pulled you out of a snowdrift, I sure didn't expect we'd still be together a week later. As a matter of fact, I spent the first couple of hours wondering who I could pawn you off on."

"That's flattering," she said.

"I know, but as far as my relationships with women go, this one must be running on Duracell batteries to have lasted this long."

She covered one of his hands with hers. "My relationships don't really have staying power, either. So, okay, ask me questions. We might as well see if you like the answers. What do you want to know?"

He sighed heavily. "I know you have family. Sisters, a father, assorted animals…"

"Yes."

"And you're close to them?"

"Yes."

"Then why haven't you told them about the accident and your injuries?"

She clasped her hands in her lap, stared down at them. She feared he would think her answer bordered on the absurd, but she said it anyway. "Because my father, who has always watched over me as if a black cloud loomed on every horizon, warned me not to drive in the snowstorm." She frowned. "He more than warned. He practically threatened."

"Turns out he was right," Keegan pointed out.

"Yes, and that makes it all worse. But there's another reason. My father is a renowned cardiologist in Fox Creek. He always kept track of my asthma. Sometimes I felt like he was monitoring every breath I took."

"That can be tough, but it's hard to find fault with a caring father," Keegan said.

"I know that, but you're supposed to see this from my point of view. I want to live my own life without the strict regimen of always taking my illness into account. I love my job, but sometimes I think my decision to work in nature was a direct rebellion against my father's constant worrying."

"I suppose that makes sense."

"He continually advises me to come home and live at Dancing Falls. If he learned about how I disobeyed him and ended up, well—" she glanced at her walking boot "—like this, we'd only argue, and who knows where that might lead."

"And you don't want to take that chance?"

"No. I can't. My relationship with my father is a long story about an even longer battle fighting for my independence. Being the baby of the family has its rewards, for sure, but if the baby has an ongoing physical condition, then the rewards are too often outweighed by the obstacles."

His hand came to rest on her nape. He gently massaged the tense muscles. "And your father never let you forget you had asthma?"

"Right. He has worried about me my whole life. He'd probably keep me in a bubble if he could."

"But you've been here a week. You've been outside, around a dog. You've experienced stress, which I've heard is a trigger for asthma. The temperatures have been bitterly cold. And you haven't avoided any of my scraggly trees."

She smiled.

"And at least to me, you seem to handle your condition very well," he added.

"I do handle it well now. But when I was a kid, I was reckless, and I had a number of problems. My father can't seem to forget those times. He was furious when I joined the Forestry Service. If it hadn't been for my mother, I probably wouldn't have pursued the career I love."

"And doesn't your mother support you now?"

"She would, I'm sure, if she could." Carrie drew a deep breath and told Keegan about her mother's illness.

"I'm sorry, Carrie," he said.

She looked into his eyes. "Don't misunderstand. I love my father. He is a wonderful, caring man who is burdened with responsibilities no one should have to face. And he feels he's the one person who must protect everyone, save everyone, even from themselves."

Keegan nodded. "And if you'd told him about the accident…?"

"He would have ignored his own welfare, set out on that cold, bitter day in the middle of a blizzard and come to get me. Instead, you found me, and, Keegan…?" She grasped his hand. "You have allowed me to be myself, the person I want and need to be. My father can't do that. To him, I am sickly. I need care and guidance."

"To be fair to your father, I know that asthma is an ongoing condition that has no cure."

"True, but it can be controlled, and I control mine. I take a daily medication and have my inhaler with me at all times. The problem with my dad stems from my childhood when I wasn't so careful. Unfortunately he has seen me in distress too many times, and he can't forget that I'm older and not so careless now." She inhaled and blew out a deep breath. "We have had some serious fights about this topic."

"I can imagine."

"My sisters are more understanding, but even they treat me like an invalid sometimes."

Keegan's eyes, the greenest she'd ever seen, stared into hers. "I hope I haven't treated you that way. I certainly don't think of you in those terms."

"No. You've been wonderful—for the most part."

He laughed. "Great. A qualified compliment. But the truth is, the day before I met you, I didn't care if I was wonderful to anyone, except maybe my son, and he doesn't count since he's so far away."

*"He counts,"* she said with a bit too much conviction. "You call him twice a week, and he knows he can call you."

"Yeah, he knows. But he doesn't."

"Maybe that will change," she said.

"Maybe. So how long are you going to wait before telling your family? Can you keep up the lie for three more weeks until you're cleared to drive?"

"No, probably not. I can't stay with you that long."

She watched his face for any sign of agreement. After a moment he said, "But your car isn't ready yet."

"No, it isn't, so there's not much I can do right now. When it is fixed, I'm still hoping to drive myself back to Michigan by using the walking boot."

"Carrie…"

"Only if it's safe," she added. "Otherwise I guess I'll have to call Larry, my supervisor, to come and get me. I won't be able to do much work in the field, but I can at least monitor some experiments I'd been working on." She grinned at him. "That's two…"

"Two what?"

"Questions. Any more?"

"The rest are personal," he said. "I'm not sure you're ready for that. Let's call it a night."

"Sure, and, Keegan…"

"What?"

"I have a hunch we'll have a terrific New Year's Eve, so get a good night's sleep."

He stood from the sofa, leaned over and kissed her forehead. "My, Miss Foster, that sounds intriguing. My reporter's mind is running on all cylinders."

Oh, dear, she might have given him the wrong idea. "Don't get too carried away," she said. "You're still a grumpy hermit, and I'm still a freeloader with a broken leg."

She fluffed her pillow and stretched out on the couch. All at once the wrong idea was starting to sound like it might just be the right one. Closing her eyes, she willed herself to sleep. Tomorrow was going to be a wonderful day.

CARRIE WAS DRESSED for the day when Keegan emerged from the bedroom at eight wearing his faded pajama bottoms and a long-sleeved thermal shirt. He didn't usually sleep so late, but Carrie was glad he did this day.

He would be well rested and cheerful when she told him where they were going.

"You look nice," he said in a yawn. "Got plans?"

He was making a joke, but she hoped she did look okay. She wore comfortable boot-cut jeans to accommodate her walking boot and a light blue sweater with a few sparkles around the neckline. She didn't want to scare Taylor by showing up in her usual sweat-pants and T-shirt.

"I might," she said, answering his question.

He clasped his hands behind his back and stretched. "Am I included, because I don't remember you going over any schedule for the next few hours." He headed to the kitchen and turned on the coffeemaker. "On the other hand, I can't imagine who else you have made plans with." Looking over his shoulder, he added, "Jeanette?"

"Don't be silly," she said. "What's for breakfast? Can I help?"

"I'll make eggs." He brought the toaster to the dining table and plugged it into the nearest outlet. "Sit. You're on toast duty." He supplied her with bread, a knife, butter and jam before he went to work on the eggs. "I noticed you avoided my question. Are we back to having secrets?"

She slid two pieces of bread into the toaster. "Keegan, get serious. I'm pretty sure you and I have many secrets yet."

Even with a view of just his profile, she could tell he was smiling. "True that," he said.

"But don't jump to any conclusions," she said. "I plan to tell you everything when the time is right."

"And since you're dressed so fancy, with all those sparkly things, am I to assume that the same is required of me? Because if it is, I'm not going to like it."

"No. You can dress in your customary Paul Bunyan clothes..." The ones she secretly adored. "But you might want to shave." *So when you give me a hug of appreciation, I won't feel the whiskers.*

They ate, as was Keegan's habit, with the TV tuned in to a news channel. He made comments about the questionable political scene, frightening world events and the many mistakes he was sure leaders were making. "Another day in paradise," he said, picking up the dishes.

"You should have stayed a reporter," she said. "That way you'd have an outlet for all these complex opinions you have. Truthfully, they're wasted on me. I happen to like most everything about the world we live in." In case she sounded too naive, she added, "Well, there are some things I would change."

He gave her a warm grin. "I just might be starting to appreciate your optimism." He hung up the dish towel he'd been using. "I'll get dressed now for what I'm guessing is a New Year's Eve celebration of drinking beer and soda at a local pub in faux, not-even-breakable crystal glasses."

She smiled. "Not even close."

He reappeared after a shower and shave wearing a roomy brown-and-tan-checkered shirt over a clean brown Henley tucked neatly into his jeans. His hair, still damp, showed signs of attempted styling. Still, strands fell over his forehead looking adorably messy and touchable. "What am I ready for?" he asked.

"A drive," she said. "And we'd better get

going. It's a two-hour drive, and we have to be there by one o'clock."

He plopped down in his easy chair and rested his hands on his knees. "Okay, that's it, Carrie. I need more to go on, so spill."

"I know you do, and I'll tell you everything when we're in the car. Can't you just trust me for right now?"

His features looked uncertain, as if he were actually debating an answer to her question. What if he told her that no, he couldn't trust her? Luckily he nodded as he rose slowly from the chair. He moved forward as if his next steps might lead him into a pit of quicksand.

Carrie sympathized with him. A life as a reporter in the most dangerous locales must have made him cynical about trusting anyone.

"Let's go," he said. "As far as we'll get anyway."

She pointed him east toward a major interstate highway when they left the campground. Carrie kept up an animated conversation about the scenery, the weather, speculation on what Duke and Delores were doing today, what plans her family might have, and general questions about how Keegan had spent previous New Year's celebrations.

After more than an hour had passed, he said, "I'm not going another mile without knowing our destination Carrie. It's not that I think you're part of some guerilla army planning an ambush, but my past has taught me to expect what might be in the road before I get there. So tell me where we're headed."

She sighed, knowing she had to tell him now. He'd been more than cooperative. She consulted the GPS on her cell phone. "Okay. Take exit twenty-three and head south toward Riverside Drive."

"Riverside Drive? That's the address of the airport. We didn't drive all this way just to watch planes take off and land, did we? 'Cause I have to tell you, Carrie, I'd rather be watching football."

"No, of course not. We're only here to watch one particular plane land."

"What plane? What are you talking about?" His hands tightened on the steering wheel. "Who's coming in on that plane?"

She'd been so sure, so confident of her plan. But suddenly his eyes, suspicious, alert to a potential problem, his mouth, curled downward into a frown of anticipated trouble, made her think that just maybe Taylor's arrival wouldn't go as she'd hoped.

She clasped her hands tightly in her lap and stared at his profile, trying not to concentrate on the muscles in his temple throbbing. "The plane is coming from Seattle, Keegan. It lands at one fifteen, and Taylor is on it."

He swerved off the road but quickly righted the Tahoe. "What did you say?" His glare made her want to shrink into the seat. If they hadn't been going sixty miles an hour, she might have considered jumping out.

# CHAPTER TWELVE

HE MUST HAVE MISHEARD. That was the only explanation Keegan could come up with. Carrie didn't even know Taylor. She didn't know how to contact him. And even if she did, Marta would never agree to... He ground his teeth. Marta had surprised him before. She could do it again.

Keeping his eyes fixed on the road, Keegan tried to think. There was no point in turning around. His son was coming in. He had to deal with it.

After a few moments, a meek voice croaked, "Surprise."

He risked a glance at her face, centered with the sweetest smile he'd ever seen on a person. Yet that flirty grin was completely inappropriate for the conniving little princess who had interfered in his life in the most dramatic and personal way.

He had to say something. They were only

about a half hour from the airport. Soon they would be greeting an arriving plane, one that had brought his son all the way from Seattle. "You're serious?" he said for lack of a better opener. "Taylor is coming here?"

"Yes. Aren't you happy? I mean, he's your son…"

"I know who he is, Carrie! And because he is my son, *mine*! I know you had absolutely no right to play any part in my relationship with him. Where do you get off thinking…" He couldn't go on. Her eyes were glistening with moisture, and he figured she was seconds away from a full-on deluge.

"I just thought this would make you happy, help to repay you for all you've done for me."

"So you repay me by pulling the rug out from under me? By sabotaging any plans I may have had to see my son this summer? By interfering in a family situation that is delicate, to say the least?"

"Keegan, it's only delicate because you two…"

"No. Don't tell me anything about me and my son." He blew out a long breath. "You can't work people according to your whims, Carrie. We're not trees or plants that you can water and fertilize until they come out the way you want them to."

"I know that! But aren't you being just a bit ridiculous?"

Ridiculous? She thought he was being ridiculous? She was forcing a meeting between him and Taylor without giving him any warning, without realizing the possible consequences. And he was being ridiculous?

"I mean," she went on. "You don't have any plans for the weekend. And as far as your family situation is concerned, I've heard your conversations with your son. I would have to see DNA results to know you two were even related."

"That's just my point!" he said. "We're not buddies. I love the kid, yeah, but he's one type of person and I'm another. He's into sports, music and books and…" Realizing he was totally incapable of describing his son's interests, Keegan clamped his mouth shut. "I don't even know what he's into, frankly," he said after a moment of fuming over his own insecurities, this woman's interference, and who knew what else.

"Then you'll use this weekend as a time to get acquainted with him," she said, as if all the problems of the world could be settled with a plane ride and a few days of forced bonding.

"Did you also purchase a return ticket?" Keegan asked. "Taylor is in school. His grades are important…" *At least I think they are.*

"Naturally, I did. He's going back on Tuesday. Marta would never have allowed him to come unless I assured her when he'd be back."

*So now she's even claiming to know what's going on in Marta's mind.* "That's another thing," Keegan blustered. "How did you talk her into this? Marta is the most protective mother you'll ever meet. She doesn't allow Taylor to cross the street without an escort."

"He's thirteen, Keegan," Carrie said. "I'm sure she allows him more freedom now than she did when he was a toddler."

"She's never let him come to see me," he said.

"How many times have you asked?"

He hadn't. At least not often and not for

over a year since he'd moved into the campground. What kid would want to spend even an hour in such a forsaken, miserable place as Cedar Woods?

"He wanted to come," Carrie said. "He asked his mother. I talked to Marta. Taylor still had some time left on his winter break. We all agreed..."

"Oh, so you all agreed? How nice. Didn't any of you think, for even one moment, that another person was involved? And maybe that other person should have a say in this little adventure?"

"That's not how surprises work, Keegan," Carrie said.

"You convinced Marta to go along with this surprise? I can't believe it!"

"She was fine with it," Carrie said. "Everyone is fine with it, except..." She pointed up ahead. "Take the next left toward the sign that says Short-term Parking. I think we should park and be in the terminal when Taylor comes out of the gate area."

He had totally lost control—of this woman, his son, this entire situation. And he was stuck, so he put on his left blinker and slowed for the turn.

"If we get close enough to an entrance, I won't need my crutches. I can just use the walking boot."

So here he was, a man who had survived five days in the Superdome without sanitation or decent food, a guy who had dodged bullets and pulled injured bodies from numerous wrecks, a fellow who had reported on the devastating effects of earthquakes and tsunamis. And now he was darting around a nearly full parking lot with a woman who was playing the role of ruthless dictator over the next few minutes, not to mention days, of his life.

"There's a spot," she said. "Oh, shoot, a motorcycle. Go down, turn right, take the next level. There's a spot up ahead."

After fifteen minutes of riding around, Keegan finally pulled into a narrow parking place with barely enough room to open the Tahoe doors. "I hope this will suit, Your Highness," he said as he got out of the car.

"It's fine. I knew we'd find something." With some effort, Carrie managed to get out of the Tahoe without mishap. She met him at the back of the vehicle and grabbed his arm. "Hope you don't mind. I wouldn't want to trip."

He started toward the elevator.

She chuckled nervously. "Everything all right, then?"

They got in the elevator, and Keegan took a deep breath. "I'm not ready for this, Carrie," he said. "Any time I'm going to see Taylor, I prepare."

She stared up at him with those wide, bottomless blue eyes. "You have to prepare to see your own son?"

"I tried to tell you before, we have nothing in common, Taylor and I. We get together for a few days a year, usually in a place where entertainment abounds..."

"So you don't have to talk to him too much?"

He grimaced. She was such a smarty. "We spend some time seeing exhibits or going on rides, and then I take him home where his mother probably checks him out for damages or contraband."

"I doubt that."

"I told you she was overprotective."

"Yes, and I told you... I've had some experience with an overprotective parent, and even I would say that your opinion of Marta is exaggerated. She's very nice, and she was quite willing to let him come."

He smirked. "Yeah. And your vast experience with an overprotective parent is why you haven't called your father since you got in your accident."

"I've called him," she said. "Several times. I've just let him think that I'm still in Michigan."

"So when do little white lies start turning into darker, more serious ones?" he said as the elevator door opened to the airport's arrival deck.

She grabbed his arm to step out. "This day isn't about me. Quit turning everything into my problems. Today is about solving your problems."

"And the particular problem I have that you are attempting to solve is what, exactly?"

"Your strained relationship with your son. You need to see him more often. He needs to see you, to get to know you. You only have one son. He only has one father. You both are missing a great opportunity. I'm hoping you will come to realize that for the price of one round-trip ticket, you could set up these days together many times during the year."

They walked slowly into the airport—her because she was navigating on her walking boot, him because every instinct told him to turn around and run back to the car. Patrick Breen, who'd seen it all, written about it all, hadn't prepared to see his son, and he was scared to death.

Carrie stopped to check the arrival board. "Gate C-6," she said. "This way."

He followed, his footsteps heavy, his heart racing, his breath coming in short gasps. She was right. He didn't know his own son, at least not in an intimate, closed-up-in-a-cabin kind of sense. It was one thing to take an exuberant kid to Disneyland and watch him have fun. It was entirely another to bring him to the boonies of northern Ohio in mid-winter and have to talk about things. What if his son didn't like the man he was cooped up with for three days? What if they didn't like each other?

From a bank of windows Keegan watched a large superjet taxi toward the terminal. Was it going to gate C-6? He paused. Having no alternative, Carrie paused next to him.

"Come on, Keegan. Don't you want to see him come down the escalator?"

"Carrie…" He swallowed a huge lump in his throat.

She stared up at him with eyes so full of sympathy that for a moment he considered that he might do anything she asked of him. "Keegan, pull yourself together. This is your son we're meeting."

"What if we can't think of anything to say to each other? What if he's totally bored at the cabin? What if he truly doesn't like me anymore? I mean he used to…"

"I'm sure he loves you, just as you love him."

"I don't know if he does. And I don't have your confidence."

"Keegan, I've had problems with my father all my life. He doesn't understand me. He thinks my lifestyle is foolish and dangerous. But so what? I adore him. He's my dad. I wouldn't trade him for anyone in the world."

"But that's you," he said.

"No. That's kids. Most kids, anyway. We get the father we're dealt and generally we're happy with the arrangement."

"I wasn't."

"I'm aware of that, but you're the exception. Your father walked out on you, and that was totally wrong. Surely you can't believe that Taylor thinks of you like you thought of your father?"

He realized they'd been standing frozen in one spot, and he took a few steps forward. "I didn't walk out on him," Keegan said. "I was working. I came home when I could, and I always provided for him."

"Of course you did. I have an idea," she said. "We'll stop at one of those superstores on the way back. We'll pick up a couple of games, some pizzas, another pair of cross-country skis if you both think that's a good idea. We'll find out what Taylor likes to do."

She squeezed his arm, and even through the thick fabric of his heavy winter jacket, he appreciated the comforting pressure. His breathing returned to normal. Maybe he could do this. But maybe he couldn't. By Tuesday he didn't know if he would want to strangle this woman for interfering in his life, or thank her for putting his relationship with his son on track. But now wasn't the time to worry about Tuesday.

People began coming down the escalator, one after another, until his son, fair-haired like his mother, tall and lanky, with a young teen's awkward swagger, appeared with nothing but a jacket over his arm and a bulging backpack holding his weekend possessions. Keegan had to smile. At least in this respect, he and his son were alike. Keegan had often traveled the world with nothing but a backpack on his shoulders.

"HI, DAD." TAYLOR stood about three feet from Keegan, his shoulders slightly slumped, hands in pockets, his legs bent at the knees—a typical teenage slouch, Carrie thought.

Keegan put both hands on his son's shoulders and pulled him toward his chest. Taylor's feet didn't move, so Keegan relaxed his hold. "Good to see you, Taylor," he said.

"Were you surprised?"

"Sure was. I didn't know you were coming until about an hour ago when this lady informed me we were on our way to the airport." Keegan nodded to Carrie. "This is Carrie Foster, but I know you've already talked to her."

Taylor stuck out his hand. "Yeah, how you doing?"

"Fine. How was your flight?"

"Good. Saw a movie, listened to music."

Carrie noticed the earbuds dangling from his shirt pocket.

"Is this it?" Keegan asked. "No other bags?"

"This is it. Got my jacket, a hat, two pairs of jeans. Is it cold outside?"

"About twenty-five degrees today," Keegan said. "Always feels colder with the wind blowing off the lake."

"Shoulda' brought gloves," Taylor said.

"I've got spares."

Carrie waited for one of the guys to speak again. Neither did, so she figured a discussion of the flight and the weather was about all she was going to hear for now. She tugged them both away from the bottom of the escalator. "We're sort of in the mainstream of traffic, fellas," she said.

"Might as well go to the car," Keegan said. "We've got about a two-hour drive."

He took Carrie's arm to help her. She lumbered her way to the exit.

"What's wrong with your leg?" Taylor asked.

Whew. A conversation starter. By the time they'd reached the car, she'd told Taylor about her accident, his father's rescue and kindnesses since. "I'm just waiting for the leg to heal and my car to be fixed so I can go back to my job in Michigan," she said. "I'll never be able to thank your father for all he's done."

Keegan opened the back of the Tahoe and tossed the backpack inside.

"That's cool, Dad," Taylor said. "Mom wondered if maybe you and Carrie were… Well, you know—if you had something going on."

Both Carrie and Keegan said a firm and overly loud "No" at the same time. "We're just friends," Carrie added. "I don't know what I would have done if your dad hadn't found me in that snowdrift."

No one spoke while Keegan navigated the congested airport traffic and headed west toward Sandusky. Once they were rolling along smoothly, Carrie did her best to keep up a conversation.

"What do you like to do, Taylor?"

"What books do you like?"

"What movie did you see on the plane?"

After hearing the boy's short answers she didn't argue when he stuck the listening devices in his ears, put his head back on the seat and closed his eyes. His fingers made drumming gestures on his thighs, so she knew he was into the music.

Keegan was staring straight ahead.

"It's going great so far, don't you think?" she said.

"Just dandy."

"You've hardly said a word," she pointed out.

"Haven't had the opportunity."

"Why? Because I'm talking so much?"

He shrugged.

"Someone has to keep the conversation flowing. If I waited for one of you to introduce a topic, we'd all have gray hair!"

About a half hour from the campground, Keegan pulled into the parking lot of a supermart which carried everything from food to athletic equipment and games.

"What are we doing here?" Taylor asked.

"Carrie and I were thinking that it's kind of quiet out at the campground. Figured you might want to pick up a few things to pass the time. Games maybe. Plus food. I don't really know what you like to eat. Does your mother have you on a health food diet?"

Taylor smiled. "Yeah, but she's not here."

Thirty minutes later they exited the store with a loaded shopping cart. They'd bought Scrabble, Pictionary, two movies and enough food and soda to feed four teenagers for a week. The word *no* didn't seem to be part of Keegan's vocabulary. In fact, he kept asking, "Do you like burritos? How about tacos?" It was a good thing Carrie liked Mexican food and pizza in all of their varied forms.

Taylor's introduction to the cabin was underwhelming. After tossing his backpack on the sofa, he looked around briefly. "Is this all there is to it?" he asked his dad.

"This is it," Keegan said. "I'm only here temporarily. Soon I'll be moving on."

"Where to this time?"

Carrie couldn't ignore the bitterness in Taylor's tone. Obviously Keegan had "moved on" a lot.

"Oh, here and there. I haven't decided yet."

"What will happen to this place then?"

"I'll sell it," Keegan said. "I already have an interested buyer. We're just waiting for the weather to clear so the buyer can get a good look at the property. But the cabin will be torn down."

Taylor looked at the wood walls, beamed ceilings, stone fireplace. "And this is where my great-grandfather lived full-time?" he asked.

"That's right. Even after my grandmother died, he stayed on, running the campground as long as he was able. Eventually it just got to be too much for him."

Taylor nodded, a subtle gesture just like his father's. "Sure, I understand. Not much here for an old guy to do...or anybody for that matter." He walked over to the fireplace where Keegan had built a respectable blaze. "It's kind of nice, though. I mean, with the right person..."

Carrie quickly averted her gaze when Keegan stared at her.

"How about that pizza?" Keegan said.

They ate dinner, played a game of Scrabble and watched an action film. Tired and ready to suggest turning in, Carrie went into the bathroom to get ready for bed. The sleeping arrangements had been discussed and agreed upon. She would continue on the sofa, and the men would take the bed and an air mattress on the floor. By nearly eleven o'clock, the tension between Keegan and Taylor had mellowed to a comfortable level of almost wary companionship, and as she slipped on her nightie and robe, Carrie was cautiously optimistic about the future for them.

When she came out of the bathroom, she found the main room empty. Where had the men gone? They had left the television on, and it was tuned to a network showing Times Square as the clock ticked toward midnight. She'd almost forgotten it was New Year's Eve. She walked to the door and opened it a crack to peek outside.

Keegan and Taylor stood across the road at the edge of Lake Erie. Both men were huddled into their winter coats and had stocking caps pulled low over their ears. They stood together but apart, just looking out at the waves crashing on shore in the cold wind. Occasionally one would turn to the other, say something, and receive a response.

After a few minutes Keegan stepped sideways and as naturally as a mother bird might cover her young with her wing, he slipped his arm around Taylor's shoulder. They remained that way for several minutes just looking out at the vastness of a wintry waterscape.

Carrie's cell phone rang, interrupting the peaceful scene across the road. She answered to hear her sister Jude's fantastic news. She had received an engagement ring from the second love of her life, Liam Manning, and she was giddy with joy. Carrie was happy for her, just as she was happy for the father and son she'd helped bring together. She had no more doubts. She'd done the right thing when she called Taylor. She would remember this New Year's Eve forever because of the joy she'd shared with others.

"Hey, guys," she called after disconnecting. "It's almost midnight. You don't want to miss the ball drop, do you?"

"Heck, no," Keegan said. He turned, waited for his son, and together they crossed the snow-blown road.

# CHAPTER THIRTEEN

MONDAY MORNING KEEGAN reminded Carrie of her doctor's appointment at ten o'clock. "Just enough time to grab breakfast at the diner first," he said.

The day was sunny and cold, the sky brilliant blue. A perfect winter atmosphere. Keegan asked Taylor if he'd like to rent some skis and try the slopes at Happy Valley later.

"Not really," the boy said. "I'm okay just hanging with you and watching movies."

Keegan glanced over at Carrie and raised his eyebrows in acceptance of Taylor's decision.

At the diner, the few people who recognized Keegan stared when he entered with an entourage. Jeanette wasn't there, but an older gentleman came to the table, asked about Duke, and pointedly waited for an introduction. Their waitress was equally curious, and Keegan figured that by lunchtime, everyone in the county would know he had a son who, according to the waitress, was "cute as a button."

It wasn't as if Keegan hid the fact that he was a father. There had just never been a time to announce Taylor's existence to his neighbors, who from the beginning, and like everything in Keegan's life, were only temporary. And besides, if left to himself, Keegan would never have thought to bring his son to this remote lake area.

They continued to the hospital where Carrie was taken in for an X-ray. The doctor who had set her leg met with them in his office.

"Everything looks good, Mrs. Breen," he said. "That's good, considering you've already stopped using the crutches."

Keegan had forgotten to tell Taylor that Carrie had introduced him as her husband when she'd been treated after the accident. He glared his son into swallowing a squawk of surprise.

"The leg is healing nicely," the doctor added. "In fact, I'm going to send a therapist to your place tomorrow to suggest some beginning exercises. You can remove the boot as he advises and try a few simple stretches. Where do you folks live?"

"The actual address is 660 Shorelake Drive," Keegan said. "It's an old campground."

"A campground, eh? Can't say as I've ever had a patient who lives in a campground." The doctor quipped that modern GPS devices can find any old place these days. "Keep that walking boot on at all times," he said, "unless you're sitting in the shower."

Carrie asked when she would be able to drive, and the doctor muttered some old adage about putting a cart before a horse. "Not until I give you the all clear."

"Are you sure I can't drive with the boot?"

"Not unless you want to risk ruining all my good work."

They left the doctor's office and drove back to the campground. Keegan expected Taylor to bring up the "Mrs. Breen" comment as soon as they got in the car, but he merely attached his earbuds and listened to music.

Once at home, Keegan asked Taylor to help him replace some shingles on Duke's trailer. "He's got a leak over his bed," Keegan said, "and I promised to patch it."

"Sure, I'll help," Taylor offered. He stared at the platter of scones Delores had left this morning. "Maybe we should take these in case we run out of shingles."

They both chuckled, and before going out the back way, Keegan reminded Carrie to take it easy. She had found a comfortable spot on the sofa and had picked up a book.

"I suppose this fits your definition of taking it easy," she said.

"Call if you need anything. I may not hear you over the hammering, but I guarantee Delores will."

They stopped at the shed for tools and supplies before trekking back to Duke's trailer. Keegan set his ladder against the front siding. "Let me go up first," he said to his son. "I'm sure it's safe up there, but I wouldn't want your mother calling to ask me why I let you fall through a roof."

Once they were both on top, Keegan located the trouble spot and spread out the shingles they would use. He put the necessary nails in his work belt and started hammering. Taylor held the shingles in place as Keegan pounded them in.

They'd only replaced a couple of pieces when Taylor said, "So, what was all that at the doctor's office, Dad? The doctor called Carrie 'Mrs. Breen.' If you guys are married, don't you think that's something I should have known?"

"If we were married, then, yes, definitely," Keegan said.

He sat back on his knees. "Of course I'm not married. There's a perfectly good explanation for why the doctor called Carrie Mrs. Breen." Keegan smiled to himself. *Only if lying were a good explanation.* He proceeded to tell Taylor the whole story of Carrie's need for a convenient husband.

"I figured it had to be something like that," Taylor said. "Besides that look you gave me, I already figured that Carrie's way too young for you. She's a lot closer to my age than she is yours."

Keegan scowled. He remembered thinking Carrie was too young for him, as well. Heck, he still did at times. But then he'd kissed her, and all thoughts of her immaturity had vanished. But he certainly didn't want his son thinking he would rob a cradle. "For your information, she's seventeen years older than you," he said, striking his hammer down.

"No way! She looks like she's twenty or something."

"Maybe she does, but she's not."

A few minutes went by when neither one spoke. Then Taylor said, "So is something going on between the two of you? I mean, I know about the accident and everything, but are you interested in her?"

"Nothing's going on," Keegan replied, a bit more forcefully than he'd intended. "I found her on the road in a snowstorm and helped her out. I had no idea I would be having a houseguest for this long." To further define his independence to Taylor, he added, "If anything, as nice as she is, she has been something of an inconvenience." Keegan looked up at the clear, cloudless sky, grateful that a storm wasn't approaching now. If he were struck by lightning on this roof, he would deserve it for telling a whopper worse than any Carrie had told.

Taylor picked up another shingle and held it in place. "She's pretty, don't you think?"

"She's okay." Keegan stopped working long enough to give his son an earnest stare. "Now that you know her age, you're not getting any ideas, are you, Taylor?"

"About her and me?" Taylor laughed. "No way. She's way too old. I'll admit she's pretty well preserved for her age, but geez, Dad, she's thirty, right? I wouldn't be interested in any girl who could send me to my room for misbehaving."

"Wait until you hit forty, son," Keegan said. "Not to mention forty-one, like I am. You'll realize that preservation doesn't come so easy. It's a constant battle to keep ahead of the clock."

"Yeah, for you," Taylor said. "You've been to all those awful places. Cold and hot, and sun and desert."

Keegan didn't think he looked all that weathered. Sure, he had a few wrinkles, a few scars. His beard, when he used to let it grow, was sprinkled with a few gray hairs. But he'd avoided the typical middle-aged potbelly. And he still had all his teeth and hair. He wondered now at the way his son saw him versus the way he viewed himself in a mirror. Was he only fooling himself?

Was he showing the ravages of a dangerous life and Father Time? Would a sweet, young thing like Carrie think of him as a kindly old uncle? But he'd kissed her, and he was quite certain that Carrie had enjoyed kissing him back. Still, he'd always been a realist, and he'd do well to keep his imagination in check now.

"Can I ask you something, Dad?" Taylor said.

"Sure. Anything."

"Why did you take those assignments, the ones that took you to all those dangerous places?"

Keegan put down the hammer. He'd known this question would come up eventually, and he wondered what Marta had told their son about his reasons for writing about the most troubled spots in the world. Had she made him out to be a purely selfish thrill-seeker? And if so, was she completely wrong?

Taking the easy way, he said, "What did your mother tell you?"

"Mom always said you were brave."

*Okay. Not bad.*

"But sometimes she added 'stupid' to that.

Mostly she just said you were a good man but not so great a husband."

"I wasn't."

"I know you always sent money," Taylor said.

"Being a good husband isn't about money. At least, that's not the only thing."

"So why did you go to those places?"

Because he couldn't *not* go, but would his son understand that illogical, self-centered reasoning? Could he make Taylor understand that he went because he had to see for himself what a messed-up planet this earth had become? He had to try to understand what made cruel people tick and natural disasters crumble major cities to rubble? And he had to attempt to put into words the feelings and conclusions he reached on each assignment?

No, these didn't seem like good enough reasons for a thirteen-year-old to accept why he was left without a father so many times. So he said what was also true. "The money was good, Taylor. I was a journalist, and taking these jobs was a way to make more money than I could have at a regular nine-to-five job."

The boy nodded as if he understood. "Okay."

"And another thing," Keegan said. "I had the best darn photographer in the business. Butch Slattery was fearless. He and I went anywhere there was a story that needed to be told. There was no picture he wouldn't take, no situation that could make him drop that camera and run for his life. If there was one more shot, one more image to burn into people's minds, Butch would take it.

"We were obligated to each other," Keegan continued, remembering his old friend fondly. "We were responsible one for the other. And maybe we even thought we were invincible. I don't know. Some of Butch's photos hang in the White House. Pretty impressive, eh?"

Taylor nodded.

"He was the best, and together we were the best ever. People get addicted to all sorts of things, Taylor. Butch and I were addicted to getting the story no one else could. Was it selfish? Yeah, it was, and I lost a lot because of those years. You, in a sense, your mom, my friends and, even though you might not understand, even part of myself."

Taylor's eyes were wide as he said, "You could have been killed, Dad."

"Yep, I could have. Almost was a time or two." He smiled. "But the most dangerous thing I do now is replace shingles on an old trailer."

"Do you miss it?"

Keegan wanted to say an unqualified no, to put his son's mind at ease. But he couldn't, because sometimes he did miss it. His writing was helping him cope with what he'd seen and experienced. But too often the inactivity made him itchy in a way that even he didn't understand. Would he go back? By all that's holy, he hoped not. He hoped he had more sense now.

"That's all behind me now, son."

"Good. I know you and I may never live close to each other, but I don't want to think of you in those dangerous places."

"We're done here, Taylor. Thanks for your help."

When they'd put the tools away, Keegan and Taylor stood outside the cabin as both seemed to survey the property from his own perspective. For the first time, Keegan experienced a twinge of regret that he would have to make Duke move. He started to feel the hint of loss that he wouldn't have Delores's "shingle scones" to make him chuckle in the mornings.

As if reading his mind, Taylor said, "This place isn't so bad, Dad. I'll bet it looks a lot better in the summer."

"It does for sure." Keegan turned, stared down at his son. "Are you saying you'd want to come back?"

Taylor smiled. "Oh, no. I'm not saying that at all. There's nothing to do. It's miles to the nearest town. I'd be bored to death."

Carrie's sketches popped into Keegan's mind. "You might not say that if you knew what Carrie wanted to do with the campground. She wants to turn it into a resort almost."

"Well, that's different," Taylor said. "You add a tennis court, mini-golf, a game room and a swimming pool, I'd come back for sure. In fact, thinking about cute girls in bikinis, I might even offer to be your lifeguard."

Keegan laughed. "Not going to happen, son. The next time, if there is one that you come here, you'll see a five-story hotel and a parking lot."

"I wonder what my great-grandfather would think of those plans."

Keegan weighed his answer for a long moment. "He might be disappointed, and I'm not basing that on Granddad's love of bikini-clad teenagers."

Taylor smiled.

"Granddad loved this place. He and my grandmother were friendly people who liked welcoming guests and planning activities for folks. I'm afraid those genes didn't pass down to me."

"Then why have you stayed here?"

It was a good question. Why had he stayed so long? Originally, he'd arrived at his inheritance intending only to take a quick look around, put the property up for sale and move on. But something about the memories of his childhood and now the solitude of the place beckoned to him, and so he stayed, longer than he'd ever thought he would. He'd started writing. He'd started healing and coping with what he'd seen. But now it was time to go—where, he wasn't sure. Not someplace crowded, but someplace near a larger city where he could be busy, do things, appreciate things. He looped his arm over Taylor's shoulders. "I suppose I stayed because it was easy," he said. "I could kick back and smell the roses, you know."

"This is the perfect place to do that," Taylor said. "Though I haven't seen a rose."

"Nope. No flowers at all anymore. But if Carrie had her way..." His mind wandered again to those sketches. She wouldn't have her way, and that was kind of sad, but America was flush with dirt and forests, so she'd find plenty of places to plant and groom. "Let's go check on her," he said to Taylor. "We need to figure out what kind of pizza we'll serve up tonight."

TRAFFIC WAS STILL heavy at nine thirty Tuesday morning when Keegan and Carrie circled the Cleveland airport terminal and headed west for their two-hour trip back to the lake.

"Hard to believe Taylor will be home in Seattle a couple of hours after we get back to the lake," Keegan observed.

"And Marta will be there to pick him up?" Carrie asked.

"Yeah." Keegan sighed. "He's so grown up. Didn't even want me to park so we could go into the terminal with him."

"He's thirteen, Keegan. I doubt he needs his parent to escort him to his gate. Besides, the prospect of acting the experienced traveler is something most kids his age would prefer."

Keegan rubbed the back of his neck.

"What's wrong?"

"Nothing," he said. "It's just that, well, I missed so much of his growing years. He was always this little boy, who giggled and ran around and hugged me good-night. Now all of a sudden he's ready for high school and then it'll be college."

"Can't stop the passage of time, Keegan," Carrie said.

"I know that, but I wish… I wish I had been there for him for the tough times. I only saw him when we had vacation days planned, and every hour was jam-packed with rides and games and fast food. I let Marta carry the load of raising a responsible boy who did his homework and ate his vegetables, while I got him for the fun times."

Carrie paused before responding. "Pardon

me for pointing out what's obvious here, Keegan," she began. "But I'd say a kid just entering his teen years might still have some tough times ahead, times when he'll need his father. And I think you opened some windows these last few days, if not a door, to communication. I watched you and Taylor in your quiet moments, and it seemed to me that some genuine bonding might have been going on. Your fathering days are not over."

Keegan glanced over at her. "I suppose."

"You can thank me anytime, you know."

He stared at her. "Don't pat yourself on the back too quickly. You still overstepped your role as houseguest by about a mile."

"How can you say that? Everything turned out great."

"It did, yes. But a happy ending certainly wasn't written in stone, Carrie. You spoke to my ex-wife, for heaven's sake—something I rarely do. You paid for a plane ticket without consulting me. You put two awkward males together, and one of them had little more than a half hour's notice to prepare."

She crossed her arms over her chest in a

smug gesture. "If I had told you ahead of time, you would have just stewed."

"Maybe, but that wasn't your call. None of this was your call. At least admit it, Carrie. You interfered in a situation which you had little knowledge about. This whole trip could have backfired."

"I knew it wouldn't," she said simply.

"How could you know?"

She pulled the hexagonal crystal pendant from under her blouse and showed it to him. "See this piece of quartz? My mother gave it to me, and I've always believed that maybe it guided me. I just felt bringing Taylor here was the right thing to do."

Keegan darted a quick, skeptical look in her direction. "Oh, well, that explains a lot. I didn't realize that you were using hocus-pocus to bring Taylor and me together."

"I know you're being sarcastic," she said. She thought back to some tough times when she'd needed good judgment, like the night she realized she wasn't ready to make a serious commitment with Jeff.

"Look, I admit that I'm at least a partial believer in fate," Keegan said. "I could have taken a direct hit from a bullet or an IED many times when I was only grazed. Maybe some lucky star was watching out for me. And maybe your mom's special faith in you has made you a wiser woman somehow, but you still went too far by arranging this visit."

She cleared her throat until he looked over at her. "Well, overstepping or not, my cynical friend, at the end of the day, only one question really matters."

"And that is?"

"Are you satisfied with Taylor's visit? Are you, deep down, grateful that I brought him here?"

He frowned over at her, but she could tell he really wanted to smile. "That's two questions. Yes, I'm satisfied, more than satisfied, but am I grateful to you for butting in and taking a chance that this little 'meet up' of yours would work the way you wanted it to? No. Taylor could be flying back to Seattle right now thinking up excuses why he won't see me again."

"Do you think that's what he's doing?"

"No, but he could be."

"But he's not." She let the silence settle comfortably in the car before she said, "You don't have to tell me, but I hope that whatever you and Taylor discussed helped you to understand each other."

Keegan nodded. "It did. Taylor asked me some serious questions about my past, my plans, the occupation which kept me away from him and his mom for long periods. I almost felt like I was talking to an equal, an adult who would understand my lame answers, or at least try to."

Carrie sat forward in her seat, straightened her spine and said in her most queenly tone, "Well, then, that sounds like gratitude to me!"

Keegan took a hard right off the two-lane road they were traveling and sped toward a forested rest area up ahead.

"What are you doing?" Carrie demanded. "I don't need to use the facilities."

# CHAPTER FOURTEEN

KEEGAN DROVE INTO the nicely landscaped park but passed the restroom building and kept going to a picnic area which currently had no picnickers and probably wouldn't until at least May. He parked his Tahoe, settled his left arm over the steering wheel and just stared at Carrie.

She narrowed her eyes at him. "Why did we stop here? What are you doing?"

He kept the car running, heating the interior comfortably. "You want to talk so badly... Well, let's talk."

She sat a bit straighter. "I don't know if I want to talk anymore. Why don't you take a crack at it?"

"Okay, I will." He angled his body so he was closer to her, his knee practically touching her thigh. "First of all, Carrie, are you for real?"

"What's that supposed to mean?"

"Sorry to be so blunt, but you are a combination of so many contrasting characteristics, that sometimes you make my head spin. One minute you're this creative environmentalist who hates to see one acre of land go to waste…"

"Well, is that so bad…"

"No interruptions. This is my time. The next minute you're a sunshiney do-gooder who believes the world is a beautiful place and who is determined to make everyone happy, improve everyone's situation, whether they want you to or not. And then there's the Carrie who runs around hugging trees and who has probably seen fairies in the forest."

"That's ridiculous. I've never seen a fairy."

He was almost surprised she hadn't. "Okay, but what about the rest of it? You manipulated Taylor and me into your idea of happiness. You talk to your sisters as if you alone can make them see the positive side of everything. Let me tell you something, Carrie. The world can be a cruel and challenging place. A lot of bad things happen because of a lot of bad people and the whims of an extremely vengeful Mother Nature. I've seen it all. I've lived it."

She clasped her hands in her lap and stared at them. For a moment he thought she might be close to tears. Well, too bad. Someone had to tell this woman that lies of convenience, like inventing a husband when you needed one, claiming you were in Michigan when you were recuperating a few hours from home, often didn't work out the way you wanted them to. And making a world look beautiful with trees and flowers didn't make it so. And manipulating lives to suit your expectations of how people should act could get you in a heap of trouble.

Was he sorry she'd brought Taylor here? No, as it turned out, he wasn't. Was he still angry at her for taking such liberties with their lives? Yeah, he was. She had no right to tamper with his personal business and to manipulate a future she didn't know would work.

He cleared his throat, refusing to let his guilt for being so blunt infuse his words now. "Aren't you going to say something?"

"Sure." She looked up at him. Her eyes

glistened with moisture, but her mouth was set in a determined line. "I feel sorry for you."

"Okay. Many times I've felt sorry for me, too."

"You have your outlook, and I understand you've come by it honestly, by seeing the horrors of war and devastation. But you chose that kind of life. I chose my life as well, and I have my outlook, too. I've come by it by trying to make the world a better place."

He harrumphed. "And so have I in my way. But I'm a realist, Carrie. You're a…"

"I know what I am! Go ahead, be cynical. That's all you've been in years. But no one forced you to follow every trail of destruction, to witness lives shattered, homes destroyed, futures ruined." She glared at him, an inner fire now lighting her eyes. "You were a good reporter. Heck, you're even famous. But here's what I think. I think you got some kind of high out of seeing the awfulness of mankind. And it confirms what your dark, brooding soul has always believed— that our world is a miserable place, and those who live in it are miserable, too. And that,

Keegan Breen, is sad, and that's why I feel sorry for you."

"You know what I think, Carrie?"

She scowled at him. "Yes. You've made it quite clear."

He smiled because in truth he was enjoying this moment more than many he'd experienced in a long time. He more than liked this fighter Carrie. He more than admired her. "I think we've pegged each other pretty accurately. We haven't been together two weeks yet, and we know each other as well as if we'd been friends for years."

She almost smiled back at him but at the last moment got control of her lips and frowned. "Do you even have any friends, Keegan? Do you really think of me as a friend?"

"A few. And no. I don't think of you as a friend. I'm not quite sure what I do think of you, but a buddy, a pal, isn't it." He reached across the space between them and put his hand on her knee. "The other night I kissed you, remember?"

She rolled her eyes. "Of course."

"I'm going to do it again. I've been thinking about doing it all three days that Taylor was here. Heck, I've been thinking about it since I pulled you out of your car."

Her eyes widened. She took in a sharp breath. "I can't imagine why you would want to. I mean, if we're oil and water…"

"I can't imagine, either," he said, drawing her close to his chest. His hand caressed the side of her face. He tucked a strand of hair behind her ear. "You baffle me, Carrie. You confuse and destabilize me." His lips brushed hers. "But dang, if you don't make me look at the world a little differently."

"Well, that's a good thing, isn't it?"

He smiled. "Not always for an eternal pessimist, but right now, yes."

His mouth covered hers, and he tasted sweetness and goodness and hope. And most of all Carrie, the brightest ray of whatever fate or angel or mischievous heavenly entity had sent her into a snowdrift that day. His chest expanded with the effort of keeping his heartbeat in rhythm.

Her lips softened against his. He moved his head, seeking more of her, drawing her into whatever might still be decent in his soul. She moaned, a gentle responsive sound that made him deepen the kiss until there was nothing but the two of them, the subtle hum of the car heater and this brilliant winter day.

MARTIN STUDIED THE reports from the geriatric specialty doctor and the neurologist. Both professionals had been to Dancing Falls today. The neurologist had left a comprehensive report and the geriatric doctor was still standing by Maggie's bedside.

Looking up from reading the report, Martin said, "You've looked at these, Ron?"

"I have."

"What do you think?"

"You're a doctor, Martin. You know as well as I do what those reports..."

"Don't try to sidestep giving your professional opinion, Ron. We've known each other too long. And you're the geriatric guy, the one who sees his patients through end-of-life situations." He paused long enough to take a deep, steadying breath. "How long does she have?"

"I don't know, Martin. A few days, maybe a few weeks yet. You know that sometimes death is a slow and difficult journey."

There was much to prepare, so much Martin had refused to take care of while he still maintained some hope for a miracle. "Your best guess, Ron," he said in a hoarse voice.

Dr. Ron Norton sighed. "Okay, leaving out the stats which you can clearly read for yourself—the slowed pulse rate, the diminishing brain wave activity—we have other signs that Maggie is entering the last phase of life. You told me that she has a hard time swallowing and will only take ice chips or Popsicles. Her skin is thin and colorless. There are liver spots on her hands and feet and all her extremities are cool to the touch."

He stared down at the patient he had been visiting regularly for over two years. "But her breathing is stable. There is movement behind her eyes. Her legs and arms are still limber, and most importantly, there is no evidence of pain. She's peaceful, Martin. You should be thankful for that."

"What are you talking about?"

Both men turned as Jude came into the room. She walked on bare feet, having obviously left her boots and socks downstairs. "Dr. Norton, you make it sound as if Mom is dying."

Martin put his arm around Jude. "Honey, you knew this time would come…"

"But not now. We're not ready."

Martin put his hand on the side of Jude's head and pressed her face to his shoulder. "No, Jude, not now. She's not dying now. But we have to accept…" His voice faltered. "It could be soon."

Jude stood straight and walked to the bedside. In her typical attire of jeans and an old plaid shirt, she looked like the young tomboy daughter he'd never quite understood, Martin thought. But at least he could take comfort from the fact that Jude had found her happiness after years of trials and sadness.

"I have to call Carrie. She needs to be here," Jude said.

"There's time, Jude," Dr. Norton said. "Your mother's death isn't imminent."

"But Carrie would want to know…"

"We'll alert her when it's necessary," Martin said. "Let's not disturb her work until we know something more definite. There's nothing she can do anyway. And Alex is close by. Maybe she'll come for the weekend."

Jude took her father's hand. "But, Daddy, what about you? I want to help you through this, but I don't know how. I don't know what you need."

"You girls are what I need—when the time comes. You three and your mother are all I've ever needed."

"At least let me call Aurora," Jude said. "She would want to be with you."

"Yes, she probably would, and there's no doubt Aurora would be a comfort to me, but right now she is suffering from the loss of her son." He smiled at his daughter, though his lips trembled with the effort. "I'm going downstairs with Dr. Norton, honey. Why don't you sit with Mom for a while? It will help you find some peace with what is going to happen."

She nodded. "Wesley is in the kitchen. Don't tell him, Daddy. He still thinks his grandma is sleeping. He still reads her stories and picks out TV shows for her."

"I won't tell him." He followed Dr. Norton to the door but stopped and turned back to his daughter.

"Jude…"

"Yes, Daddy?"

"You are a help to me every day, even if I don't tell you as much as I should. Each of my girls is special, but you're the strong one. I depend on you, Judie. You've always stood up for what you believe in, no matter the consequences. Your strength has seen you through many heartaches, and a simple man of science like me can learn a lot from you."

She ran a finger under her nose and sniffed. "Thank you, Daddy."

## CHAPTER FIFTEEN

IN THE WEEK since Taylor had returned to Seattle, Keegan experienced a level of comfort he hadn't enjoyed in years. His conversations with Taylor had been more intimate as they shared details about their lives and relived the conversations they'd had while Taylor was at the campground.

Keegan's writing had taken on new meaning. He was writing faster now, thinking way ahead of the pace of his fingers. And he'd discovered one distinct change in the attitude he reflected on the monitor. His words had become less cynical about the world as he discovered renewed empathy and compassion for what he had seen as a reporter. Deep inside he didn't hurt any less. Maybe that would come in time. But in many ways the hurt he was feeling now was good, cleansing and blessedly normal for a man who had witnessed the worst of mankind.

Sometimes, very often in fact, he paused and reflected on what had changed in his life, and the answer was always the same. Carrie. And more and more his thoughts lingered on her. She had opened his eyes without ever expanding his current world, which was now confined to seven lonely acres. But he'd lived in a world in which he'd buried his hands in the muck of human suffering for so long, he didn't think he'd be able to live as a contented man.

He didn't regret what he'd done with his life. True, he felt a continuing guilt over what his obsession with his work had done to his son, but maybe he was taking steps to close the gap he'd allowed to grow while he was away. But regret over what he'd seen, the words he'd written? No. His reporting had been top-notch, an eye to the miseries of injustice. His award-winning words had brought millions of dollars to the world's oppressed who needed it. His articles had made people more aware of their own good fortune and perhaps more aware of the darker nature of man's soul.

Keegan didn't kid himself that he was healed, that the dark side of his own psyche had been purged. He was a realist, and he knew that the events he'd witnessed would be with him always, a continuous beast clawing inside his breast to break free. But he was changing, little by little, and he was better because of Carrie.

So where did they go from here? The last seven days had been experimental. They'd spent their time pursuing their own interests, coming together for meals and conversation. And then, in the evenings, they would nestle side by side on the sofa watching a movie, or they would take drives over nearby snow-dusted roads. They lived wonderfully normal lives, whatever that meant. He'd all but forgotten.

When Keegan held her hand, he felt connected to something better than himself. When he kissed her, he imagined himself as he was in the nineties when he'd accepted that his family was basically dysfunctional and turned his attention to sports and girls. It had been an innocent, uncomplicated time then, and it was so now.

Carrie's stay at the campground was coming to an end. Her car was fixed and sitting outside on the gravel lot. Her walking boot would be cast aside in a week if her X-rays were positive. She'd stayed in touch with her fellow tree lovers in Michigan. They understood her plight but wanted her back.

Could he let her go? Of course, if that was what she wanted. And she should want her old life back, not this temporary one with an embattled hermit of a man whose demeanor was as different from her pleasant, hopeful attitude as anyone's could be. She "could do so much better." That old phrase entered his thoughts with regularity because it was true. She deserved better than him.

He checked the clock. Three in the afternoon. Maybe he'd decide what they'd have for dinner. He walked to the back window and looked over his yard where Carrie sat in the middle of it all sketching. She'd taken to doing that again, adding details, drawing plants and trees, maybe in hopes of changing his mind, maybe to make beautiful what had grown wasted. He sighed. She'd given him so much more than he could ever give her.

When a knock sounded at the front door, he went to open it. "Well, hello," he said.

Jeanette stood on his threshold wearing a light jacket, appropriate for the day, black leggings and a dark blue sweater.

She came inside, not waiting for an invitation.

"So, you are still alive out here," she said. "I was beginning to wonder." She pulled off her gloves and shrugged out of her jacket, tossing everything on the closest chair. Then she went to Keegan and put her arms around his neck. "Missed me?" she asked, a note of flirtiness in her voice.

"We haven't gotten together in a long while, Jeanette. I thought you'd moved on," he said, backing away from her.

"You don't still have your houseguest, do you? It's been three weeks, for heaven's sake. She should have gone by now."

He resented her tone, as if no one could stand to be around him for that long. "She hasn't moved on. Not yet. She broke her leg, Jeanette. It takes time to heal."

Jeanette's gaze swept the small area. "Then where is she?"

"Outside."

She strode to the window. "What's she doing, drawing pictures?"

"Yes. She likes to do that."

Jeanette went to the nearest chair and sat. "I've got to tell you, Keegan. You've really surprised me. I never saw you as the type to willingly minister to someone's needs like this."

He couldn't argue that point.

"I mean...if I thought you were getting other benefits from this arrangement, but you're just boarding and feeding her...aren't you?"

Keegan frowned. "She's not a horse, Jeanette. She's a guest."

Jeanette stared up at him with a coy smile. "So, are there?"

"Are there what?"

"Other benefits."

"No! Nothing like that is going on."

"Well, good, because she's just a kid, isn't she? I mean, is she old enough to vote?"

"Yes, she is."

"Doesn't she have family? Why aren't her parents taking care of her instead of you?"

"It's a long story and frankly, none of your concern."

"Fine. It's you and me that I'd like to be concerned with." Jeanette rose from the chair and walked to him. "I've missed you,

Keegan. You aren't always fun in the usual sense, but you're always entertaining." She looped her arms around his nape again. "How much longer is she staying?"

He fastened his hands on her forearms with the intent of pushing her away. "I don't know. As long as she needs to."

A blast of cool air enveloped them, and they both turned to see Carrie on the back threshold. She tried to shut the door quickly, but the wind caught it. Keegan dropped his hands to his sides. Jeanette backed away slowly. Carrie's mouth opened, then closed again. "I'm sorry," she mumbled. "I didn't mean to intrude."

"Well, hi, honey," Jeanette said. "How are you feeling?"

"Pretty good, thanks. I won't be staying much longer."

Keegan closed his eyes, drew in a deep breath. She'd heard Jeanette, and had probably even seen her arms around him.

"Don't hurry on my account," Jeanette said. "You wouldn't want to rush the healing process."

When he opened his eyes, Keegan allowed his gaze to settle on the floor. He could imagine what Carrie was thinking, and she wouldn't be wrong.

"Is there anything I can do to help?" Jeanette asked. "Do you need anything, hon? Things I could pick up at the store for you? I see you're walking on that boot. Maybe we could have a girls' day soon. Would you like that? Maybe go to lunch?"

Keegan's gut clenched. Jeanette was talking to Carrie as if she were twelve years old. He couldn't look at her to see the hurt he knew would be in her eyes.

"No, thank you. I won't be staying long enough to have a girls' day."

Jeanette picked up her coat and gloves. "Okay, then, just call if you change your mind. Kee has my number." She headed for the exit. "You two behave yourselves, and, Kee, call me."

She exited the cabin, leaving a deathly silence behind her. Keegan wished there were a hole in the floor so he could disappear for a while. His relationship with Jeanette was what it was, and he'd always accepted that they gave and took from each other in equal measure. But nothing he could say to Carrie now would make up for what just happened. But he had to try.

"I'M SORRY," SHE said again after a moment. "I had no idea…"

He took a step toward her. "It's not like it seems, Carrie."

She brushed past him, determined to hide her pain and shock behind cool indifference. "You don't have to explain to me, Keegan. I realize you had a life before I got here…"

"Not much of one," he said in a hoarse whisper.

"I should have known you had to have had at least one good friend. It seems Jeanette has filled that place for you."

"I met her soon after I arrived at the campground. She was at the diner and came over to introduce herself. She said she was alone and…lonely. I could relate."

Carrie disregarded his explanation with a flippant wave of her hand. "You once told me you didn't live here as a monk. This is no surprise really."

"Will you let me finish?"

She shrugged. She already knew how this

story would end, and she wanted to hear no part of it.

"When I came here I was tense, trying to unwind. I would have done anything. Jeanette said she could see the pressure building inside me. She said she could help."

"How nice that she was able to," Carrie said.

"Look, I'm not going to lie to you," Keegan said. "The whole situation escalated. It just happened, and darn it, Carrie, it felt good to talk to a woman again. It felt good to be touched. Did I love her? No. Not even close, but for a time I needed her, and then, even when I didn't need her so much anymore, I didn't send her away."

Carrie swallowed the lump in her throat. "The life of a hermit isn't really so bad, is it, Keegan?"

"Carrie, please..." He reached for her hands, but she stepped back. "Jeanette didn't change my life. Each time when she left, I was happy to see her go. I could go back to work, back to being the anonymous, quiet guy who lived in the campground."

"So you used her?" Carrie said.

"We used each other. We never established claims one on the other. We never talked of a future. It was a sort of relationship, I guess you could say, but it never went beyond…"

Carrie held up her hand. "I get it, Keegan. It's fine. I don't need to hear any more details, and you certainly are not obligated to tell me any."

As if noticing the tablet in her hand for the first time, he tried to take it. "Let me see what you've done."

She clutched the papers to her chest. "Not now. I'm tired. If you don't mind, I'm going into the bedroom to lie down for a few minutes."

"Okay. Do that. I'll call you when dinner is ready."

"I'm not hungry. Fix it for yourself."

She went into the bedroom intending to stay there until morning.

*Four years earlier…*

*"I'm going to give you one solid piece of advice, Carrie."*

*Carrie sat down next to the woman she'd come to admire since she'd arrived at the remote location. Virginia Marcos had been with the Forestry Service for twenty years.*

*She had requested the locale in the dense forest of northern Minnesota and had stayed for years. Virginia was happy here. She was a true forest native. Now Carrie had been assigned to the place for a short period to complete her training.*

*Anxious to hear what her mentor would tell her, Carrie said, "What is it?"*

*"Don't date any of the guys in the Service, at least not the ones who are stuck here in the wilderness."*

*Carrie almost laughed out loud. "Why not? They're all so nice."*

*"No, they're not, not all of them. And I've seen you at lunch with Jack Martin."*

*"Are you telling me that Jack isn't a nice guy?"*

*Virginia rested her chin in her hand. "I don't like to speak ill of anyone in the Service, so let me just say that he has something of a reputation."*

*"Oh, well, you mean he's dated a lot? I don't mind that. It's understandable. He's very good-looking, and women seem to like him."*

*Virginia chuckled. "Oh, they do, honey. They do. Until..." She tapped her finger on the table. "Choose wisely, Carrie. I've warned you. That's all I can do."*

*Carrie hadn't dated anyone seriously since Jeff, and she was ready to take a risk. She was lonely and fearful that she would never find the happiness her sisters had. She knew she had hang-ups about men. Maybe Jack was just the guy to help her through those. He was charming and rugged, and shared the same interests Carrie had.*

*She accepted the first few dates with him and couldn't find any reason to heed Virginia's warning. She and Jack went to movies and diners. They hiked along the local rivers. They fished for trout in clear streams. They kissed and held hands and sat long hours on the porch of Carrie's temporary employee cabin while Jack played the guitar.*

*When he asked her to spend a weekend camping with him, she carefully considered the implications of that invitation. She explained to Jack that she didn't know if they had gone together long enough for that kind of adventure.*

*"Hey, we're both adults," he'd teased. "I*

*think we can spend a couple of nights in the wild."*

*"As long as we don't get too wild," she'd said.*

*"I understand," he'd assured her. "You bring your sleeping bag and I'll bring mine."*

*Carrie was only a few hours into the weekend trip when she started to regret accepting the invitation. Jack seemed to find the most isolated locations in the woods. He wasn't satisfied to cozy up to a fire. Instead his hands roamed freely over her parka. Carrie had forestalled any advances with gentle warnings and stern reminders of her qualifications in accepting the weekend date.*

*When they returned to the training site, Carrie hurried to the door of her cabin.*

*"Look, Carrie, I'm sorry," he said, stopping her from going in. "I should have known you weren't ready for an intimate relationship. You told me often enough. But to be honest, all I could think of was getting closer to you. I hope you won't let this weekend spoil what we have. You're the girl I want, Carrie. I feel like I've waited my*

*whole life for you, and I don't mind waiting a little longer."*

*And so she accepted another date. This time they went to a roadhouse where Jack seemed to know many of the patrons. When she went to the restroom, Carrie overheard several girls talking through the bathroom stalls.*

*"Jack's got a new one."*

*"She'll learn soon enough."*

*"Are you talking about me?" Carrie had asked when they came out. "What is it I'll be learning?"*

*The girls faltered a moment, but then opened up. "We're members of the Jack Martin has-been club," one said.*

*"He's only interested in sex," another warned. "Don't take Jack at his word."*

*Carrie looked from one to the other of the group. "And you all know this firsthand?"*

*One of the girls laughed. "Yeah. We were all new to the camp like you are now. You seem like a nice kid, so of course you can do what you want, but you're the catch of the day, and Jack's likely to throw you back when the next recruit comes along."*

*Carrie returned to her table and asked Jack to take her home.*

*"What's going on?" he asked when he dropped her off.*

*She told him what she'd heard, being careful not to sound judgmental. After all, everyone was different as far as values and choices were concerned. Jack immediately became angry, calling the girls at the roadhouse unflattering names and accusing Carrie of childish behavior.*

*She never went out with Jack again, and when they ran into each other, as they often did, he would always ignore her. Within two weeks he had another girl on his arm...*

Carrie pulled the throw at the end of Keegan's bed to her shoulders and punched her pillow. She'd become so comfortable with Keegan. There had been no games, no dating disasters, no attempts to coerce one person into doing what the other wanted. Keegan had been sullen at times, but Carrie had never questioned his honesty. She'd begun to hope that maybe, finally, this man would be the one she could give herself to.

She was thirty years old, and she'd never... Maybe she never would. Maybe her hang-ups about guys would keep her from ever having a happy ending in her life. Keegan didn't owe her an explanation for his past, and yet still she was disappointed in him. They'd grown so close, and yet while she'd been in his yard, a few steps away, he'd had his arms around another woman. He'd admitted that their relationship went far beyond friendship.

Nothing was more important than trust. She trusted Keegan more than anyone she'd known outside her family. Maybe she shouldn't have. Maybe she should never trust anyone. Maybe she should accept that she would never be ready to commit to a man.

## CHAPTER SIXTEEN

"YOU'RE DOING GREAT, CARRIE," the physical therapist said the next morning. He stood beside her as she took a few tentative steps across the cabin floor. This was the first time she'd attempted to walk more than a foot or so without the boot.

She winced slightly as a pain shot up her calf.

"Too much?" the therapist asked. He grabbed her arm. "Don't rush it."

"No, Lou, I'm fine. Really." She silently berated herself for showing weakness. She had to convince the therapist that she was ready to drive.

Lou led her back to the sofa and made sure she was safely seated. "Minor pain is normal," he said. "You'll see the doctor next week, and I'm guessing he'll let you resume all your regular activities soon."

"And I can throw this boot away?" she asked.

"If he okays it, sure." He smiled. "Maybe you should keep it just in case you run into another snowdrift."

"I'm never doing that again," she said. "Trust me."

Lou stuck out his hand. "It's been great working with you, Carrie, but I'm going to send in my final report on you. Just keep doing the exercises I showed you, and you'll be fine."

Carrie shook his hand. "Thanks for everything, but before you go…"

"Yeah? What is it?"

"I really feel as good as new," she said. "Honest opinion…what do you think would be the harm in rushing this recovery a bit?"

His brow furrowed. "What do you mean, 'a bit?'"

"I'm ready to drive now. I know I can. I'll be careful."

"You mean today?"

She nodded.

"What's the matter? Isn't your husband taking you where you need to go?"

She bit her lip to keep from correcting

the lie she'd told. "That's not it," she said. "I have work to finish up in Michigan. I have to go there, and I feel confident I will make it with no problem."

Lou sat down beside her. "If you're expecting a recommendation, Carrie, you can forget it. I saw the pain you experienced a few minutes ago. You're not ready. You might not be ready in a week. A doctor has to advise you on that, not me." He remained silent a moment. "What's your hurry? Why do you want to get out of here so badly?"

"I told you. It's my work."

"Everything's all right here at home?"

"Of course." She hadn't handled this well. She hadn't intended to raise alarm bells. "Don't worry about it, Lou. I'll be patient." *For another few hours anyway while I pack up.*

"Patient about what?" Keegan asked, coming in the back door. "How'd she do today, Lou?"

"She did well, but she's talking about driving already."

"Really?"

"Claims she's got some pressing work in Michigan." Lou stood, looked at Keegan. "It's not a good idea for her to drive, Mr. Breen. We've come a long way in a few weeks, and she'd be putting our progress at risk if she tries too much too soon."

"She's likely got a case of cabin fever," Keegan said. "Can't blame her for that."

Lou put on his jacket. "Nope. It's lonely out here in the winter." He opened the door. "You folks take care now. And Carrie, I expect you to do the right thing."

Lou closed the door, and the room was filled with an awkward silence. Carrie looked around for something to read or fidget with or basically command her attention. And then Keegan spoke.

"When were you planning to leave, Carrie?"

She stared up at him. "Today. I'm quite able to. Lou is just being cautious. My car is fixed. I'm fixed. There's nothing to keep me here any longer."

"Nothing except a broken leg."

"I told you. It's fine. I can drive."

He began pacing. "You might be able to, it's true. You might start out fine, drive an hour or two and then stop because the pain has gotten so bad. Or you might have to brake suddenly, and your injured leg won't cooperate with the stimulus from your brain, and you could end up rear-ending somebody at sixty miles an hour."

"You paint a very negative picture," she said.

He stood still, spread his legs. "Look, I know you're upset with me. I don't know what you think you saw through the back-door window, but…"

"It doesn't matter," she said.

"It does matter. You think I kissed her, and I didn't. But I can't blame Jeanette. She was just behaving as we have in the past. But that was then, this is now."

He looked into her eyes, obviously wait-ing for a reaction. She maintained a stony indifference.

"This is nuts," he said, pacing again. "I feel like a teenage boy who's been caught behind the bleachers. I've had women be-fore, Carrie. I'm forty-one years old. I've been around the block. I shouldn't have to make excuses for the way I've lived."

"No, you shouldn't. And I shouldn't make excuses for why I'm leaving tonight."

"You're not leaving. That's ridiculous."

"You can't keep me here if I want to go. I appreciate all you've done for me. You have been a considerate and helpful friend..."

"Friend? I thought we'd determined that of all the things we are to each other, friend isn't the only one."

He seemed on the verge of anger, and she couldn't help feeling a small victory inside. Maybe he wasn't too stoic to feel emotional hurt. "I'm sorry, but that's how I think of you."

"Does a friend kiss you the way I do? Does a friend put his arm around you and hold you close? Does a friend make you feel how I make you feel?"

The answer to all those questions was no, but Carrie couldn't admit to the emotions churning inside her. No one had ever kissed her or held her like Keegan had. Keegan, with his maturity and strength and experience. He could have been the serious partner she'd always wanted. But her eyes had been opened yesterday. Jeanette made her face the truth—that Keegan had lived too differently from her. He'd lived fast and recklessly, without ties and probably without conscience. Carrie had never lived that way. She couldn't any more than Keegan could follow her path.

"Carrie, I told you once that you baffled me, and it's true. Do you know how many times I've thought about the day you would leave here? And each time I wondered how I could go back to the way things were. I don't know what's going on between us, but something is. You're not like any woman I've spent time with.

"The point is…being with a woman like you is like treading water in the middle of the ocean to someone like me. I know I want to live. I know I want to grab on and not let go, but I'm not sure which direction to take or where I'll end up."

He picked up her hand from her lap and rubbed the knuckles with his thumb. "You can't blame me for not knowing how someone like you might fit into my life. And you can't blame me for the women who have been in it before you showed up."

She stared into his clear green eyes. "You keep saying 'someone like me.' What does that mean, Keegan? What is it about me that confuses you? I'm about as simple as any person could be. And you…you've done so much in your lifetime."

"That's just it," he said with sadness in his voice. "It scares me to think that maybe I've done too much. But I think we owe it to each other to see where this might go. First, though, you've got to forgive me for having a past."

He chuckled softly. "Heck, you've pointed out to me often enough that you're not a child. You're thirty years old. I'm sure you've had your share of boyfriends and relationships. You've had experiences with men. A woman doesn't get to be your age without leaving a few broken hearts in her wake. There must have been many men who've loved you and you loved back…"

He stopped talking. His gaze sharpened and fixated on her eyes. His jaw dropped just slightly as he drew in a long breath. She knew what he was thinking. Her features must have given her away.

"Carrie, you have been in relationships before, right? I mean, serious ones? You have… You're not inexperienced in…"

He took his hand from hers, sat back and

stared. "Help me out here, Carrie. Tell me you're not a…"

She began frantically groping for the end table. "Get my inhaler. I'm having an asthma attack."

# CHAPTER SEVENTEEN

WITHIN A FEW minutes Carrie had calmed enough to let Keegan lead her to the bedroom. But those first few minutes had frightened him almost as much as the most terrifying bombing activities in the Middle East. There was nothing he could do. In a situation like this, her lungs simply didn't work, and he was helpless to alleviate her suffering. For the first time, he could see her father's point in wanting to safeguard her. What father could stand by and watch this happen to his child?

Luckily, she knew what to do. She took steps to open her airways and didn't argue when he said she should rest. Keegan took off her shoes and socks, loosened her blouse a few buttons and tucked her into bed.

"I'm going to get you some water," he said when she seemed to be out of danger.

"That would be helpful. Thanks."

He came back with a full glass. She had a few sips.

"What else can I do, Carrie?" he asked. "Should I take you to the hospital?"

She waved off the suggestion with a vigorous shake of her head. "That's the last thing I want." She sat up in the bed. "Sitting a bit higher helps for a while."

"You scared the…out of me," he said, omitting the word he would normally use for an emotional reaction like this one.

She smiled. "I'm sorry. This was a bad attack, but it's happened before. I'm fine now, really."

"Your father has seen you this way?"

She nodded. "I suppose you're going to say he has a good reason for wanting to keep me in a bubble."

"Not a bubble, exactly," Keegan said. "But he definitely has an excuse for wanting to protect you. What brought this on? The fire was nearly out. The dog wasn't in the yard. I wasn't smoking a cigar." He smiled at the last one.

"Asthma attacks can be caused by many things. This one must have come on by stress."

"Stress? Something I did? Something I said?"

She took his hand. Her palm was warm, so he felt her forehead. No fever.

"I guess I reacted this way because you discovered my secret." She laughed softly. "Leave it to a nosy reporter to uncover the very details a woman tries to hide the most."

He knew what she was referring to. He was still recovering from the shock—both of the dramatic revelation and the result. A virgin? And Carrie was beautiful, sweet, smart…and thirty.

He sat on the edge of the bed and tucked her head in the crook of his neck. "Oh, baby, it's all right…"

"Don't call me that. It's bad enough that I'm the baby of my family. I don't need to be reminded that I've never had an intimate relationship with a man."

He grinned against the top of her head. "Let's see… I can't call you baby. I can't call you princess. I certainly can't call you a ruined woman. I'm running out of options, Carrie."

They sat that way for several minutes, neither one speaking, and Carrie breathing with a blessed regularity. She placed her hand on his chest, and he covered it with his.

"You know, it's a good thing I didn't follow my instincts a couple of times this week. It's no secret that I'm starting to consider you my girlfriend..." He cocked his head to try to see her face. "I'm allowed to use that one, aren't I?"

"I suppose. It's better than any of those other names."

"Infinitely."

She leaned back. "Keegan, I think I could eat something now. If you'll help me up, I can make it to the kitchen and fix it myself."

"Good. I was beginning to worry about your refusal of the last two meals I offered."

"I don't blame you for having a past," she said. "You're a very interesting man, you know."

"I am?"

"Oh, yes. My reaction to Jeanette was due to my sudden and unexpected discovery of the kind of man you are versus the kind of woman I am. Naturally I figured you had had experiences—you've been married even—but seeing Jeanette with her arms around you brought it all into a clarity I wasn't ready for. It's safe to say that I've had problems with men in my life."

"Do you want to talk about it?"

"Not until I've eaten, okay?"

"Right."

He left the bedroom and began to tremble. He hadn't had the shakes since he'd left the last war zone, but Carrie's attack had scared him senseless. Wrapping his arms around his midsection, he went into the kitchen. *Get a grip, Breen*, he said to himself. And then the simple words she'd spoken a few minutes ago came back. "The kind of man you are versus the kind of woman I am." She was right. He was not the kind of man she needed, and she was not the kind of woman he deserved.

"What do you think you're doing, Breen?" he said aloud. *Even thinking of bringing a sweet thing like Carrie into your muddled world is crazy. You could spoil the best thing that ever happened to you.*

But what was he going to do? The truth was, he was falling for her. His terrifying fear during her attack convinced him of that fact. But was he good for her? Was a man who'd seen it all, done it all, witnessed the worst, good for a woman who communed with trees? It didn't seem bloody likely.

JUDE CALLED SOON after Keegan went to the kitchen. Carrie took a deep breath, cleared her throat and answered. "Hi, Jude. How's everything?"

Jude's voice came across as anxious and high-pitched. "You've had an asthma attack!"

Jude could tell that from hearing four words? "I'm okay. For heaven's sake…" Deep breath. "Don't always assume the worst."

"Then why is your breathing staggered? Why is your voice hoarse? Have you been coughing?"

Carrie had put up with this concern all her life, and sometimes it was difficult to find excuses for where she worked and how she felt. "I have a slight cold, that's all."

"I hope you're telling me the truth. Maybe you need to see a doctor. Asthma can be worse if you have any kind of infection."

"You think I don't know that? I'm fine!"

"I'll believe you, but if you aren't, I'm coming to Michigan to get you."

"Don't do that. Waste of gas." She paused

for another breath. "What's going on at home?"

"I'm engaged, but you know that. I just never get tired of saying it."

"Have you set a date yet?"

"We're aiming for the spring. But there's so much to do. We have to decide where we'll live. I can't expect Liam to drive an hour each way to work. Maybe we'll find something closer to Cleveland where I can keep a horse or two and my one remaining goat. Obviously, his Lakeshore Drive condo won't work."

Carrie laughed. "Obviously." She asked about Jude's son, Wesley, and their sister Alex's family before getting around to her parents. "How's Mom doing?"

There was a slight hesitation before Jude said, "The same, unfortunately."

"Is there something you're not telling me?"

"No, no. Daddy's adjusting his hours at the hospital to be able to stay with Mom more."

Carrie was surprised. Martin Foster loved his duties as the head cardiologist at the hospital. But then again, he would want to spend as much time as possible with his ill wife, especially if the inevitable…

"But Mom's okay?" Carrie asked again.

"Yes, but…"

"But what?"

"It's just so sad, you know."

"We all know, Jude. You'll tell me if anything changes. And in the meantime, go outside and hold your finger up to the sun. The glint off that new diamond should cheer you."

"I love you, Care-bear."

"Back at you. Talk soon."

Keegan came in the room with a tray. "Everything okay?"

"Yes. I was just talking to my sister. Did I tell you she got engaged a little over a week ago? She's over the moon. No one deserves such happiness more."

Keegan put the tray on the bedside table. "Good for her. I brought you two sandwiches and more water. You're supposed to drink lots of water."

Carrie smiled at him. "My goodness, has someone been doing research?"

"Could be."

He pulled a chair close to the bed and sat.

"Are you making sure I clean my plate?" Carrie teased.

"Something like that. Mostly I just like looking at you."

"Keegan Breen, is that charm I see oozing out of your pores?"

"Couldn't be," he said. "I lost all my charm in the first grade and never managed to find it again."

"Then you must just enjoy watching someone breathe normally again."

He grinned. After a moment he said, "So many times I've listened to you interact with your family. It's nice that you are so close to them."

Around a bite of sandwich she mumbled, "Uh-huh."

"Both sisters?"

"Yep. We're all different, but we love each other, just as I do my wonderful nephew and talented niece. And did I mention one brother-in-law who is actively involved in community service at the governmental level? And a soon-to-be brother-in-law who has a gift with numbers and making one very sad lady smile again." She took a long sip of water. "Then there's my mother.

We all wish we could make things better for her."

"I remember. Very tragic."

"And my father is the most self-sacrificing man I've ever known, besides being a pain in the butt about my asthma."

"But you love him, too."

"I do. He has put up with so much from my sisters and me, yet he's handled everything with patience and understanding...for the most part." She tore off a bite of grilled cheese and brought it to her mouth. "But I'm still not going to let him rule my life."

"This place where you grew up, Dancing Falls you call it?"

"Yeah. It actually has a waterfall at the back of the property. Not a large one by true mountain standards, but it's pretty nonetheless. At dusk, when the sun is setting, the water looks like it's dancing over the rocks. We all go there when we have problems. It's the Foster thinking place."

"It sounds like you miss it."

"Sure, but that's normal. Everyone should miss their home. Otherwise something went terribly wrong with their childhood. Mine was almost ideal. Loving parents, great place to live, lots of opportunities to learn and grow." *Not to mention an abundance of adoration from male classmates—not that I handled their attention very well.*

"But for me, getting away from home and doing what I love was more important than staying where everything was comfortable and secure. I had all that, in spades, and I needed to strike out on my own." She gave Keegan an earnest stare. "Besides my asthma, everything came fairly easy to me. I made good enough grades, had lots of friends. I was never tested in the way I should have been until I found what I wanted to do with my life. I like the challenge of turning wasted land into something beautiful and enduring."

"Like this campground?"

She smiled so he wouldn't misinterpret her words as another plea for him to keep his land. "I can't deny it. This property is like an empty canvas to me. I can imagine vibrant colors and usefulness and stability for years ahead." She sighed. "But a girl can't have everything she wants, now, can she?"

"No, I guess she can't." He looked at her plate. "Are you finished?"

"It's all gone, isn't it? Don't know how I managed to eat all that while talking a mile a minute. Suppose I must be feeling better."

"I'm glad." He picked up the tray. "If you don't need anything else, I'm going to work at my computer for a while. I want you to rest."

"No problem." He left the room, and Carrie settled into the covers. A smile drifted across her face when she closed her eyes. She'd never talked so freely with anyone as she had with Keegan. It felt so good to bare her soul. It felt just right doing it with him.

THE WORDS WOULDN'T COME. Keegan stared at his blank computer monitor as images from his childhood took front and center in his mind. His upbringing couldn't be any more different from Carrie's. He hadn't known he and his mom were poor until he was ten years old—unless suffering from a lack of parental affection was a by-product of poverty.

His father, who Keegan had come to realize had problems beyond mere discontent, had taken off when Keegan was five. After that, he and his mother had lived on paychecks Sonya Breen earned working part-time waiting tables at a restaurant. And when she wasn't working, she was out looking for someone, anyone, who could make up for her sad life by supporting her now. She found him when Keegan graduated from high school. She married and died four years later. But at least she'd begged the new husband to help her son get through college. After his mom died, Keegan thanked the man who resented every dime he gave him and never saw his stepfather again.

The only bright spot in Keegan's life had been his summers at this campground where his dad's father had taught him to use tools and fix things and basically be a man. His granddad had done for Keegan what he'd failed to do for his own son. But the summers always ended, and Keegan always had to go back.

How does a man talk to the woman he was thinking of going through life with when they were so different? Carrie came from a loving, supportive family. She still enjoyed tight bonds with her sisters and other family members. Her father loved her—often confusing his protective instinct for love, but still…

Besides his grandfather, no one had loved Keegan, really loved him, until he'd met Marta. She would have done anything to make him happy, even travel to dangerous parts of the world to accommodate his assignments. But then she'd become pregnant and all bets were off, and all plane tickets canceled. Marta had been in training for motherhood, and Keegan was on his own.

He could have stayed with her, taken a nine-to-five job, watched his child grow day by day like other conscientious dads did, probably like Dr. Foster did. But, no. A rootbound life was not what he'd trained for, not what his psyche yearned for, not what his creative juices thrived on. After having so little, he wanted it all.

So, what was he going to do about that innocent, lovely, kind woman lying in his bed? Carrie had probably never had a cynical thought in her life. She'd never thought that mankind was doomed for its aberrant behavior. Keegan had never believed in the goodness of man. He never hoped for a better outlook for the world. He couldn't. His experiences were real and bitter and cold. His dreams, even the simple ones, had died when he was five.

What could he give her? These lousy seven acres of neglected land? And then if they tried to build a future together, could he stay here? He was a man who'd never stayed anywhere. And though comfortable financially, he wasn't a rich man. Money mattered, yeah, but he'd written many articles that paid very little. Honest storytelling was more important than riches. He needed a job or the profits from the sale of the campground to support himself down the road. Which road? He didn't know. He only knew his plan had been to leave here as soon as he'd finished his book.

Keegan leaned back in his chair and stared at the bedroom door. What lay beyond that door was everything pure and good. He suddenly felt all used up, as if he were decaying from the inside out. He couldn't bring Carrie down to his level, and he sure as heck didn't hold any illusions that he could rise to hers.

# CHAPTER EIGHTEEN

CARRIE WAS ENJOYING a break from cold temperatures the next morning. Sitting in the forty-degree weather, she could almost imagine her drawings coming to life. How different these seven acres would look with flowers and trees and blooming shrubs. She'd decided to stay with Keegan until her next doctor's appointment in seven days, but that only gave her more time to dream and sketch a natural paradise that wasn't hers to plan.

But there was another risk in her decision. She believed what Keegan had told her about Jeanette; she was falling so hard for him that she could convince herself to believe anything he told her. For a woman like Carrie, that could be a dangerous path. Her past was littered with mistaken trust.

Sipping her second cup of coffee, Carrie noticed the door to Delores's trailer opening. The elderly woman stepped outside, her coat bundled around her and a plate in her hands. She headed toward the cabin.

Carrie smiled. More scones.

"Good morning, Delores. How are you?"

"I'm fine, dear," she said. "But I'm afraid I have to disappoint Keegan. I was missing one of the ingredients I needed to make my scones, so I'm forced to substitute blueberry muffins today." She raised a napkin from the platter and offered a muffin to Carrie.

Carrie took a tentative bite and then a much larger one. "These are wonderful," she said, thinking that if the woman's scones were half this tasty, Keegan might have married her.

"Thank you. They're okay, I guess, but my scones are my specialty. I like bringing a taste of jolly old England to the colonies." She laughed at her humor.

Carrie pointed to the chair that Keegan used when he joined her outside. "Can you sit a minute and talk to me?"

"Love to." She settled into the deep canvas seat and took a muffin for herself. "How's our boy doing this morning? How is his mood?" Chuckling again, Delores said, "I don't need to ask that so much anymore. Your presence has changed Keegan's demeanor."

Carrie smiled. "Do you mean made it worse?"

"Oh, no. Surely you can tell, Carrie, but Keegan definitely fancies you. All you'd have to do is bat those long eyelashes a few times, and I'll bet you'd have a wedding to plan."

Carrie almost choked on her muffin. "Whose? Mine and Keegan's? You're kidding, right?"

"Not at all."

"Sorry to disappoint, Delores, but my eyelash-batting days are over. I've gotten into too much trouble with the wrong men."

"I can see that you'd be cautious," Delores said. "I could tell right away that you were smart as well as pretty."

"Well…"

"And at first you must have been watchful of Keegan's behavior. I mean, he was always so scruffy and gruff. But he's changed. Both Duke and I have noticed." Delores managed a sly grin. "I might even consider paying him some rent now."

"Delores! Have you been able to afford it all along?"

"This is girl talk, Carrie. And there is a bond between girls. I'm far from wealthy, but I have enough that Keegan might deserve a few shillings."

Carrie smiled and shook her head.

"What are your plans, Carrie? You should be able to go without the boot soon."

"One week. I go to the doctor this coming Friday. I'm sure he'll recommend that I walk without the boot."

"And then?"

Wasn't that the question of the day? What would she do? Drive back to Michigan, she supposed. She loved her job. Maybe not as much as she would love staying put somewhere and making a few acres her own to beautify and cultivate. For a year or so, Carrie had been feeling the need to establish roots somewhere, not with her father watching over her, but maybe someplace close to him, a place where she could monitor the triggers to her asthma and learn to more effectively live with the disease.

And ironically, she'd crashed into the perfect property a few weeks ago, and now she hated to leave. Lakefront, potentially lush and lovely, Keegan's land was a dream come true to a reforester like Carrie. But some dreams were destined not to come true, and in a year or so, this fertile land would hold a multistory hotel and asphalt parking lot.

"I'll return to my job," she told Delores. "I'm lucky they haven't replaced me."

"And what will Keegan do?"

Carrie reminded herself that Delores and Duke didn't know of Keegan's plans to sell the land out from under them. "He'll stay here, for a while at least," she said.

"And be all grumpy again." Delores stood. "I'll be sorry to see you go, dear. But you never know what can happen in a few days."

"No, I guess not."

"I'll take these muffins to Keegan now. Afterwards I promised Duke I'd mend his curtains."

She shuffled toward the cabin's back door, leaving Carrie to ponder what an odd little group they all made. Two elderly people who Carrie had thought were practically indigent, an old dog who loved snow more than any creature ought to, a brilliant and previously

famous reporter, and an optimistic but somewhat sickly tree hugger.

Carrie sighed. What would happen to that
optimism when she drove away from this
place, and Keegan, a week from now?

"THANKS, DELORES," KEEGAN SAID, taking
the plate she offered. "These look good."
He paused, sniffed the muffins. "I mean
they really do."

"You enjoy them."

He peeked around her shoulders. "How's
Carrie doing out there?"

"Oh, all right. She's having what we used
to call an air bath and quite liking it."

"Did she have one of your muffins?"

"She did. And again, I'm sorry I didn't
bring scones."

Delores headed back to her trailer. Keegan
set the plate on the table and grabbed a muffin to sustain him while he went back to
work on his computer. His thoughts were
flowing more easily now that Carrie had
agreed to stay for the next week. Funny
how she was affecting nearly every aspect
of his life. He wondered what he had done
for her. Fixed a few meals, given her some

rides and a place to sleep. That was about it. Her worldview didn't need changing, and if he tried, he would only pollute it.

After a few minutes Keegan heard a car pull up to the cabin. He got up and went to the front door. A stocky man, a couple of decades older than Keegan, got out of a rusty SUV.

"It can't be," Keegan said aloud. A smile broke across his face as he opened the door. "Butch Slattery! What are you doing here?"

The two men embraced the moment Keegan's beloved photographer crossed the threshold.

"You were hard enough to find, Pat," Butch said. "A campground somewhere in Ohio? That was all I had to go on, but a good reporter never gives up."

Keegan took Butch's coat, tossed it on a chair and went to the kitchen to brew a fresh pot of coffee, the beverage the two men had lived on for days at a time, when they weren't sipping whiskey.

"I should have contacted you," Keegan said. "Though you're just as hard to locate. Where have you been?"

Butch pulled out a kitchen chair and sat

at the table. "Been at my daughter's place in Indiana. She's a sweetheart, you know, believes I need looking after. But the boredom has gotten me down. Do you realize there's not a whole lot to do in central Indiana?"

Keegan chuckled. "About as much to do as there is in northern Ohio, I imagine."

"How do you put up with it, Pat? After the lives we led, looking out for each other, dodging trouble. Don't you miss the excitement of the old days?"

Butch was the one person Keegan could answer with complete honesty. "Yeah, sometimes. I came here to collect myself, find some peace, think about my future. But after more than a year, my future doesn't seem any more clear than it did the day I arrived."

Butch smiled, showing he hadn't yet replaced a couple of teeth he'd lost in Iraq. "I knew I hadn't made a mistake in coming here."

Keegan brought him a mug of coffee. "What are you talking about?"

"Have you been watching the news?"

"Sure." Keegan sat across from him. "Can't change your stripes."

"That civil war in northern Europe is a

fascinating piece of business," Butch said. "Almost tribal in its ferocity. So many factions fighting for domination, so many folks fleeing for safety. Refugee camps are springing up everywhere."

Keegan nodded. "I've been following the story."

"Bet you've been writing it in your head, too."

Keegan smiled. "Like I said about stripes…"

"I haven't seen one bit of reporting that seems to capture the desperation in that area, the human interest stuff, the struggle to survive in those conditions."

"It's got to be tough."

Butch took a long sip of coffee, stared at his friend and remained quiet for a few moments. Then he cleared his throat and said, "Let's go, Pat. Let's hop a plane before all the airports are closed over there and do what no other two guys can do as well as the two of us. Tell it true."

Keegan tried to ignore the tremors in his chest. His heart was beating hard enough to make him sit straight and take a deep breath. "Are you serious, Butch? You want to get involved in these messes again?"

"I do. And I want you with me."

Keegan tried to cover his surprise with a forced chuckle. "I don't think so. Those days are behind me now."

"They don't have to be."

Keegan leaned toward his old friend. "You and I should be thanking our lucky stars that we made it out as many times as we did. I've got the scars to prove the close calls, and so do you. If we go back, we'll just be tempting fate, and this time we might lose."

Butch frowned. "I can't believe this is Patrick Breen I'm talking to."

"It isn't. I go by my middle name, Keegan, now. Patrick left his past on some remote desert."

"I'm not about to call you any name other than the one that made you famous. Reporting's in your blood, Pat. You know it is. The excitement, the thrill, the adrenaline rush. I know you, son, and you can't live without it any more than I can."

Keegan nodded toward his computer. "My life has taken a new turn, Butch. I'm writing my memoir, not that anyone will read them, but I'm getting them down. It's been a healing experience for me."

"Well, fine. But your life story isn't over by a long shot, Pat. You're what? Only forty, forty-one, right?"

Keegan nodded. "Feel older, though."

"Nonsense. You've got more stories to tell. You just have to live them first."

"It's not simply the writing, Butch." Keegan's thoughts focused on Carrie. "I've met someone."

"You're in love?"

Butch asked the question as if the concept were impossible. Keegan wasn't so sure the old guy was wrong.

"I didn't say that," Keegan answered. "I don't know what I am." He stood. "Get up, follow me." He walked to the window and made room for Butch to look outside. Carrie's back was to them, her stocking cap pulled low over her head. "That's her. She's recovering from a broken leg and has been staying with me since I rescued her from a snowbank."

"So you've had yourself a sweet deal for a while."

"No, it's not like what you're thinking. I'm just getting to know her. She's… Well, she's not like anyone I've ever connected with before. She's…" He stopped. Revealing more might compromise Carrie's trust in him.

Just then Carrie turned toward a sound in the bushes. Her profile became visible to the two men.

"What is she, eighteen?" Butch said.

"She's thirty," Keegan said, the same defensive tone in his voice he'd used before.

"She looks like a kid," Butch said, laughing softly. "A sweet, innocent kid. What's she doing with a hard-nosed renegade like you?"

Keegan stepped back from the window, aware that he'd had the exact same thought too many times. What was Carrie doing with him? And what made him think she would stay? He expelled a deep breath. "I don't want to talk about her anymore."

"Okay, okay. Let's talk about you and me and getting back into action. I want you with me, Pat."

A few minutes passed. Finally, Butch said, "Give me a piece of paper." When he had the scrap, he jotted down a phone number. "My cell. Call me anytime. Think about my offer, what we've been through—the scrapes, the narrow misses, the victories. We're not over the hill, Pat. We can make a difference over there, one last bit of action before we put ourselves out to pasture. This may be the last chance we'll have, together anyway. I'm not getting any younger."

He pushed the paper scrap into Keegan's shirt pocket and patted the outside. "Hope to hear from you. I know I'm a good photographer. And I know you're the best with words. Don't wait too long. I'm going to book air travel by Tuesday. Time isn't on our side."

Keegan watched his friend get into his SUV and drive off. He couldn't pretend that his blood wasn't flowing like rapids through his veins. He pressed his palm over his chest as if he were keeping his beating heart from bursting through his shirt. Just one more time. Could he do it? Did he want to?

The story of the civil war had captured his imagination and held him spellbound. He'd thought of all the angles, the big stories, the little ones, the ones that would make a difference. Still, he'd relegated those yearnings to the back of his mind where they belonged. Patrick Breen was gone. He was lucky to be alive.

But now he could only shake his head.

Butch had made him think about all the angles of his life, as well—the isolation, the solitude, that sweet woman in his backyard who'd be better off without him. Maybe Patrick was back for one last hurrah, and Butch Slattery had shown up at just the right time.

"I HEARD TALKING," Carrie said, coming in the back door. "Did you have company?"

"Ah, yeah, a fella I've known for a while."

"That's nice." She glanced at the kitchen table. "You made coffee? And I see that most of the muffins are gone."

"They were good. Two men can polish off a plate of muffins pretty easily."

She sat on the sofa, removed the heavy boot from her calf and massaged her leg. "I'll be so glad when this last week is over and I can throw this thing away." She sighed. "And I've got to start making some serious plans for what to do next." After a pause, she added, "Maybe we should talk."

She stared at Keegan's back as he rinsed the coffee mugs in the sink. He didn't respond. In fact, he seemed almost indifferent.

"Keegan?"

He turned to face her.

"Is something wrong?"

"No. What could be wrong?"

She heard his words, but his face conveyed a different message.

Later, after she'd had her shower, she snuggled next to Keegan on the sofa. He slipped his arm around her and breathed deeply.

"Your hair smells good," he said.

His hand on her arm, his thigh touching hers, she felt the same warmth and security she'd experienced with Keegan from the start, but now...most amazing of all, she felt loved. He hadn't used the words yet, but Carrie sensed the deep feelings growing between them. How incredible that this gruff loner of a man who had taken her in, as if it were the last thing he wanted, could become the central force in her life. He didn't treat her as if she were ill. He treated her as if she were well, and that meant more than words could say.

He was nothing like the men—boys really—she'd known and trusted. The ones who'd led her on because of what they wanted from her. The ones who'd made her wary that most men had an ulterior motive.

Keegan was solid, strong and, once she'd gotten past his wounded soul and stubborn exterior, he was caring, compassionate.

And he'd changed her. Made her more confident, more ready for an adult relationship. Like the living things she nourished, Carrie had blossomed in this wintry clime. The woman who'd been fearful of giving herself to any man wanted this one with an ache that had been growing for weeks. The realization that she looked forward to this kind of commitment made her tremble with anticipation at the same time her heart swelled with an abundance of emotion. She wanted Keegan to be her first. She wanted him to be her last.

Since Keegan knew the truth about her, he probably wouldn't be the one to initiate an intimate relationship. She would have to show him she was ready. She laid her hand flat on his chest and felt his muscles tense. "My leg is feeling especially well tonight," she said.

His hand stopped moving on her arm. "That's great."

With her index finger, she traced the buttons on his shirt. He shifted on the sofa.

Thinking he was inviting her to do more, she slipped the first button by his throat clear.

"Carrie, what are you doing?" His voice was hoarse.

She leaned up and kissed his cheek while her deft fingers freed the next button. "Keegan, you know about my past." She smiled. "Or perhaps my lack of a past is more accurate. But you should also know that I care deeply for you. We've been together for weeks now. There is no one I trust with my feelings more than you." She gently gripped his chin and turned his face to hers. When she kissed him, she hoped to convey the desire churning inside her. She kissed him deeply and thoroughly.

He closed his hand over hers, preventing her from baring his chest to her fingers. "Carrie…"

She sat straight, her gaze locking with his. His eyes seemed troubled, uncertain, while for the first time in her life, Carrie was absolutely positive about what she wanted. "Take me into the bedroom, Keegan. I don't want to sleep on the sofa any longer."

He cleared his throat. "Carrie, I'm not sure this is what we should be doing."

"Because it's my first time?"

"Yes, that, and other factors."

"You don't want me?"

He groaned, a sound so sad and somehow desperate that she put a few inches between them and settled her hand on his thigh. "What's going on, Keegan? I thought... If you don't have feelings for me, or if they aren't as strong as mine are for you, then you have to tell me."

"It's not that," he said. "I do have feelings for you."

"Then what is it?"

"I don't know if you should give up to me what you have saved your entire life for some special man."

Her voice dropped to practically a whisper. "I believe you are that man."

"I wish I were, Carrie. I'm afraid that I'm not and never will be. The differences between us are vast and fundamental..."

"No, stop." She turned away from him, locked her gaze on her hands clasped on her lap. "I get it."

"I'm not sure you do." He stood. "We'll

talk tomorrow. I'll try to explain. But right now I need a walk in the cold air. You take the bed tonight."

She listened to his footsteps as he went to the coatrack by the front door. She heard the rustle of fabric as he slipped his arms into his jacket. She felt the cold blast of winter air when he opened the door. And she jerked at the finality of the sound of that door closing.

## CHAPTER NINETEEN

"How did you sleep?" The question, so common and natural between the two of them, suddenly sounded forced and rehearsed. Keegan cleared his throat. "Well, I hope."

"Sure. Great."

Dark blotches under her eyes told a different story. "I've been thinking," he said.

"Not just yet, Keegan, okay? I need coffee."

Thank goodness. Preparing the cup the way she liked it gave him something to do, something to cut the tension that had filled the kitchen when she came out of the bedroom. He set the coffee in front of her.

"I've got to run an errand," he said. "I'll be back before long. Will you be all right?"

"Of course." She didn't look at him. Just drank her coffee as if she weren't really tasting it.

"I've got my cell phone. Call if you think of anything you'd like me to pick up."

She shrugged one shoulder, a dismissal of his offer.

Once outside, Keegan hurried to his vehicle and climbed inside. He really didn't have anywhere to go. Oh, he'd stop at the closest market and buy a couple of things so his story would look convincing. But mostly he had to make a phone call. He drove to a roadside park, empty during the winter months and especially in the light dusting of snow falling around him this morning.

Checking his watch, he determined the time was appropriate for this call. He'd always heard doctors were early risers. Speaking to his Google search app, he requested the number of a Dr. Foster in Fox Creek, Ohio and dialed.

The phone rang and was answered by a woman. "Hello, Foster residence, how may I help you?" she said.

"I'm looking for Dr. Foster," Keegan said. "Is he home?"

"Yes. He's having breakfast."

"Would you mind disturbing him for a

moment? I need to speak to him about a matter of some urgency."

"You cannot call him at his office?"

"I really need to talk to him now." Keegan clenched his hand into a fist. *Please, hurry.* He knew his resolve was slipping, and he had to get this done. This was the only way he could think of to keep Carrie safe and healthy, even if she didn't forgive him. In fact, her life would be easier if she carried hatred in her heart for what he was about to do.

"Just a minute," the woman said. Keegan heard her footsteps retreating into the house.

A minute later, an alert voice said, "This is Dr. Foster. Can I help you?"

Keegan drew a fortifying breath. "My name is Keegan Breen," he said. "You don't know me…" He considered that Dr. Foster would probably know him by his professional name. Most people who were even somewhat aware of world events knew of Patrick Breen.

"Are you a patient, Mr. Breen? I don't recall the name."

"No, sir. I'm actually a friend of your daughter's."

"My daughter? Which daughter?" Foster's voice had assumed an edge of wariness. Obviously any discussion of one of his offspring brought an immediate alert reaction.

"Carrie."

"Is she all right? Has something happened?"

"She's fine," Keegan quickly assured him. "But there is something you don't know about. A few weeks ago, Christmas Day to be exact, Carrie had a car accident near my home."

"A car accident?" Foster said. "On Christmas?"

"That's right," Keegan said. "I realize she didn't tell you about it."

"No, she didn't. I remember that day well. We were having blizzard conditions around here. I told her not to drive. Where are you?"

Keegan had looked up the distance between the campground and Fox Creek. At most a two-and-a-half-hour drive. "I'm not far from Sandusky," Keegan said. "Yes, there was a blizzard here at Lake Erie also."

"What was Carrie doing on the road? What sort of accident did she have? Why didn't she tell me? I've talked to her at least a dozen times since the holiday."

As briefly and yet with as much detail as possible, Keegan explained about Carrie's slide into the snowbank, her broken leg and the fact that she had been staying with him since she'd been released from the hospital.

"Staying with you?" The doctor was alarmed. Why wouldn't he be? His youngest daughter had been living with a stranger for almost a month. What father wouldn't question everything about this story, especially the man telling it.

"Again, Dr. Foster," Keegan said, "Carrie is fine. I've seen that she got to her doctor's appointments. She's healthy, except for the leg, and it's practically healed now. It wasn't a bad break." Keegan tried to put himself in Foster's position. He had to ease the poor man's mind. "I can imagine what you must be thinking," he said. *That I'm some sort of nut who has been holding your daughter captive for who knows what nefarious purposes?*

"I can assure you that I've treated Carrie fairly and with respect," Keegan said, hoping to convince the man.

"That girl," Dr. Foster said under his breath. "Where are you exactly? Give me an address."

"I intend to do that, sir, but there is more you should know."

Dr. Foster drew in a sharp breath. "Go ahead."

"Carrie didn't want you to know about what happened."

"Obviously. That doesn't surprise me. She knew I'd come and get her immediately. She's vulnerable and prone to illness. Did you know that, Mr. Breen?"

The question was put to Keegan almost as a challenge. "Yes, sir. I know about her asthma, but she's done well here. Only a couple of incidents."

"She's a stubborn girl," Dr. Foster said. "Sometimes I wonder if she even knows whether she's doing well or not. All her life she has fought me..." Dr. Foster paused, took another breath. "Never mind about all that. Tell me where you are, and I'll be there as soon as I can."

"You'll need another driver," Keegan said. "The damage to Carrie's car has been repaired, but the doctor doesn't want her driving until he's convinced the leg has healed properly."

"Of course he wouldn't." Dr. Foster coughed, calmed himself. "That's the only thing in this whole scenario that makes any sense. Now come on, young man, we're wasting time. I need to get Carrie's sister to drive with me. There are other matters besides this one that require my attention."

Keegan recalled the doctor's attention to his ill wife. He gave him directions to the campground using such familiar landmarks as the old lighthouse and the rocky outcropping across the road.

"Tell her I'm on my way," Dr. Foster said.

"All due respect, sir," Keegan said. "That would be a bad idea. If you want her here when you arrive, maybe we'd better keep this between ourselves."

For the first time, Dr. Foster relaxed. In fact, he almost chuckled. "I see you know her well, too, Breen. Good idea. She's coming home, though, rest assured."

Keegan made one more phone call before he left the park. He called his friend, Butch Slattery. "I'm in," he said when Butch answered.

"Great! I'll make reservations tomorrow. There's a plane leaving JFK on Friday for Latvia. We can get two of the last seats. And then it's just a few hours' drive to where the fighting is. I'll let you know what time to be at the Cleveland airport for our flight to New York."

Keegan didn't respond at first. Butch's enthusiasm was genuine, and he knew he couldn't match it with his own.

"You there, Pat?"

"I'm here."

"This will be a wild, wonderful ride, maybe the last we ever have together. We can sell our stories and pictures to the highest bidder and sit back and enjoy our retirement." Butch laughed. "Or not. I know you have other irons in the fire, but I haven't figured out a way to end a great career yet."

Keegan disconnected. He would go to Cleveland Thursday. He had plenty of time to pack a few belongings. After all, he'd lived for years out of one duffel bag. He'd leave the property in the hands of a Realtor who would have the job of getting the best price for the place once the snow melted.

He stopped at a local market, picked up

a few things and then just drove. East and west along the lakeshore route, stopping for moments at a time to watch the waves or gather his thoughts. He'd be home when Dr. Foster arrived.

Saying goodbye to Carrie was suddenly made simpler since he knew he betrayed her trust. Once she saw her father and put the pieces together, she'd be more than willing to leave. Keegan didn't want to end it this way, but what else could he have done? He couldn't leave her here in the dead of winter. How would she even get to the doctor on Friday? And what if her leg wasn't healed and she couldn't drive?

Though frustrated by him, Carrie loved her father, and once she was safely in his care for the remainder of her convalescence she would know that Keegan had done the right thing. He had protected her by making the ultimate sacrifice. And then she could continue her life without the influence of one very damaged, cynical middle-aged man named Patrick Breen who would only bring her down with him. The gray hairs on his head had reached all the way to Keegan's soul, and maybe this way, he could prevent Carrie from having to see them.

But when the doctor arrived... When Keegan had to look into Carrie's trusting eyes, could he bear one last heartache? Could he withstand the force of her bitter disappointment and even, possibly, her hatred? He had to. Once he was on that plane to JFK, once he'd truly given in to the person he used to be, once he'd buried Keegan for the near future, he would know he'd done what he had to do for Carrie.

CARRIE WAS READING when Keegan came in from his errands. She didn't look up.

He set a grocery sack on the kitchen counter. "Can I get you some lunch?" he asked.

"I already ate," she said. *If a trail mix bar could be considered a meal.*

"How about some tea?"

"No. Thank you. If I need anything, I'll let you know."

He sighed heavily. "I'm ready to talk now if you want to discuss what happened last night."

"Nothing happened last night," she said. "Your honor is intact."

He'd never been the victim of her sarcasm, and she wondered if her words had stung.

"Besides," she continued, "I'm at a good part in this book and don't want to stop." She tried to read the same page for a third time.

He puttered around in the kitchen putting a few canned goods in the cupboard. When tires crunched outside on the gravel lot, he jerked his head around. Carrie thought she heard him say, "Too soon."

She set the book on her lap as Keegan went to the door. He opened it, stuck out his arm to shake hands with whoever was on the threshold.

"Nice to meet you, too, sir," Keegan said.

And then her father came through the door. His gray hair was mussed from the wind. His eyes were bright and alert. And for that moment, his shoulders seemed broader than ever. And since she was so close to crying anyway, the tears rolled from her eyes.

"Daddy…"

He came to her, kneeled by the sofa and embraced her. "Sweetheart, what kind of a mess have you gotten yourself into this time?"

When the tears didn't stop, he pulled an inhaler from his pocket. Daddy, always prepared. "In case you need this, honey."

"Hello, Care-bear," came a second voice.

Martin moved out of the way so the sisters could greet each other. Carrie hugged Jude like she never would let her go.

"Hey, what's this?" Jude said, patting the dang boot that had been Carrie's companion for weeks. "I believe I said you should come home for Christmas. I didn't know you'd risk those delicate bones to do it."

"I've risked a lot more than my bones," Carrie said through her sobs.

These first moments of emotional highs were reactionary. Carrie didn't have time yet to be angry. She was hurting from Keegan's rejection. Her heart was breaking, and when that happened, no one was better than family. No one knew her like her sister did. No one cared like her father did. In fact, no one had ever cared for Carrie the way this family did. She'd thought, she'd hoped that maybe Keegan... But no, and so she let her tears fall. After a minute or so, she dried her eyes, looked at each of the three faces in the room and sagged when the awful weight of knowledge, newly realized, pressed on her shoulders.

Staring at her father, because looking at Keegan would hurt too much, she said, "He called you."

"Thank goodness," Martin said. "At least this man had the sense to do what you should have done weeks ago. I'm a doctor, Carrie! Didn't that thought enter your head?"

She almost smiled. That thought had never left her head since her fifth birthday when a pediatrician had diagnosed her asthma and told her parents that an ongoing condition of their youngest, frail daughter "needed watching." Her wonderful, well-meaning father never stopped reminding her that, whatever her age, he knew what was best for her.

Martin had entered the cabin with an air of loving authority, and his command of the situation continued. "Jude, help your sister pack." He pointed a finger at Carrie. "Gather your things, whatever meds you're taking for the leg."

"I'm not taking any…"

He nodded at Keegan. "I owe you a debt of

gratitude. Your call this morning was overdue, but nevertheless you have my thanks. My daughter looks well."

"She is well," Keegan said. "I've tried to take care of her."

At this moment Carrie wanted to punch him or kick him or do something equally demonstrative of her broken heart, but she couldn't argue with him. He'd taken excellent care of her without treating her as if her next breath could be her last. He had betrayed her, used her secrets to serve his own motive to be rid of her and, maybe worst of all right now, made her offer last night seem small and even childish. But he had never made her feel like an invalid.

"Daddy," she said. "Could I please have a few minutes alone with Keegan? Maybe you and Jude could sit in your car or walk over to the lake. It's not so cold today."

Martin looked at Carrie and then transferred a wary gaze to Keegan. He didn't respond.

"I'm not going anywhere except home with you, Daddy," Carrie assured him. "Just give me a moment, please."

"Okay." Martin took Jude's elbow. "Come

on, Judie, we'll wait outside. Give me the keys to that toy car of yours, Carrie, and we'll make sure she starts up."

Once her father and sister had left the cabin, Carrie sank heavily into the sofa and waited for Keegan to raise his face and look at her.

"I'm sorry, Carrie. I hated to do this but it was a last resort. I know you told me about your relationship with your father in confidence, but you also told me you loved him and wouldn't want to hurt him."

"How wonderful," she said in a hoarse whisper, "that no one was hurt today."

A muscle in his temple throbbed. "I deserve your sarcasm, your anger, whatever you want to throw at me. But I need to explain…"

"You don't get to talk now, Keegan. You get to listen. As a reporter, you must find it easy to listen, especially now that you've gotten your way and relieved yourself of an awful burden."

## CHAPTER TWENTY

HIS FACE WAS drawn and tight, his lips pressed together. For the first time since she'd known him, Carrie decided Keegan looked less than comfortable with who he was, what he'd done. Maybe he felt bad about calling her father. He deserved to feel like the biggest heel in the universe.

"Four days, Keegan," she began. "With any luck, or even without any, I would have been out of here on Friday. Whether or not the doctor gave me permission to drive, I would have gone." She took a deep breath. "You couldn't wait four days?"

He started to speak. She held up a finger. "You made your position perfectly clear last night. You don't want me, and like a desperate, lonely woman, I made a foolhardy play for you. I wish I could take it back, but I can't."

He blinked hard. "Carrie..."

"No! I'm not finished. It's not so much that you don't care for me. It hurts…" Her voice cracked. She took a moment to compose herself. "I could have accepted that you didn't care. We were on two different pages, I misread all the signals. You know I'm not experienced in the ways of relationships. A pitiful lack of practice, I guess."

He looked tired, sad somehow. Why? She didn't know. He'd gotten what he wanted. "But why, Keegan? Why couldn't you have practiced even a small percentage of the patience you've obviously shown over the last four weeks? Why couldn't you have let me leave on my own terms in four days, gone back to Michigan, continuing the life I had before running into a snowbank?"

"And why, oh, why did you kiss me? Not once but many times. I suppose I'm just too naive to understand that kisses don't mean all that much. Maybe they are just a form of adult entertainment, one that the least experienced of us take much too seriously."

He bit his bottom lip, holding in words that she knew he wanted to speak. But she wasn't done.

"I suppose I should be most angry about

the way you took my innermost secrets about my illness, my family, and used them to your own advantage, so you wouldn't have to feel any guilt for last night, for today. But you know what? I'm not that angry after all. The two people who came in your door today love me, truly love me. Perhaps I don't always agree with the way they show that love, and maybe I am the most needy person I know right now, but I'm at least smart enough to know that I need their support. And I'm grateful for it."

He brought a chair close to her, straddled it backwards and sat. He reached across the space that separated them and tried to touch her knees. She twisted away from him.

"Are you still practicing your skills on me, Keegan? Because I'm not practicing. I'm facing reality. It's not pretty, but I'm facing it."

He expelled a breath he'd been holding. "Is it my turn yet?"

Her lips quivered. She couldn't break down now. "I owe you a turn, I guess for the weeks you took care of me. So, yes."

HE THOUGHT HE'D seen it all, experienced the most dreadful lows of anyone's lifetime. But nothing quite compared with what he was facing now. His own personal, intimate and devastating failure.

He inched his chair closer to her. She didn't look him directly in his eyes. Those beautiful blue eyes that had taken him on the most remarkable journeys the last weeks.

"There's something you don't know," he said. "Remember the other day when a friend came by to see me?"

She kept her gaze focused on him and nodded.

"That was Butch Slattery. He's a photographer, the best in the business. We worked together on quite a few stories. I wrote, he snapped the pictures. I depended on him, counted on him. I wouldn't be here today if it hadn't been for Butch."

"Why are you telling me this now?"

"Because he came to me with a proposition, one which I thought I would turn down. But ultimately I didn't. His enthusiasm was so powerful, so genuine. He wants us to cover the civil war in the Baltic states. I told him I would go. We fly to Latvia on Friday."

Her eyes rounded, focused intently on

him. "I see. I'm surprised. I believed this part of your life was in the past. After you saw your son..."

"I know. I thought so, too. But the adventure is still smoldering in my blood. Maybe not as much as it once did, but the adrenaline still pumps, the desire to tell a story still exists."

"Have you told Taylor?"

"No. Good God, Carrie, if I haven't told you, I certainly haven't told him." He shook his head. "It's all just a bit fast, I know. I should be proud to tell my son, but I'm not. I'm embarrassed, perhaps. I told him I was through with that life. But when Butch came, it all descended upon me—the thrill, the escapes, the almost impossibility of succeeding. It's hard for me to explain, but in spite of my inner reaction to going one more time, the pumping of blood through my veins, I didn't think I could disappoint Butch."

"So you will just disappoint Taylor."

He stroked his hand over his jaw. "I suppose that's a good possibility."

She sighed. "All right, so you can take the reporter out of the war zone, but you can't take the war zone out of the reporter. Is that it? The excitement, the danger, the thrill of just one more headline always exists."

"I think so," he said, feeling the strongest hint of regret at his decision. Why would he tempt fate one more time? Why would he risk what he had here, in this old campground, with this wonderful woman? And then he remembered. Because he was who he was—deeply scarred, perhaps unfixable, and close to tarnishing every good thing that came his way. In his cockeyed view he was saving Carrie for something much better than him, just as she'd been saving herself.

She stared at him with warm, endlessly deep eyes. He felt her sympathy, her understanding for the sacrifices he'd made for the written word. She would probably never understand that he was doing this for her. And he would never tell her.

"Keegan…"

She let him touch her hand. He felt its warmth to his shoulder.

"I can accept much of what you say," she said. "But why did you call my father? You wouldn't have had to betray me. You could have gone and left me here in the cabin until Friday. I would have gone to the doctor. Chances are, I would have been cleared to drive my car back to Michigan that same day, fully intending to reassert my independence, and fully capable of doing it."

"I couldn't leave you here," he said. "I couldn't not know your future. I couldn't go without assuring myself that you were safe."

"But what you did was a violation of my privacy. You shattered my belief in you, my trust, by taking it upon yourself to manipulate my life."

He smiled, and her eyes narrowed. "Much as you did to me?" he said. "Without my knowledge, didn't you arrange for my son to come here, to face me, to challenge our relationship?"

Her lips curled just slightly. "I guess I did. Maybe it's good that we are parting after all, Keegan," she said. "We seem to be a pair of manipulators above all else."

He raised her hand to his lips and kissed her knuckles. At this moment he could only question his resolve to let her go, to feed his own need for adventure, to pay a debt to an old friend and to play a martyr for her. His book remained unfinished on his computer. But he now knew that Carrie Foster would have her own chapter, one that perhaps would paint him as a better man than he was. Maybe by letting her go, he was finally beginning to heal.

He spread her fingers and kissed her palm. "I have never been more enchanted by a manipulator in my life, Carrie. From the day you declared to all the world that I was your husband, to now, it has been an amazing journey."

Her eyes glistened, her lips trembled. She rose from the sofa. "Tell my family I'm ready," she said. "And please, Keegan, take care of yourself."

AFTER SOME DISCUSSION, Carrie convinced her father to let her ride in her own car with Jude as the driver. Jude chuckled, obviously trying to make light of a serious situation, about all the "frozen Christmas gifts" still in the back compartment.

"Okay," Martin said, "but I'm following you girls in case you have any trouble."

They weren't a mile away from the campground before Martin called Jude's cell phone. She smiled at her sister. "What's that, Daddy? Say again."

She put the phone on speaker.

"I said, watch that lead foot, Jude. This road is notorious for speed traps. And you have an injured passenger in the car. I expect you to drop your speed by at least ten miles an hour."

"No problem." Jude disconnected and stared for a moment at Carrie. "We might be home by tomorrow morning at this rate."

Carrie tried to appreciate the humor in Martin's typical fatherly warning. Unfortunately, she hadn't seen the humor in anything the past twenty-four hours, and she didn't know when she would again.

A few somber miles later, Jude said, "So, maybe you want to tell me how my sweet little sister, who for the last five years has viewed every man in her life as having an agenda, came to stay with a stranger for nearly a month."

Carrie smiled. "I admit it seems a stretch, especially for me. But aside from the fact that on Christmas Day with snow piling up by inches an hour, there weren't too many options for an injured motorist..." She paused, thinking about Keegan, the first moment she saw him, the surprise and shock she'd experienced.

"I don't know, Judie," she said. "I just believed I could trust him. There certainly wasn't anything about his appearance that day that would lead me to think that." She chuckled. "He was gruff, bearded and scraggly..."

"A true Prince Charming," Jude said.

"Right. But he was also calm and comforting and strong where I was obviously weak. He took charge of my situation and stayed with me until I could make decisions."

"And again, your decision was to move in with a stranger?" Jude said.

"Yes, but by then he wasn't a stranger. I know he didn't want me in his life. He was living alone and liking his hermit lifestyle. I was a burden and a chore, but he took care of me." She sighed. "And, maybe, just a little, I took care of him, too. I wasn't the only one who needed comforting and healing."

"Why did he need to heal?"

Carrie stared across the seat at her sister. "You didn't recognize him?"

"No. Should I have?"

"He looks different now, but his real name is Patrick Breen. He goes by his middle name…"

"Patrick Breen!" Jude practically squealed the name. "The correspondent? The one who went to the Middle East and Afghanistan and Haiti?"

"And everywhere else there was a story," Carrie added.

"Oh, my gosh, Care-Bear, he's famous! A famous guy has been taking care of you all this time. Does Daddy know?"

"I don't think so. It was enough for Daddy to see me living with a man without me piling on too much information."

"Probably wise. I'm sure Daddy would view him as a worldly man, one with many experiences, and one who certainly could spell trouble for his youngest daughter."

Carrie smiled with a recurrent memory of warm nights by the fire, grilled cheese sandwiches and embraces when one or the other of them needed one. "He was a gentleman the whole time, Jude," she said. "I couldn't have asked for a better person to take care of me, to comfort me, to…" She stopped, not wanting to say too much.

"Oh, Carrie, sweetie, you're in love with him."

There being no point in denying what was obvious to the person who knew her best in the world, Carrie nodded slightly. "Let's keep this between ourselves, okay? I don't need anyone to attempt to clarify my feelings for me, or, even worse, to feel sorry for me."

"So, what happens now?" Jude asked.

"Now?" Carrie repeated. "I'm doing it. I'm going home to Dancing Falls where I will finish recuperating, and then I suppose I will go back to my job if I still have one." She expelled a long breath. "There are always trees that need me."

"And Keegan? What about him?"

"He's on his way to another civil war in another desperate country. It seems that there is always a story that needs to be told, and he's determined to tell it."

"He doesn't love you? Does he know you love him?"

"I think he knows how I feel. And maybe

he does love me a little, but certainly not enough."

Jude reached over and patted Carrie's hand. "How could he not love you enough? You are the sweetest, kindest..."

"Stop," Carrie said. "You're describing the problem. I'm the innocent girl who communes with nature while trying to hide her fear of giving herself to a man. Keegan is the spontaneous, passionate man who records the stories of the world's greatest disasters. My wounds, if you want to believe I've suffered any, are on the surface. Keegan's go so deep I can never reach them, and possibly he'll never recover from them.

"This is hard to explain, but, in a way, Keegan is afraid of me, afraid of changing me, bringing me down. The very qualities he likes about me are the ones that are keeping us apart."

Jude shook her head. "How did you get so smart? I thought Alex was the one with all the brains."

"She has most of them," Carrie said. "But when you have almost a month to sit on a sofa and contemplate what went wrong with all of your relationships, you eventually come up with answers. Not all of them," she added. "But some."

"I just want you to be as happy as I am," Jude said. "Why is it that when things are going so right for one of us, the other one or two must suffer?"

"But I am happy for you, Jude. Truly I am. I want to hear all about the wedding you're planning for the spring at Dancing Falls. I want to hear every juicy morsel about the fabulous Liam Manning. I want to hear about my wonderful nephew."

As Jude talked, Carrie listened. She could find contentment in the happy endings her sisters had discovered. People could be happy for others if not for themselves. Carrie had lost at love. She'd lost Keegan, but there could still be joy in her life. So why did she concentrate on the passing landscape out the passenger window?

So Jude couldn't see her tears.

## CHAPTER TWENTY-ONE

"HOW LONG HAS she been like this?" That evening Carrie sat by her mother's bedside and held Maggie's hand. The sun was low in the sky, coloring the room with a soft pink glow, terribly sad, yet somehow peaceful.

"Not long," Jude said. "Daddy didn't want to alarm you before we really knew what was going on."

"She's so thin," Carrie said. "All I can think about is how Mom loved to cook. She fixed the most creative meals and taught us all how to do the same. We Fosters have always been such good eaters, and now…"

Jude put her hand on Carrie's shoulder. "You have to be strong for Daddy, Care-Bear. Remember, the Mom you're talking about has been gone for a long time." She touched Maggie's cheek. "I think Mom is ready to go now, and we have to let her."

"Does the doctor say when that could be?"

"A matter of a few days to a week or so," Jude said. "Believe me, Care, we would have let you know in plenty of time to come home and say goodbye."

"What have you told Wesley?"

"Not much. He knows that his grandma is getting weaker, but at only six, he can't handle too much information. He never knew his grandmother the way we did. She showed the first signs of dementia before Wes's first birthday. But amazingly he has always related to her in his own way. He reads to her and finds programs on her television he thinks she'd like. He'll miss her."

"Does Aurora know?" Carrie didn't know their neighbor as well as her two sisters did, but she knew that Aurora had been a source of inspiration and comfort for their father.

"Yes, she knows. She's been to the house and has sat with Mom a time or two. That pleases Dad, knowing that the two women in his life had a chance to get acquainted, even in this limited way."

"Woman in his life?" Carrie said. "That's how you describe Aurora?"

"Not literally. Dad is all about Mom right now, but you've heard how caring Aurora is. Dad depends on her." She paused before adding, "Actually, Carrie, they depend on each other. Aurora's son died recently, and Dad was there for her when she needed him. They both are grieving right now, and that's a strong connection."

Carrie nodded. "Most of you have depended on Aurora at one time or another. Lizzie stayed with her when she had that awful fight with Alex. You said Aurora was instrumental in getting you to go to the hospital and demanding to see Liam." *I wish there was some way our fairy godmother could help me*, Carrie thought.

"How's everyone doing?"

Both girls turned to the sound of their father's voice in the doorway.

"Fine," Jude said. "There hasn't been a change in Mom since this morning."

Martin walked over and stood between his two daughters. "I don't know about that," he said. "I think she might be smiling, just a little bit. Like she knows on some level that two of her girls are here." He bent to kiss the top of Carrie's head and put an arm around Jude. "It's been a long day. Your Mom and I are turning in."

Both girls glanced at the narrow twin bed next to Maggie's larger one, where their father slept each night. This was their cue that he wanted to be alone with his wife.

"I'm tired, too," Carrie said, adjusting her walking boot before standing.

"Me, too," Jude said.

"Go on with you," Martin teased. "I know you'll be up for hours talking. And you know what? It makes me happy just thinking of you doing that."

They each kissed their father and left the room. "So how about those wedding plans?" Carrie said. "What do you and Mr. Dreamy have in mind?"

Jude smiled. "We're both wearing cowboy gear and riding into the ceremony on horseback..." She paused to look at Carrie's horrified expression. "You are so easy to fool, Care-Bear!"

THE CABIN WAS COLD, empty. Keegan hadn't even bothered to light a fire. He told himself he was preparing his body and spirit for the poor conditions he'd be facing soon. That was a lie, of course. He was punishing himself for pushing away the kindest woman he had ever met. He deserved to freeze. He deserved to stare at lonely corners of his room, to eat a simple meal by himself.

How had it happened that he'd fallen so hard for sweet, innocent Carrie Foster? He'd never been attracted to that type of woman before. But, then, he'd never made a relationship work before either. And he hadn't made one work this time.

She'd practically said the words many men long to hear, but the very ones he feared. She couldn't love him. She was too good, and he was almost all bad. He'd come to believe that the life he truly deserved was one where he unrolled a sleeping bag and bedded down in a blown-out hut in a rural part of nowhere only to face anger and discontent in the morning.

His future before Carrie had been uncertain. He intended to sell his land and use the stake to start over somewhere far away from Ohio, the memories of his youth and the only adult who had ever loved him when he was growing up. Keegan was satisfied with not knowing where he would be a year from now. He would survive. He always had.

And then a terrible blizzard had sent him

a chance for redemption. For Carrie's sake he didn't take that chance. Her roots were as deep and solid and pure as the trees she loved. His were still stretching into the darkness, searching for something he never would find.

And so he sat this night on a hard wooden chair in front of a meal of cereal and toast and thought about what might have been. He considered having a drink or two...or three, but he never took the bottle from his cupboard. Like he had so many times in the past hours, he remembered that Carrie would be disappointed in him.

Even though he'd sent her away, he still thought about pleasing her. In the past month she had been easy to please, but deep down he knew that someday, maybe soon, maybe years from now, he would quit trying to please her. That was just the sort of man he was. Marta knew that. Or maybe she would become impossible to please, and that would also be his fault.

Missing her hurt, but he would get through this night and the next two and then he would fly to New York with Butch and reenter a world that accepted him for who he'd become. He would put his book away for a while and tell his new stories. Devastation and despair were embedded so deeply into his spirit now that he feared he could only survive when everything around him crumbled.

And that's how he felt tonight. Like he was disintegrating bit by dusty bit. Like he'd lost his soul in order to save another's.

# CHAPTER TWENTY-TWO

MAGGIE ELIZABETH FOSTER passed away on Wednesday, two days after her daughter Carrie arrived home. When the doctor determined that Maggie's time was near, Martin called his oldest daughter, Alexis, and all three girls were at their mother's bedside. She slipped quietly into the next world with each of her daughters proclaiming that they, too, could see the smile their father claimed to have seen on Monday.

Aurora Spindell was called to the house, and the four women cried and laughed and comforted the man Maggie had left behind. Aurora had never known the Maggie that the family knew, but because she loved Martin, a fact that she kept secret from the family but Carrie knew right away, Aurora understood and appreciated the kind of woman Maggie had been.

Preparations were quickly organized for a

funeral two days later, on a beautiful, sunny Friday. Pallbearers were members of Martin's medical community, his son-in-law, Daniel Chandler, and his future son-in-law, Liam Manning. Maggie's two grandchildren, Lizzie and Wesley, walked somberly behind the casket, followed by their mothers and aunt.

Aurora offered her home, the charmingly renovated Victorian bed-and-breakfast, for an after-funeral brunch. With nearly one hundred people from Fox Creek and surrounding areas attending, the home could not accommodate all who wanted to express their sympathy to Martin. The well-wishers spilled out into Aurora's yard and sunroom until the winter sun began to fade.

Guests left, temporary help tidied the mess and soon only the immediate family remained to see Martin through the rest of this difficult day. Standing in the entrance to the sunroom, Carrie was the only one to see her father's hand slip without ceremony into Aurora's comforting grasp as they stood looking over the acreage in the dusky shadows.

Aurora's Attic, the place was called, and

Carrie found comfort surrounded by the charm of old china settings and images of angels on the walls. Perhaps Aurora was an angel herself. She had helped her sisters find their loves, and she would help her father through his grief. What more noble purpose was there for an angel?

By six thirty the sky was dark. The family thanked Aurora and prepared to go back to Dancing Falls.

"I'd like to stay for a while, Daddy," Carrie said. "I have my car, and I'll be home soon."

"I shouldn't let you drive when you're still wearing the boot."

Carrie shook her head. "You know I could quit using the boot anytime, and besides, it's less than half a mile."

He looked to Aurora for consent, and his friend nodded. "I think Carrie and I need some time alone," she said.

"If you're sure, Carrie," Martin said.

"Yes, Daddy, I'm sure." Since the funeral had been planned at the same time as her doctor's appointment, she had rescheduled for Monday. What difference would one more weekend make in her recuperation?

She'd been conscious of the boot all day as if relinquishing it in three days signaled an end to much more than simply a broken leg.

When the house was quiet, Aurora made tea and served it in delicate china cups in her parlor. At the last moment, she went to a cabinet and withdrew a bottle of brandy. "It's the best quality," she said. "I've never opened it, but bought it months ago thinking there might come a time." She took off the cap. "I don't know about you, dear, but I think that time has come."

The two women sat in comfortable silence for minutes until at last Aurora spoke. "I never knew you as well as I did your sisters. I regret that. Sometimes I felt that you needed your mother more than the other two did. I know your pathway with Martin hasn't always been an easy one."

Carrie smiled. "No, it hasn't. My mother understood my desire to be independent and follow my dreams. Daddy never quite got that. No one did, really, until…"

Aurora set her teacup on an end table. Her shoulders relaxed with a deep exhalation of breath. "Do you want to talk about him, Carrie? I am very happy to listen."

She did want to talk about him, and in the waning hours of a trying and sad day, she told Aurora her story.

AT FIVE O'CLOCK on Friday afternoon, JFK Airport was as bustling as Keegan had ever seen it. People rushing to weekend destinations, people heading somewhere hoping to find something better than they were leaving, executives going home after business trips. Keegan figured few of the multitude were adventurers hoping to get the last remaining seats on the last remaining flight to a civil war.

The flight was boarding in a half hour. Butch had gone into a bar to either pump some liquid courage into his blood for what they'd be facing, or to accentuate the thrill he was feeling at being back behind his camera. Keegan had passed on bar time. He'd probably drain a couple of ounce-sized liquor bottles on the plane and then try to sleep for the eleven-hour flight. Once they landed, renting a decent car and traveling into hostile territory would be the real test of their commitment to this story.

Boarding the flight from the Cleveland

airport the day before hadn't been easy. Keegan remembered his last trip to the airport, when he and Carrie had met his son. He recalled his frustration at Carrie for interfering in his life, and later his gratitude that she'd done it. Waiting to connect to JFK, Keegan recalled, too, his last conversation with Taylor. "It's just one more time, kid, I swear," he'd promised. "I wouldn't be doing this except I owe Butch a lot."

"More than you owe me, Dad?" Taylor had said. "You promised you were done with this life."

"I know. I'm sorry. This is the last time. I'll call you when I can."

Now, sitting in an uncomfortable vinyl chair waiting to sit in an even more uncomfortable narrow seat with little leg room, he contemplated his relationship with his son. He'd have to make this up to Taylor. And then his mind strayed to his worst infidelity, his betrayal of Carrie.

While in Cleveland, his mind had played tricks on him, causing him to imagine where she was, what she was doing. He'd looked up her hometown of Fox Creek and knew it was close to the airport. He could forget this whole thing with Butch, rent a car and be looking into Carrie's eyes again in less than a half hour.

And then his rational side took over. He was leaving because of her, because he wasn't what she needed in her life. They had no future. She needed someone who would share her beliefs in the goodness of man and the powers of nature. Keegan Breen wasn't that person, and the sooner he cut off ties with her, the better her life would be.

But damn, he loved her. And now, sitting for the last few minutes at JFK, the doubts haunted Keegan once more. He closed his eyes tightly. Her face, so beautiful, so serene, appeared in his mind. Who really knew what the future held? If people waited for secure, guaranteed futures, would there ever be marriages or children? Could love be enough? What could he offer her to show he could be a changed man, that he had, in fact, already started the difficult journey toward normalcy because of her influence?

Didn't he owe it to himself to try? He wasn't such a lost cause that he didn't deserve one chance at a future that held promise. One last trip to a battle zone paled in comparison to the shot at a lasting future he never thought he'd have.

He thought about what he could give her, how he could show his devotion and his willingness to try. And he smiled when he decided upon the exact thing he could offer her. Maybe it would work. Or maybe she didn't want to see him again. But he had to try. Even if he failed, he would know he had tried. With a great burden lifted from his shoulders and a spark of his own optimism burning inside his chest, Keegan hitched his duffel bag over his shoulder and strode to the bar.

Butch looked up from a half glass of ale. "Time to go?" he asked.

"I'm not going," Keegan said.

"What? What are you talking about?"

"I'm sorry, Butch. You're the best friend I've ever had. We've been through a lot together, but I can't do it again…"

"It's that woman, isn't it? The one drawing the pictures?"

Keegan nodded. "I don't know. I think so. I just have to see what the future could hold with her. I always thought I could handle loneliness, but these last few days showed me what loneliness really is. And I didn't handle it all that well. If she'll have me, I want her back."

"I'm sorry you're not going," Butch said. His voice held no hint of anger, just an edge of disappointment. "I'm not surprised, though." He chuckled. "Well, since we are at the airport just minutes away from taking off, maybe a little surprised. I don't know where I'll find another reporter."

Keegan put his hand on his friend's shoulder. "When you get there, just lead with your name. There isn't a word jockey anywhere in the world who wouldn't jump at the chance to work with you."

"What are your plans now?" Butch asked. "You going back to that campground?"

"I just might be," Keegan said. "It really isn't such a bad place to live." He grinned. "Needs a few more trees, though."

The two men embraced, and Keegan strode off to the nearest ticket counter. He bought the last seat on the first plane back to Cleveland and had to run to catch the flight.

WHILE WAITING ON the tarmac for the plane to take off, Keegan used his phone to locate

Dr. Martin Foster. After storing the address, he pressed Connect to phone the home. He'd considered not calling first, but there were too many variables. What if Carrie wasn't home? What if she didn't want to see him? What if his last surprise had left her suspicious of anything he might do again? Since he didn't have Carrie's cell number, he hoped to reach her this way.

"Hello." The voice that answered was that of a child.

"Hello," Keegan said. "Is Carrie there?"

"You mean Aunt Carrie?"

Keegan smiled. "Yes, that's right. You must be Wesley."

"I am. Who are you?"

"I'm a friend of your aunt Carrie's. I'd really like to talk to her."

"She's next door at Miss Aurora's. It's one of those places where people sleep and then get a free breakfast."

*Ah, a bed-and-breakfast.* "When will she be home? Do you know?"

"No. Maybe she'll sleep there and get the breakfast. Everyone's sad today because my grandma died."

Oh, no. Carrie was dealing with her mother's

death. The timing couldn't have been worse. Carrie was carrying a burden of grief as well as the emotions she must be experiencing about him. But at least she was among people who loved her.

"I'm sorry to hear that."

The flight attendant walked down the aisle, telling passengers to disconnect their electronic devices.

"I have to hang up," Keegan said.

"Okay, bye." The line went dead. And since he was already on the plane and they were in position to take off, Keegan decided he'd take his chances with a surprise visit. Finding a bed-and-breakfast next door to Dancing Falls shouldn't be too difficult. He leaned his head back and closed his eyes. Could be worse. If Carrie wouldn't see him, at least he'd have a place to stay and a free breakfast.

# CHAPTER TWENTY-THREE

CARRIE AND AURORA had switched to decaffeinated tea around eight o'clock. Plus they'd raided the pantry and refrigerator for samples of desserts brought by well-meaning friends today. And between them they'd managed to make a dent in Aurora's expensive bottle of brandy.

"I don't know about you, Carrie, but this cherry cheesecake is hard to top."

"Speak for yourself, Aurora. I'm sticking with chocolate mousse pie."

"We can't give up now, dear. There are at least a half dozen cakes and pies we haven't tried yet."

Carrie smiled. "Between all the tea we drank and all the sugar we're consuming, neither of us will sleep tonight."

"I don't mind," Aurora said. "Sleep is overrated."

Carrying their plates, they went back to

the kitchen to scavenger for more sweets. Aurora set a few dishes on her long farm table. "I'm sorry it took such a sad occurrence for us to become friends," she said. "I'm so grateful to have had the opportunity to get to know you better." She scooped a chunk of blueberry cobbler onto Carrie's plate.

"I know," Carrie said. "But I feel like I've known you for my entire life. My sisters told me they think of you as family."

"As I do them."

"And you've helped them with their problems. You were so kind to Lizzie and Alex, and it was you who talked Jude into going back to the hospital to see Liam. I don't know if either one of them would have found their happy endings if it weren't for you."

"I wish I could do the same for you, Carrie, but your man sounds like a difficult fix."

Carrie sighed. "He is, and I absolutely must stop thinking about him. It has been four days and not a word. He was due to leave today, and I'm sure he's no longer in the country by now."

"You'll meet someone, or maybe when this young man returns..."

"I won't count on that," Carrie said. "I told you a bit about my past with men. Someday I'll fill in the details, pitiful as they are, but Keegan was different. I sensed from the very beginning that I could trust him. He didn't make demands or act disappointed when he didn't get his way."

Carrie sat at the kitchen table and pushed her plate of cobbler away. "I really doubt that I'll find that kind of connection again, Aurora. Keegan erased practically all my doubts and fears. With him I would have, I wanted to…" She sighed deeply. "It doesn't matter now."

She glanced at the clock on the wall. "Oh, my, it's almost nine thirty. You must be exhausted, Aurora. And my family must be wondering when I'll be home." She stood. "I'll just grab my coat."

A knock at the front door halted all further discussion.

"Who could that be at this hour?" Aurora said.

"Do you have someone scheduled as a late check-in?"

"No. Some skiers are coming tomorrow

but no one tonight. You stay here, dear, and I'll check it out."

"No way am I staying here. We'll go together. It's probably just my father, but in case it's not, there is safety in numbers."

Carrie locked her arm with Aurora's and smiled. Did she imagine the sparkle in Aurora's eyes when she mentioned that the caller might be Martin?

When they reached the front door, Aurora peeked out the leaded-glass side panel. "I don't recognize him."

"Hello!" a familiar voice called. "I'm looking for Carrie Foster. Is she here?"

Carrie's heart stopped beating for a few wonderful, terrifying seconds. She clasped her hand over her mouth and spoke through trembling fingers. "It's him. It's Keegan."

"Well, my goodness, will wonders never cease?" Aurora started to open the door.

"No, wait!" Carrie said. "I'm not ready to see him. I don't know why he's here. And then there's my mother's funeral today. And I've probably had too much of your brandy." She began trembling and grabbed hold of an antique hall stand to steady herself. "It's too much."

"Hello!" Keegan called again.

"I can't just leave him out there, Carrie," Aurora said. "It's cold outside. And besides, he saw me looking out."

Carrie took a deep breath. Her next words came out of her mouth at a speed she didn't think possible. "Give me a minute. I don't think he saw me. I'll run to the kitchen. You can open the door, tell him I'm not here. Tell him I went away and you don't know where."

Aurora gave her a look that was part sympathy and part exasperation. "Carrie..."

But Carrie was already across the room and heading for the kitchen. She shut the door all but a crack and gave in to the temptation to listen.

Aurora opened the door. "How can I help you?" she said.

"My name is Keegan Breen," he said. "I'm a friend of Carrie's. I'm aware that it's late, and because of the events of the day, this may not be a good time, but someone in her father's household told me Carrie might be here. I really need to speak to her."

Carrie heard the subtle creak of the door as Aurora opened it more fully.

"Come in, young man. You need to warm up."

He stomped his shoes on her mat. "Thank you. So…"

"Yes, Carrie and I were visiting this evening."

"Were?" Keegan said. "Do you mean she's no longer here?"

What would Aurora say? She prided herself on being a good friend to the Foster daughters, but she'd also made it known that she did not approve of lying. Her ex-husband and son had lied to her too often and she was vehemently honest now.

"To tell you the truth," Aurora began, "I don't know if she's still here or not."

"Her car is out front," Keegan stated bluntly.

Aurora chuckled nervously. "Then I suppose she's still here. Why don't you come into the parlor and warm up? I'll see if I can find her."

"Thank you."

Carrie listened to the rustle of fabric as

Keegan lowered himself into one of Aurora's comfortable chairs.

Five seconds later Aurora bustled into the kitchen. "What are you waiting for, Carrie? He's here. He wants to see you."

Carrie shifted from one foot to the other. "I don't know," she said. "What if it's something terrible? What if he forgot to tell me one of the reasons why it would never work for us, and he came here to make sure I understood? My history with men... I've always believed one thing and it turned out to be something completely opposite. At least now I'm beginning to adjust to being without Keegan. I don't think I could bear it if he came to break my heart again."

Aurora pulled out the kitchen chair Carrie had been using and told her to sit. "I've just seen this man, dear, and he looks as nervous as you do..."

*Nervous? Keegan?*

"He doesn't look at all like a man who came here to send you farther away from him. He looks like a man who realizes his mistake and regrets it with his whole heart."

"Oh, Aurora," Carrie said. "How can you possibly tell that by just looking at him?"

"Because I look at more than the eye can see," she said. "I look inside."

"But this has been such a horrible week, such a reminder to me that my instincts are so often wrong, and I'm doomed never to find happiness."

Aurora smiled.

"Why are you smiling?"

"I thought Lizzie was the one studying drama in this family. Come to find out, you're not bad at playing the downtrodden heroine yourself."

Slightly offended, Carrie sat straight in the chair. "Aurora! If you knew my past with men…"

"I don't need to know your past, honey, unless you just want to tell me. It doesn't matter. We don't live backward, Carrie. We live forward. If you've had relationships with a dozen men or zero, it all comes down to one thing—you never found the right one. And you won't find him if you sit in this kitchen and concentrate on what went wrong in the past. Your future could be waiting in my parlor right now."

"I wish I could believe it," Carrie said.

"Believe it." The voice that came from the

doorway was strong, masculine and just a bit quivering.

Carrie stared up at the man who'd stolen her heart in a winter blizzard and had warmed her ever since. She couldn't speak for fear he would leave. She couldn't breathe for fear she would die.

Aurora backed up a step, looked at Carrie, then at Keegan. "I assume you two know each other," she said with a grin.

Keegan smiled, a wonderful huge spreading of his fabulous lips that was so unlike him and yet so genuine, as if he'd just learned how to do it. "I know her," he said. "This woman is my wife—or at least I hope she will be."

Aurora's eyes widened. Carrie released a sound between a sob and laughter.

"How does it feel, Carrie Foster," Keegan said, "to have someone proclaim you to be an intimate member of the family without one word of warning?"

She found her voice. "Truthfully, it feels strange and a bit scary and wonderful."

"I know," he said. "I remember."

He crossed the space separating them, pulled out a chair and sat down, letting their knees touch. He picked up both her hands and held them in his before glancing down at her leg, still supported by the boot. "I assume you'll be able to toss that boot into the garbage bin and walk all seven acres of Cedar Woods after you've turned it into an oasis."

"You're keeping your campground?"

"I'm keeping *our* campground," he said. "Your name will be on the deed."

"Oh, my God, Keegan, do you mean it? All seven acres plus the two trailers in back?" The roots she'd so often dreamed of owning were becoming a reality. "Are you really proposing to me, or...?" Carrie almost choked. Had she really said those words?

He grinned. "Crazy as it sounds, yeah."

With a snap of Velcro fastenings, Carrie ripped the boot from her leg, stood as tall as her five-foot-four-inch frame allowed and pulled Keegan up with her. Grasping his nape, she brought his mouth to hers for a long, lingering, blood-pumping kiss that didn't leave room for doubt or fear or thinking about the past.

When she drew away, she realized Aurora had left them alone, and there was still much she didn't know. "How did you get here?" she asked. "What happened with Butch? Have you decided not to go to Latvia? Oh, I hope so. How did you know I was here at Aurora's?"

He hugged her to his chest and kissed the top of her head. "Read my book. It will all be in the last chapter."

# *EPILOGUE*

"It TURNED OUT to be a beautiful day for a wedding, didn't it?"

Martin smiled down at Aurora who looked almost as lovely as the bride in her long, pale blue skirt and white blouse gathered with ribbons at her chest. Like many of the guests today, Aurora also wore sandals, another sign that Mother Nature had done her good deed for the Foster family this day.

"You are right, Aurora," Martin said. "April weather in Ohio is always iffy. From one day to the next Maggie and I never knew if we'd be dressing the girls in snowsuits or shorts."

Their conversations about Maggie had become much more natural. Now they both talked about her as if she'd been more than the love of Martin's life. She'd also been influential in Aurora's life, and Aurora wished she had gotten to know Maggie before the illness. Already Aurora sensed Maggie would approve of her companionship with Martin.

They both glanced toward the center of the tent where the bride and groom were dancing. Jude wore a cream-colored mid-length dress embroidered with tiny yellow flowers. Matching flowers adorned her hair, which was uncustomarily tamed into a charming wavy style. The groom wore a sports coat and jeans like many of the male guests, even Liam's father, Lawrence. Martin absently brushed the lapels of his own casual jacket, grateful that he didn't have to wear a custom-fitted tux. Soon he would leave the jacket on the back of a chair and dance with Aurora.

The scent of spicy barbecue sauce permeated the tent from the warming trays. "Seems fitting for Jude to have ribs and corn bread for her wedding dinner," Martin said. "She was never one to fuss."

"And look at the other newlyweds," Aurora said, nodding toward Carrie and Keegan. She sighed. "They are so happy."

"I know, and once again I had to keep my opinions to myself where Carrie was concerned. I'd always wanted to see each of my girls married in proper style, but Carrie had other ideas and eloped. I'm surprised she even let us in on it."

"I think it's romantic," Aurora said. "And doesn't it just seem like something Carrie would do?"

Martin harrumphed. "Absolutely, it does. But flying off to Seattle for a quick ceremony with only her sisters and the two of us to witness—that's not the way it was done in my day."

"Yes, but you met your newest grandson. Taylor seems like a remarkable boy, and he'll make a fine addition to this family."

A familiar warmth crept into Martin's chest. *Someday*, he thought, *so will you, Aurora.*

"What did you think of the extra room Carrie and Keegan are putting on the cabin?" Aurora asked.

"Plenty big enough for the nursery they'll need in eight months." Martin chuckled. "Those two… It's as if they're in such a big hurry to do everything at once. I'm surprised Carrie got the dirt from under her fingernails in time to be a bridesmaid today. She's determined to have the campground open by this summer. Now I just have to get her through this pregnancy safely…"

"Martin…" Aurora's voice held a warning. "Keegan will help her with that. I'm sure he'll call if he needs you."

Martin nodded. "I'll be good," he promised. "I suppose I can stop worrying about all my girls now."

"As if you can ever do that," Aurora said. "But they are all happy and settled. Alex with her Daniel, Carrie with Keegan, and now Jude with Liam. And you have grandchildren who love you. What more could a man want?"

Martin smiled, slipped his arm around Aurora's shoulders. Only one thing, he thought. In due time.

* * * * *

*More great titles are coming from acclaimed author Cynthia Thomason and Harlequin Heartwarming in 2017.*

*And if you haven't read the compelling romances of the other two* DAUGHTERS OF DANCING FALLS— *Alexis and Jude—check out www.Harlequin.com today!*

# LARGER-PRINT BOOKS!

## GET 2 FREE
## LARGER-PRINT NOVELS
## PLUS 2 FREE
## MYSTERY GIFTS

*Love Inspired®*

### Larger-print novels are now available...

# LARGER-PRINT BOOKS!

## GET 2 FREE
## LARGER-PRINT NOVELS
## PLUS 2 FREE
## MYSTERY GIFTS

*Love Inspired®*

## SUSPENSE
RIVETING INSPIRATIONAL ROMANCE

### Larger-print novels are now available...

# WESTERN (WP) PROMISES

**YES!** Please send me **The Western Promises Collection** in Larger Print.
This collection begins with 3 FREE books and 2 FREE gifts (gifts valued at
approx. $14.00 retail) in the first shipment, along with the other first 4 books
from the collection! If I do not cancel, I will receive 8 monthly shipments until
I have the entire 51-book Western Promises collection. I will receive 2 or 3
FREE books in each shipment and I will pay just $4.99 US/ $5.89 CDN for
each of the other four books in each shipment, plus $2.99 for shipping and
handling per shipment. *If I decide to keep the entire collection, I'll have paid
for only 32 books, because 19 books are FREE! I understand that accepting
the 3 free books and gifts places me under no obligation to buy anything. I
can always return a shipment and cancel at any time. My free books and gifts
are mine to keep no matter what I decide.

272 HCN 3070 472 HCN 3070

| | | |
|---|---|---|
| Name | (PLEASE PRINT) | |
| Address | | Apt. # |
| City | State/Prov. | Zip/Postal Code |

Signature (if under 18, a parent or guardian must sign)

## Mail to the **Reader Service**:

**IN U.S.A.:** P.O. Box 1867, Buffalo, NY 14240-1867
**IN CANADA:** P.O. Box 609, Fort Erie, Ontario L2A 5X3

# LARGER-PRINT BOOKS!
## GET 2 FREE LARGER-PRINT NOVELS PLUS
## 2 FREE GIFTS!

**HARLEQUIN®**

*super romance®*

## More Story...More Romance

# READERSERVICE.COM

## Manage your account online!

- Review your order history
- Manage your payments
- Update your address

> ### We've designed the Reader Service website just for you.

## Enjoy all the features!

- Discover new series available to you, and read excerpts from any series.
- Respond to mailings and special monthly offers.
- Connect with favorite authors at the blog.
- Browse the Bonus Bucks catalog and online-only exculsives.
- Share your feedback.

*Visit us at:*
# ReaderService.com